The Island of the Gods

The Island of the Gods

An Akitada Novel

I. J. Parker

I·J·P
2015

Copyright © 2015 by I. J. Parker.

Published 2015 by I.J.Parker and I·J·P Books
428 Cedar Lane, Virginia Beach VA 23452
http://www.ijparker.com
Cover design by I. J. Parker.
Cover image by Ando Hiroshige
Back cover image: Ito Yakuchu
Publisher's Note: This is a work of fiction. Names, characters, places, and incidents are a product of the author's imagination.

The Island of the Gods, 1st edition, 2015
ISBN 13: 978-1522737360

Praise for I. J. Parker and the Akitada Series

"Elegant and entertaining . . . Parker has created a wonderful protagonist in Akitada. . . . She puts us at ease in a Japan of one thousand years ago." *The Boston Globe*

"You couldn't ask for a more gracious introduction to the exotic world of Imperial Japan than the stately historical novels of I. J. Parker." *The New York Times*

"Akitada is as rich a character as Robert Van Gulik's intriguing detective, Judge Dee." *The Dallas Morning News*

"Readers will be enchanted by Akitada." *Publishers Weekly* Starred Review

"Terrifically imaginative" *The Wall Street Journal*

"A brisk and well-plotted mystery with a cast of regulars who become more fully developed with every episode." *Kirkus*

"More than just a mystery novel, (*THE CONVICT'S SWORD*) is a superb piece of literature set against the backdrop of 11th-cntury Kyoto." *The Japan Times*

"Parker's research is extensive and she makes great use of the complex manners and relationships of feudal Japan." *Globe and Mail*

"The fast-moving, surprising plot and colorful writing will enthrall even those unfamiliar with the exotic setting." *Publishers Weekly*, Starred Review

". . .the author possesses both intimate knowledge of the time period and a fertile imagination as well. Combine that with an intriguing mystery and a fast-moving plot, and you've got a historical crime novel that anyone can love." *Chicago Sun-Times*

"Parker's series deserves a wide readership." *Historical Novel Society*

"The historical research is impressive, the prose crisp, and Parker's ability to universalize the human condition makes for a satisfying tale." *Booklist*

"Parker masterfully blends action and detection while making the attitudes and customs of the period accessible." *Publishers Weekly* (starred review)

"Readers looking for historical mystery with a twist will find what they're after in Parker's latest Sugawara Akitada mystery . . . An intriguing glimpse into an ancient culture." *Booklist*

Characters

(Japanese family names precede proper names)

Characters in Mikawa:

Sugawara Akitada   Governor of Mikawa Province
Yukiko   his wife
Yasuko & Yoshi   his children from a prior marriage
Tora (Captain Sashima)   his senior retainer and friend
Saburo (Secretary Kuruda)   another retainer
Lieutenant Akechi   Mikawa police
Oyama   coroner
Inspector Ono   investigator for the Censors Bureau

Characters involved in the murder case:
Imagawa Toshiyasu   local landowner
Hiroko   his daughter
Matsudaira Kinsada   another local aristocrat
Tomiko   his daughter and Hiroko's friend
Kintsune and Kinto   his sons
Judge Ishimura   a retired judge
Arihito   his son
Naganori   a merchant

Characters involved in the robberies and piracies:
Gonjuro   a poor farmer
Tojo Muneyasu   Tokaido station master

I. J. Parker

Prefect Ikeda   district official in Mikawa
Fujiwara Michinori   Governor of Owari Province
Iseya Sadako   traveler on the Tokaido
Oyoshi   fisherman
Michiko   his daughter

1

On the Waterfront

Tora stood beside the policeman on the rocky shoreline a couple of miles south of the provincial capital. It was dawn and promised to be another beautiful autumn day. A slight haze still hung over a steel gray sea, but the sky was already turning an improbable peach shade above them, casting a pink light over the scene while the distant horizon was still a murky blue. The colors had changed imperceptibly since Tora had arrived by horse to check out the corpse that had washed up on shore.

The policeman—his name was Lieutenant Akechi—gave the corpse a tentative poke with the toe of his boot. "Fresh!" he said.

1

Tora grunted. "Small favors from the gods. How many does he make?"

"Three, but one of them may have been an accident. The fish had chewed him up too much to know for sure." He leaned to peer more closely at the corpse of the man who lay on his stomach. He was only half in the water, but the tide was going out. He looked like the others, young, deeply tanned and muscular, barefoot and wearing only a loincloth and something like an amulet around his neck. "Strangled," said the lieutenant. "With his amulet."

Tora looked where Akechi pointed. A thin red line ran around the man's neck under the string of the small wooden plaque. He bent and brushed the hair aside. The line continued all around but had left a larger bruise near his spine. "From behind," he said.

They both straightened and regarded their find unhappily.

"Horrible!" muttered Akechi, nodding toward the dead man's hands. The right one ended in irregular stubs where the fingers had been. There was no blood because he had been in the water a while, but the cuts looked fresh.

"Tortured like the others."

"Not quite the same. The other two were whipped or beaten up. One had a lacerated back, and one broken limbs."

2

"Nasty. But this must've been worse. Slow."

Akechi grunted.

"They cut them off one at a time," Tora amplified.

"Who does stuff like that?"

"I wish I knew, but we'd better do something about it. The governor will be livid. He worries about more piracy."

Akechi sighed and bent down to turn the body on its back. Tora lent a hand. Apart from the fingerless hand there were no other wounds. The amulet had had some writing on it, but the sea had washed away the ink. Now only the vague outline of a Buddha figure remained.

"I wonder if he talked," Akechi said.

"I expect I would've," Tora said. "Nothing's so important that you'll keep it to yourself when that hatchet comes for your fingers. If he's a fisherman, he needs his hands to work. I think he really didn't know what they asked about, poor guy."

"Well, let's pull him away from the water. I'll send my constables to pick him up."

∞

Akitada, duly appointed governor of Mikawa province, listened to his right-hand man's report with a heavy frown. When Tora was done, he pushed aside the papers he had been working on, sending his writing implements skittering. "I knew it!" he said angrily as he rose and started pacing. "It's the same thing all over again. Piracy and highway robbery! I thought we'd made an end of that, but I should've known better."

Tora nodded. "At sea, they go after shipping and on land they attack transport trains. We're between the bay and the great Tokaido highway; placed perfectly for robbers and pirates. And this is the time when all those goods are being shipped to the capital. Maybe I should take some of my best men up toward the Tokaido. I bet those robbers live around there. Maybe we can flush them out."

His master shook his head. "We are stretched too thin. I've asked for more troops and a stronger police force twice now, and the government has turned me down each time. They tell me to use local men. That's like setting the cat to watch the fish." He glowered. "The situation is impossible. And now this!"

Tora's eyes strayed to the papers, several in the form of opened mail. "Any news from home, sir?"

Akitada's face darkened further. "Genba sends greetings. He writes that all is well."

"Nothing from her ladyship?"

"No!"

The "no" was curt and Tora blinked. After a moment, his master added, "My sister says she's well. There's the usual court gossip and any number of parties this time of year."

4

"Well," Tora said brightly, "The ladies are being kept very busy. And there was also the marriage of her ladyship's brother."

Akitada nodded. Yukiko's full brother, Arihito, had taken the Otomo heiress Masako to wife. Theirs had been a troubled courtship when everyone believed the bride to have a murderer for her father. Akitada had proved this false, and Masako had been officially adopted by her grandmother, old Lady Otomo. Happy as this outcome had been, it had destroyed Akitada's marriage.

His young wife, who had become disillusioned equally by her husband's lack of mettle and his sense of propriety, had not returned to Mikawa with him. She had stayed with her family until she was offered a position as lady-in-waiting to the imperial consort.

Tora knew how anxiously he awaited letters from his wife and how very rare these were. He knew that Lady Yukiko had been expected to rejoin her husband after a rest—she had been pregnant and lost their child in an attack by a madman—but this had come to nothing. Tora did not expect her to rejoin her husband and perhaps his master no longer expected it either, even if he still looked for her letters and fretted. More than five months had passed since his return, and he had become more morose with every day.

Tora changed the subject. "Speaking of parties, Hanae wonders if we are to have that banquet for the Chrysanthemum festival."

Akitada sat down again and shuffled the papers into piles. "I suppose we'd better," he said listlessly. "I owe invitations and my last year here is drawing to a close."

A silence fell as both tried to think of something else to say. Finally Akitada said, "Follow up on that dead man, will you, Tora? You and Akechi can handle it, but keep me informed. I have reports to write and there's a hearing later on."

Tora thought that in the past neither reports nor hearings would have interfered with his master's eagerness to get on the trail of villains, but he left without protest.

2

The Empty House

Akitada sat lost in thought a while longer in his office, then he gathered the private letters and put them inside his robe. The rest of the mail, all of it official communications from the capital or from neighboring provinces, he passed to his secretary with instructions to answer and then file them.

He left the tribunal hall and walked to his adjoining private home. As soon as he passed through the small gate into his garden, he was in a different world. Large trees shaded this area and many birds flitted through the branches. The sun slanted through the foliage and made golden patterns on the moss under his feet. Near the house, the trees receded, and here Yukiko had installed a chrysanthemum garden when they still shared this home.

He stopped as he always did to remember the time when they had been together. The chrysanthemum plants had grown amazingly and would soon bloom in a glory of many colors. Already they were covered with dense buds, and here and there he could see reds and golds, and purples among the green buds. As always, the sight made him sad. Yukiko had left him, and would not return. With her had gone a time when he had felt young and hopeful. He was only in his forty-fifth year, but on some days he felt closer to eighty.

Nothing was to be gained from such thoughts. Shaking his head at himself, he continued to the house and his private study.

There, he reread Akiko's letter. The contents troubled him. Her references to Yukiko were unusually sparse and concerned mainly the fact that she was well and busy. Much of the other material dealt with her own family and the description of a party given by the palace women on the occasion of a moon viewing. It had been the traditional full moon party and they had composed fitting poems. Akiko added hers: "Above the tree tops the moon hides; in the palace of our great lord the lights put it to shame."

What troubled him was that she had avoided speaking of Yukiko's life at court. When his wife had become a lady-in-waiting to the imperial consort, her husband had received many letters of congratulation. Though probably arranged by Yukiko's father, the position had been a great honor, but Akitada's first reaction had been dismay. Yukiko would certainly not be bored serving the consort. The imperial women attracted a lively attendance of young men who flirted shamelessly with their attendants.

Perhaps most upsetting was Akiko's final message. She had written, "I think it's time for you to pay us a visit." No explanation was given with this, but in view of the rest of the letter he assumed that all was not well with Yukiko's current activities.

Alas, he could not comply. With the same mail had come a letter from the office of the prime minister, announcing the visit of an investigator from the Board of Censors to check into his administration of Mikawa. This was clearly the result of the severe reprimand he had received earlier in the year for having abandoned his post to bring his wife to the capital. No doubt her recent advancement at court had irritated someone enough to push for her husband's recall. Akitada still had powerful enemies at court.

He put his sister's letter away and thought about his situation. His term of office ended with this year. If the imperial investigator found fault with him, it might end sooner than that. Leaving under a cloud, he could not expect another appointment. The fact that his wife was preoccupied with her duties at court and his sister thought he ought to visit was neither here nor there. Yukiko was by all accounts in good health or he would have heard from her father. No, this time he must do his best for himself and his children.

He thought of the latest troubles. Piracy on Mikawa Bay and along Mikawa's southern coast had flourished for centuries. Often its activities had been carried out by the same families who had passed that way of life from father to son. They would certainly not talk. It was only when someone from the outside came and tried to take a share that trouble ensued and the authorities became aware of it. The tortured bodies washing up on the coast suggested that this might be happening. If so, they should soon get some information. The trouble was that he did not need this worry when he expected to be investigated.

He was still pondering his predicament when Saburo put his head in at the door, "Sorry, sir, but you need to get ready for the hearing."

Akitada sighed, but he rose obediently and, with Saburo's help, changed into his formal black robe and the small silk hat he wore with it. There had been a time when he had looked forward to hearing and adjudicating complaints. In fact, during his first post as governor, he had quaked secretly while facing hostile and shouting crowds. These days matters were less dramatic, the audience friendlier, and the cases dull. Most of the provinces now had judges to hear the serious criminal cases while governors dealt with land disputes and taxation. Akitada, with his legal training and experience was comfortable with such matters, but that did not mean he particularly relished them. It had occurred to him before that he had become involved in so many criminal investigations precisely because property cases tended to offer little beyond a lot of work in the archives, checking old documents.

Saburo was silent, perhaps in deference to his master's abstraction. Eventually, Akitada recalled himself and thanked him. Looking at his official secretary more closely, he asked, "Are you content, Saburo?"

Saburo was startled but said with a smile, "Quite content, sir. Thank you."

"What I meant was have you made plans for your charges? We will soon have to leave Mikawa."

Saburo, whose heavy beard and mustache disguised his scars, was embarrassed. "Umm, I've been thinking about that, sir, but I haven't decided."

Saburo was five years older than Akitada and still a bachelor, but he had taken into his home a woman and her young daughter, both former slaves from the North Country. Akitada had been distracted by his own marital problems, but Tora had kept a gleeful eye on the couple and reported that they seemed to be living together as man and wife.

Akitada now said, "She's a nice woman, Saburo, and she's welcome in my family. I hope you understand that."

Now the embarrassment was quite obvious. Saburo turned away, pretending to busy himself with draping Akitada's discarded robe over its stand. "Thank you, sir," he said in a tight voice. "I wasn't worried about that, but there is my mother to be considered, I'm afraid."

"I see your point," Akitada said drily. Mrs. Kuruda would not take kindly to such a daughter-in-law and had already indicated that she intended to rule any woman her son married. "Well, we all have to make our choices."

"Yes, sir."

Akitada checked the small silver mirror to see if his hat was on straight and then took up his baton of office. They walked together across to the tribunal and to its reception hall which served as the governor's courtroom today.

3

The Hearing

The guard threw wide the door and shouted into the room: "His Excellency, the governor! All kneel!"

Akitada walked in, Saburo at his heels. He saw that only a small group of people attended. Most of them were elderly men or women. In the middle of the day, most able-bodied males were at their work and property squabbles did not hold much appeal in any case. They all bowed down at his entrance, touching their heads to the floor. Akitada thought that they looked contented and cheerful enough. The mood of the population was a measure of a governor's management of the province. Of course, this satisfactory state of affairs was due more to generally peaceful conditions than to any actions on his own part.

And there was at least one unhappy face among them. A middle-aged, plainly dressed man knelt in the front row, looking very anxious.

Scanning the room, Akitada noted that two constables stood in front of the dais in case arrests were to be made, and that all the exits had provincial guards posted. All quite proper.

He took his seat in the center of the dais overlooking the room and rapped his baton on the floorboards, announcing, "The hearing is now open. The senior scribe will call the first claimant."

There were three scribes present. They were seated on the dais to either side of him, their desks and writing materials in front of them.

The senior scribe rose. "The farmer Gonjuro, from Toyohashi village, Aomi district, Mikawa province, has come here to have a great wrong righted by your Excellency."

"Where is he?" Akitada asked.

"Here." The unhappy looking man in the front row raised a hand, and having attracted Akitada's eye, bowed low again with his forehead touching the floor.

"Sit up and explain!"

The man straightened up and cleared his throat. He looked nervous and seemed unable to find the words. Akitada gave an inward sigh. In a gentler voice he said, "You've come a long way to be heard, Gonjuro. It must be important to you."

The man nodded several times and finally managed to croak, "I paid him, sir, I swear it by all the saints."

One of the constables snapped, "You will address the governor as 'Your Excellency.'"

Gonjuro shrank into himself and murmured, "Sorry. Your Excellency."

Akitada shot the constable an irritated glance and asked the farmer, "You owed someone this money?"

"Yes, you see, I'd borrowed it, sir . . . Your Excellency. For seed rice. The harvest having been bad and the taxes being so high." There was a titter in the audience. "And I paid it all back. I first paid fifty pieces of silver, and then another fifty. But Tojo says I never paid the first fifty and he won't give me back the contract I signed."

Akitada was beginning to grasp the situation. "You did not get a receipt for your first payment?"

The farmer shook his head. "Tojo gave his word and I gave mine. He agreed to take half after the first harvest and the rest after the second. But when I paid him the second time, he wanted still more."

Akitada turned to the senior scribe, "Get the information about the dates, amounts, and people involved." The scribe bowed. Akitada asked the farmer, "Were there any witnesses to this agreement or to your payments?"

"No witnesses, no. I went to Tojo's house alone. But we had an agreement. I had his word. I kept my word, but he didn't keep his." The injustice of this brought tears to his eyes.

Akitada suppressed another sigh. "Who is this Tojo?"

"He's a horse dealer, sir, Your Excellency. In Akasaka. Tojo Muneyasu."

Akitada's brows rose. "In Akasaka? You mean in Owari province? Why are you coming here then? You should make your complaint to the governor of Owari."

The farmer wailed, "I went to the prefect of the district but he said I should've asked for a receipt. He called me a fool and laughed at me."

Not surprisingly this caused more titters from the audience. Akitada rapped his baton. "Silence! Did you go back to this Tojo to demand your receipt?"

"No, your honor. I was afraid."

"Afraid? Why?"

"Tojo doesn't like it when people make trouble for him. He sends men to beat them up."

It was an impossible situation. Akitada said, "Well, I'm not sure what we can do, Gonjuro. You may have been cheated out of your money. But give the scribe all the information and I'll think about your case. That's all for now."

The scribe rose again. "There is another case, your Excellency. Mrs. Ishimura claims a piece of land her neighbor Kawakami is selling belongs to her."

That should be easily ascertained, Akitada thought. The Mikawa archives were well-maintained and all land sales had been recorded for several centuries. He said, "Have the parties approach the dais."

The scribe called the names, and a neatly dressed young man came from the audience, knelt, and bowed. He was joined by a middle-aged female who looked angry. She kept her distance from him and knelt also.

Not waiting to be asked her name, she announced, "This person is Ishimura Takao, landowner and widow of Ishimura Jiro."

Akitada nodded and looked at the young man.

The young man said, "This person is Kawakami Yoshio, farmer."

Akitada asked him, "Do you have the title to the land you're selling?"

"Yes, your Excellency. The land has been in our family for more years than anyone can remember." He took a document from his robe.

"He's lying," the woman snapped. "And whatever he's showing you, your Excellency, is a forgery."

Akitada's brows rose. He decided he did not like the woman. Akitada had noted that her opponent had waited for her to speak first. He nodded to the constable. "Hand me the document."

The young man presented it with both hands and bowed again, and the constable took it to Akitada. It was quite old, but the paper was good and whoever had done the writing had had a clear hand. It looked authentic, but before Akitada could read it, the widow cried, "Look at that seal, Excellency. That's not even the correct seal. It must be a forgery."

Akitada looked at the red seal. It was much clearer than some of the writing it covered. He waved the scribe over. "Do we have a sample of this seal here?"

The scribe hurried back to his desk, picked up a document, and brought it to Akitada. One glance proved the woman right. The two seals were indeed different. Akitada sighed.

"How did you come into possession of this deed?" he asked the young man.

"My father died during the second month, Your Excellency. I have only just begun to look at our documents. But I cannot believe that Mrs. Ishimura is right. My father would never have forged a document. He was an honorable man." The son was flushed and sounded upset.

The widow said, "Pah!"

Akitada peered at the two seals again. "There is a similarity," he muttered, "but the seal on this old deed looks almost like a new seal."

"Exactly," said Mrs. Ishimura triumphantly. "Thank heaven Your Excellency has sharp eyes or that one would have gotten away with it. Anyone can see that the seal is a fake."

"Perhaps," said Akitada, frowning down at her. "Do you have a title to the land?"

She shook her head. "We've had a fire that destroyed all of our papers."

"Hmm." Akitada pulled his earlobe thoughtfully. "This document is certainly old. The date on the deed is Kampyo 6. It means it was drawn up about one hundred and fifty years ago."

The young man said softly, "My ancestors have always lived here. Our family name is on the deed."

Mrs. Ishimura cried, "What does that prove? He could've taken some old paper and written it out himself."

"That's true." Akitada compared the seals again and began to smile. "Ah!" he said, "I think I've got it. The seal was new when this was drawn up. In all those years of use it has become worn and the shape of the characters has changed. We shall check the archives to confirm it, but I think Mrs. Ishimura, knowing that you were unfamiliar with your family papers, has tried to trick you, Mr.Kawakami."

"That's not true," the woman cried. "That seal's nothing like the documents we have."

"I thought you said that all your own documents were lost in a fire?"

She sputtered in confusion, and Akitada rapped his gavel. "The archives will prove if the deed is authentic. They will also show if the land was sold in the past. If it turns out that you have no claim to it, Mrs. Ishimura, you are warned about bringing false charges against your neighbor in hopes that we won't be checking."

"Sorry!" The woman bowed. "Sorry! How was I to know?"

Akitada ignored this and closed the session with a sigh of relief. He saw that Tora had come into the hall and wondered what brought him.

A short time later in his office, Saburo said, "That was a good guess, sir. Who would have thought a seal could ever change?"

Akitada took the official seal of Mikawa from its box, glanced at it, and handed it to Saburo. "I was guessing, but I was right. This was carved from jade, but time and heavy use will wear down the hardest stone."

Tora joined them, grinning. "Good job, sir. That Ishimura female has a bad reputation for trying to cheat people."

Akitada asked, "What brings you?"

"That body, sir. The coroner's had a look and confirms the man was strangled. His fingers were chopped off while he was still alive. Nothing to tell who he is or where he's from, but after the coroner washed the body, he found a small tattoo on his shoulder."

"A tattoo? He was a criminal then."

"Maybe, sir, but it's not that kind of tattoo. I've never seen one like it. It looks like a circle with three leaves."

Akitada rubbed some ink, then handed Tora a piece of paper and his brush. "Make me a picture of it."

Tora did, somewhat clumsily, and handed the paper back.

Akitada said nothing for a moment. Finally he asked, "A circle with three leaves? Are you certain they were arranged like that?"

"Not certain. It's small. But it looks like that. Like a seal of some sort."

"Not a seal. A kamon, a family emblem. I'm not sure, but it probably marks the dead man as a servant or slave. That particular kamon is a Matsudaira one. They are a local clan."

Finding that the emblem of a clan had been used to mark the murdered man spelled trouble. Why had a man with the Matsudaira mark been tortured and then killed? Akitada felt as if the ground under his feet were shifting. Had he been too complacent about his peaceful province?

Saburo said, "Wasn't there some trouble years ago, some tale about a Matsudaira revolt?"

"Yes, indeed." Akitada grimaced. "It was a long time ago, but that's all we need, another clan war."

Tora looked eager. "The man was tortured. I think we shouldn't ignore it."

"No. We'd better not. Perhaps it will be best to ask some cautious questions in the city. If there are secret activities afoot, someone must have taken notice. You and Saburo better spend a few days finding out what you can. Saburo will look in the archives, and you can check in the city. Report back, even if it seems unimportant."

They nodded. Tora said, "I think I'll walk to the market and chat up some people."

"Yes. Do that. Saburo, you'd better see to it first that the archivist locates the documents for that young man Kawakami. And find out who this Tojo Muneyasu is. I'll send a letter to my colleague in Owari and ask him for information about the case, but I expect that farmer was right when he said he was turned away because he had no receipt."

"What can we do about it, sir?" Saburo asked.

"I don't know. Maybe nothing. But I don't like it when our people are being cheated by someone in another province."

4

Another Body

Tora and Saburo departed, and Akitada sat at his desk, wondering if they would not be better employed dealing with more immediate dangers in the form of the visit by the official investigator. But the regular business must also be handled, even if solutions were hard to find. He decided to look over the provincial documents himself to make sure all was in readiness for the investigator.

By late afternoon, he had made some progress along this line, gratified that his capable staff had left little to complain about, when Tora returned.

"Sir," he said, excited, "I heard there's been another murder. A young woman who seems to belong to the good people. I thought you should know."

"What in heaven's name is happening?" Akitada asked, not expecting an answer. "Who is she?"

"I don't know, sir. At least not yet. She was found in a rice paddy right outside town by the peasant."

"Then how do you know she belongs to the good people?"

"The constable described her clothes. And her hair and her hands. Not a peasant, this one. I told them not to touch anything until you'd been notified."

"Did she drown?"

"No, sir. There's no water in the paddies this time of year. She was strangled, I think."

Akitada sighed. Putting aside some document boxes, he rose. "Lead the way!"

Tora grinned. "I'm glad you're coming yourself, sir."

The governor did not as a rule attend crime scenes. The local constabulary, police, and someone from his staff generally handled murders and other serious crimes. But Tora had rightly assumed that the murder of a member of one of the good families was significant enough for Akitada to become involved. For Akitada it was not the fact that the victim was of higher status than an ordinary person, but rather that crimes involving one of the powerful families could well lead to unrest in the province.

They rode, attracting little attention since Akitada was without official retinue. As Tora had promised, the field was just outside the city limits. The farm was part of the Matsudaira lands. The Matsudaira were proud and rather stand-offish toward court-appointed officials. Their landholdings were huge, as Akitada knew from the tax registers, and they were in the hands of the clan chief.

They could see the site from the raised road that passed through the rice paddies where the grain was tall and golden for the coming harvest. A small group of people stood among the rice plants.

They dismounted and tied their horses to one of the pine trees that lined the roadway and climbed down the embankment and into the rice field. Stepping carefully along a narrow path so as not to damage the growing rice plants, they made their way to the group of people. These turned out to be a village constable, the peasant whose field it was, and Akechi, the police lieutenant, who saluted. Akitada knew him and gave him a smile. The others, in various attitudes of bowing, got a nod.

At their feet among the rice plants lay a slender figure dressed in pale yellow silk, almost the same color as the ripening wheat. She had long, glossy hair tied with a white silk ribbon in back, and white socks on her feet. She lay on her side and her hair had slipped forward and over her face. There seemed to be few flies yet, but as the day turned warmer, they were sure to come.

Tora asked the peasant, a middle-aged man with a leathery, sun-darkened skin, "You found her?"

"Yes, Captain. The dog wouldn't come so I went to look, and there she was."

Akitada asked, "Have you seen her face? Any idea who she might be?"

The peasant, looking scared, shook his head. "Didn't touch her. Wouldn't know her. How would I know a woman belonging to one of the good families?

Amida! This will be bad luck! What was she doing in my field?"

"Good question," remarked Akitada. "Those socks are clean. How did she get here? She didn't walk."

They all looked. Lieutenant Akechi said, "Someone carried her. Her murderer."

"Perhaps, but we cannot be sure." Akitada bent to lift the hair from her neck. It was a very pretty neck, or had been. Now the white skin was marked by angry red blotches. The face was softly rounded, the face of a very young girl. "The coroner will make sure," said Akitada, letting the hair drop back, "but it does look as though she's been strangled." He touched her hand. Hand and arm were rigid, and so were her legs. He looked about. "Has anyone checked for footprints?"

"Yessir," said the constable. "First thing I did. No footprints. It's been too dry. And the killer must've used the same path you came by, Governor."

Nobody contradicted him, and Akitada nodded. He turned back to the peasant. "Is that your place behind the trees over there?"

Yes, Your Honor."

"Did you or your people hear anything during the night?"

"No, Your Honor." He corrected himself, "Only, the dog barked once early on."

"The dog was tied up or inside?"

"Inside, Your Honor. We keep him there until the harvest or he goes hunting rabbits and other critters in the field and spoils the rice plants. His lordship wouldn't like that. My wife and me, we weren't quite

26

asleep yet. We hushed him, being tired. It'd been a hard day. He'll bark at anything, though."

"I see. Thank you." Peasants tended to rise early and go to bed early also. If the dog had barked because someone had brought the girl's body, she had been lying in the field overnight. Akitada looked at Tora and Akechi. "We need to find out who she is."

They heard voices and turned. Down the narrow path came the coroner, followed by two constables with a stretcher. They made room for the coroner, who bowed to Akitada and inclined his head to Tora. He was a youngish man, slight of figure and with a narrow, pale face. Setting down his box of instruments, he bent over the corpse. "A great pity," he murmured. "So young." Like Akitada, he lifted the hair and said, "Strangled, but not necessarily to death. Been dead a while. Have you turned her over?"

"No," they muttered in chorus.

"Give me a hand then."

The constables jumped to it and turned the young woman on her back. There were several audible sighs. Akitada hoped they signified recognition, but when he asked, they all shook their heads.

She was beautiful. Even in death. Akitada judged her to be eighteen or nineteen, of middle height, and with a lovely oval face that not even the last throes of being strangled to death could distort. The side of her face that had touched the ground was marred by a darkening of the skin. Her eyes were closed and the lashes long. She was not wearing the heavy make-up of upper-class women and prostitutes. If she had been younger, too young for such things, this would have made sense, but there was a certain maturity about her face. He thought he would have liked to have known her.

There was no doubt she belonged to one of the leading families. Her clothes were of the finest silk and embroidered. And as Tora had said, her small hands had never done physical work; their nails were smooth and polished.

Why would someone kill such a woman?

And where was she killed, since the clean socks proved she had been carried here. Was she murdered in her father's or husband's house?

The coroner looked into her mouth and sniffed it. Then he did a quick check for wounds on her body. There were none. Her gowns were immaculate and there was no blood anywhere.

"Well," he said, standing up, "We'll take her back for a proper autopsy, Your Excellency, but it looks like death was due to strangulation."

"Let's wait with the complete autopsy," Akitada said. "The cause of death seems pretty obvious, and we need someone to identify her. But let me know if she's been raped."

The coroner nodded.

As they returned to town, Akitada gave Tora a glance. He looked unusually downcast. "One of your headaches?"

"No, sir. That girl! So young and so pretty, and now dead because some animal attacked her."

"No obvious signs of rape, but we shall soon know. Yes, it's a pity. I cannot imagine how a young woman like that could end up murdered in a rice field."

"She was killed someplace else and carried there. I expect the murderer had his way with her and was afraid she'd talk."

"Perhaps, but why bring her there?"

"Because leaving her body where she was killed would implicate the killer."

"Yes. But if we assume that a young woman like that was unlikely to leave her home alone, then that could well mean someone in her own family killed her."

Tora considered this. "Or she was someplace else with a servant and the servant either couldn't or wouldn't interfere with the murder."

"True." Akitada sighed. "We'll have to wait for identification. Surely her absence has been noted by now. Have the police post notices."

5

Tora Asks Questions

That night, Tora bade his wife Hanae good night and set out for work. Having duly seen to the posting of the notices, there was nothing else he could do to find out the identity of the young woman, so he decided to pursue the case of the tattooed sailor—or whatever he'd been—instead.

It was well past the hour of the rat, and the sky was overcast when he left their quarters in the tribunal dressed in his oldest clothes and with a knife hidden in his boot. He walked southward through the silent city streets. There was no willow quarter here where a raucous nightlife would still be going strong. That was not to say there was no prostitution in Komachi, but most of these women worked from assorted inns and drinking places. The higher class courtesans had their own homes and found their customers by referral, often visiting their patrons in their own homes or in houses of assignation.

But Tora was headed for a very different world. Toward the harbor was a warren of warehouses, cheap eating places, and low wine shops. This was where sailors, fishermen, and wharf workers spent their few coins. Here he had his informers.

Initially he had little luck. None of the dingy, stinking places he looked into held the kind of customer he was looking for: a small-time crook who was not successful enough at his work to afford assorted vices like wine, women, and gambling. These types were willing to sell their grandmothers for a few coins.

In the dingiest street, he entered a run-down dive that called itself the Red Carp.

A wave of odors met him, none pleasant. Sweat was foremost, with garlic, and fermented wine running it a close second. Most of the smoke from the cooking fire had escaped by this late hour. Nobody was eating. They gambled, drank, and talked when things were good. When they were not, they fought. This accounted for the fact that there was no furniture to speak of, and the floor was compacted dirt covered with so many layers of unimaginable things that it had taken on a sort of gloss.

Apparently all was still peaceful. And there, in the back corner, Tora recognized a face. He made his way to the host, an immensely fat man in stained clothes, who sat wide-legged on some sort of stump next to a vat. Now and then, he'd use a long bamboo ladle to give the contents a stir.

The vat was the origin of the sour smell. Swallowing down his revulsion, Tora asked for a large cup of wine."

His host eyed him appreciatively. "You look thirsty, friend," he said with a grin that revealed stained teeth. "It's especially good today. I got a new supply." He ladled out a serving into a dirty cup. "That'll be ten coppers."

Tora paid, saying pleasantly, "Rotgut, is it, Shiro? Will you let me sleep it off if I can't make it home?"

Shiro laughed; a strange, rollicking, wheezing sound that came from deep inside his gut and set his belly jiggling. "Sure. Why not? The rats'll enjoy the company."

Tora grinned and took his wine over to a quiet corner. The man he wanted was deep in a game of dice with three others. He was a gambler. Tora knew the information he sought could cost him dearly.

He wiped the rim of the cup and tried the rotgut, finding it barely drinkable. He hoped his man would detach himself from his game soon.

Tora knew he had been seen. They had all raised their heads to glance at the newcomer. In this sort of place it was as well to be on your guard.

The man he wanted did eventually rise without glancing at Tora. He excused himself for a call of nature and left the wine shop by the backdoor. Tora knew there was an alley out there where the fat man's customers sought relief after too many cups of the rotgut. He gave it a few moments, then he emptied the rest of his drink on the floor, rose, and returned the empty cup to the fat man.

"Come back!" said his host automatically and gave the cup a wipe with his dirty sleeve.

Tora headed out the back himself. In the dark, stinking alley he saw at first no one and cursed under his breath. The bastard had given him the slip. Then he heard a small splashing sound and made out a slightly darker shape against the wall of the building.

"Ho, Rabbit," he said softly.

"Ssh!" The figure moved away from the wall and approached. "Come this way." The man grabbed Tora sleeve and tugged.

They walked away from the wine shop, past another house, then into a storage area behind some sort of business or warehouse. All was silent and nobody was about.

Rabbit was a skinny, small-boned fellow, so named because of his large ears and protruding upper teeth. He asked, "So what do you want today, Captain? And what's it worth?"

He had used Tora's rank mockingly. Crooks, even unsuccessful ones, did not like the tribunal guard any better than they liked the police.

Tora fished a piece of silver from his sash and held it up. Rabbit peered at it in the uncertain light. "Ask!"

"We found a body washed up on shore. A male, maybe a sailor. He had a tattoo."

Rabbit sneered, "Since when are tattoos on sailors rare?"

"This tattoo is special. It's very small. Not the sort of thing a sailor gets done in some port, or a convict gets after standing trial. It's a circle with three leaves."

"So he's a bumboy. Plenty of those among sailors."

"No. This is some sort of emblem."

"No idea, Captain. You got any other questions?"

"The man was murdered, strangled."

There was silence.

"Rabbit?" said Tora sternly.

The thin man snapped, "It happens. Can't help you."

"Before they killed him, they chopped off his fingers. Five of them, one at a time. It's worth this piece of silver." He held up the coin.

Rabbit gasped. "Nothing to do with me," he squeeked. "Never heard of your tattoo. I've got to go back."

"You're lying."

"Have it your way!" Rabbit snatched the coin from Tora's fingers and ran.

Tora rushed after him, grabbing him by his shirt and pushing him against the wooden fence of the yard. "Oh, no, you don't," he snarled, bashing Rabbit's head against the fence. "You took the silver. Now you talk!"

Rabbit squealed again, then sagged. He said in a low voice, "Maybe I heard something."

"Tell!"

"Talking about it isn't healthy."

"If you cheat me, there'll be no more money for information. Then what about those friendly dice games? I bet you owe your friends back there in the Carp already. What'll they do to you if you don't pay up?"

"Don't make me tell. Ask me about something else."

"No."

"Oh, come on!" Rabbit twisted in his grip and cajoled. "I've always helped you."

"Not this time. Give it over."

Rabbit peered around again, then said, "All right. Let me go." After a moment's consideration, Tora relaxed his grip but kept a wary eye on Rabbit. The thin man straightened his shirt, then said in a low voice, "Swear you won't say where you heard this."

"I swear," Tora said, less than truthfully, since he intended to report the information and how he got it to his master.

Rabbit said, "There was a man here asking questions about something happening on Takeshima."

"Takeshima? What's going on there?"

A door opened down the alley and someone shouted "Hey, Rabbit!"

Rabbit was gone before Tora could stop him. He muttered a curse and went home.

6

Daughters are Fragile Things

The coroner reported to Akitada early the next morning. Akitada was in the habit of arriving at daybreak these days since there was no one to keep him at home. The children still slept when he rose in the dark, dressed, and walked across to the tribunal.

He had been working over the provincial documents only a short while when a servant announced the coroner.

"Good morning, Oyama," Akitada greeted him.

The coroner bowed and handed over his report, saying, "I finished late yesterday, but Secretary Kuruda said you'd retired."

Akitada nodded. He had spent the evening with the children. "Be seated and tell me yourself," he said, laying the report aside.

"Death was due to strangulation, as you could see for yourself. She probably died more than twelve hours before she was found. She was approximately seventeen or eighteen years old and no longer a virgin."

Akitada raised his brows. "Raped?"

"No, sir. In fact, there was no sign of recent intercourse. But she was handled very roughly. Her upper arms are bruised and there are marks on her body from being beaten and perhaps kicked. Some of the marks looked old. Whoever did this must have been very angry with her."

Akitada digested this. It was a complication. If she had merely been attacked, raped, and then killed to protect her attacker, the case would be simpler. Now they were looking for someone who had had a grudge, a violent grudge against this beautiful young woman. It crossed his mind that sometimes women hated each other like that and he asked, "Could a woman have done this?"

The coroner pursed his lips. "A man I would think. It's not easy to strangle a person to death, and this was a young woman who fought for her life. The killer could have been a particularly strong woman, of course."

"How do you know she fought for her life?" Akitada asked, interested.

"She scratched her attacker. There was blood and skin under her finger nails."

"Excellent work," Akitada said with great satisfaction. "That should help identify her killer."

The coroner permitted himself a slight smile. "I thought so, too, Excellency. Once you find him, or her, of course."

"Yes. Well, you can't have everything. Is there anything new on the body Tora sent you? The one of the sailor with the tattoo?"

"Nothing. But if you'll forgive me, Excellency, it is not by any means certain he was a sailor."

"Really?" Akitada was surprised. "He washed up from the bay, I was told."

"That is so, but he did not have the sorts of calluses and marks a sailor has. I thought it more likely that he'd worked on a farm and around animals."

"Strange, given where he was found. How could you tell?"

The coroner smiled a little. "Sailors work with oars and pull heavy rope. Their palms are not only calloused but scarred. They also tend to have whip marks on their backs. This man had a few calluses on his hands, but neither his back nor his palms were scarred. He did have scars on his legs as if he had been kicked by an animal, a horse perhaps."

"Thank you, Oyama. You are very observant. What did you think of the tattoo?"

"A set of leaves. I thought it very small, though finely made. In my experience, tattoos are large so people can see them. This one looks like the Matsudaira crest and is not much bigger than a large mole. It's like nothing I've ever seen."

I. J. Parker

Wondering what all this might mean, Akitada thanked the man who withdrew.

The new murder was, in its own way, as disturbing as that of the tortured man with the Matsudaira tattoo. A young woman from a good family should have long since been reported missing.

Saburo showed in the young farmer from the previous day's hearing. He said, "Mr. Kawakami came to find out about his land's title, sir. We verified that he is indeed the owner of the parcel and he wished to express his thanks."

Kawakami approached shyly and knelt. "I'm very grateful to Your Excellency. I was very much afraid that maybe I made a mistake."

"It wasn't your mistake," Akitada assured him. "It was your neighbor's. What in heaven possessed the woman to question your ownership all of a sudden?"

"My father died recently. I'm the heir, but my father and I were not close and I grew up in an uncle's household and knew nothing of my father's property. When I came for his funeral, I discovered that the place was mine. I also learned that there were many debts and the land had been left uncultivated. It was necessary to sell land to pay the debts."

Akitada nodded. "An honorable way of dealing with the problem."

"Thank you, your Excellency. But I found that my neighbor had been planting parts of our land for years. She claimed her late husband bought it from my father and that the papers had been lost in a fire. I showed her our deed, but she said it was no good."

Akitada sighed. He saw the difficulties this young man had encountered upon his father's death. "Well then," he said, "I wish you good success with the sale and also with planting your fields next year."

Kawakami smiled. "I have a buyer, Your Excellency. Thanks to you and with Amida's blessings all should be well soon." He bowed again and left.

Saburo remained. "The widow Ishimura has a bad reputation," he remarked. "He will have more trouble with her, I'm afraid."

"We must leave that to the future, Saburo. Did you send off those letters to Owari?"

"Yes, sir. They went off yesterday. We should hear soon."

"Something about that story troubles me. I'm wondering if this Tojo makes a habit of cheating Mikawa farmers out of their money."

"I'll ask the district prefect to look into it."

"Good."

Saburo hesitated.

"What is it? Some other trouble?"

"No, sir. I thought about what you said yesterday. About making plans. So I asked Sumiko if she would come with me when we go back to the capital." His bearded face split into a grin. "It appears, sir, that I've acquired a family."

"Wonderful!" Akitada rose to embrace Saburo. "My heartiest congratulations. It's about time, too."

Saburo blinked tears from his eyes. He was an unemotional man as a rule, and Akitada was moved to see him like this.

"Sumiko is . . . well, she's a very good woman for all that she was a slave once. She's kind and generous and has quite a good education. I'm teaching her and her daughter, Tokiwa, every evening when I return from work."

"Excellent! I wish you all much happiness. Perhaps Tokiwa could join my children sometimes?"

Saburo looked shocked. "Oh, that wouldn't be right. Though if Tokiwa grows up to be a good girl, she might serve Lady Yasuko."

"We shall see. It's very good to see you happy, Saburo. Surely your mother will accept your new family when she sees them."

Saburo's face fell. "That I doubt, sir, but I've made up my mind to protect them." He bowed, and returned to his own office, leaving Akitada to reflect that now he alone was without a wife or female companionship. Perhaps, he thought, he should pass an occasional night with one of the local beauties. He had not had a woman since his journey to the capital. It had been that one night when Yukiko had come him so joyfully, telling him about the child. Later she had lain in his arms with passion and love, and his heart had sung. But that night had been the last one. Perhaps there would never be another now. He thought again of his sister's letter and wondered what was going on in the capital.

∞

That afternoon late, a nobleman arrived at the tribunal. Saburo listened to him and immediately showed him into Akitada's office.

"Lord Imagawa, sir," he announced and withdrew again immediately.

Akitada, looking up, saw a tall man in a dark green silk robe and black hat. He was Akitada's age or a little older, pale, with a trimmed mustache and short chin beard, and he made Akitada only the merest bow, saying abruptly, "I'm told you found the body of a young woman yesterday."

Akitada ignored the lack of courtesy or manners. Perhaps this man was missing a family member and was afraid what he might be told. He bowed in return and said, "Yes, that is so. Please be seated. I think we must have met, but I don't quite recall when and where."

Lord Imagawa waved that aside without enlightening Akitada, but he did seat himself. "My daughter is missing," he said abruptly.

"I see. I'm very sorry. You have only now discovered her absence?"

This angered his lordship. "It's neither here nor there when I found out. Describe the body."

Akitada bit his lip. "The dead woman appears to be about eighteen years old. She was wearing a pale yellow silk dress. Her long hair was tied with a white silk ribbon, and she had no shoes."

Imagawa stared at him and said nothing for a while. Akitada, who was hoping for identification, asked, "Does this sound familiar?"

"It might be her." His visitor stood up suddenly. "Where is she?"

Akitada rose also. "I shall come with you. The body is here in the tribunal. The coroner has it."

Imagawa flinched. "She's been cut open?"

"Not yet. We were waiting for someone to identify her."

His lordship turned on his heel. "You needn't come. I'll find my way."

Akitada ignored this. He followed Imagawa out and across the courtyard to the service buildings that held quarters for the guards, a jail, and the coroner's rooms. He asked, "Had your daughter left the house on some errand?"

"I don't know."

Lord Imagawa's expression was so forbidding that Akitada decided to postpone further questions. No doubt the man was overwrought.

Oyama opened the door to them, glanced from Akitada to Imagawa, and stepped aside. The body lay on a reed mat and was covered with a length of cotton. This latter was an extravagance not usually accorded to the bodies that came here, but Akitada was glad of it.

Oyama walked to it and turned looking at them expectantly. Imagawa snapped, "Get on with it, man!"

The coroner bent and folded back the sheet to the girl's chest. He had tidied her up, and again Akitada drew in his breath at so much youth and beauty.

Imagawa said harshly, "Yes. This is my daughter Hiroko. How did she die?"

Oyama said, "She was strangled, my lord. I'm very sorry for your loss."

The bereaved father ignored this. He turned to Akitada, "Who did it? I want him arrested."

Akitada cleared his throat. "We don't know yet who killed your daughter. Now that we have her name, it will be easier to find out."

Imagawa said, "Very well! Get on with it and keep me informed. When can I have the body for burial?"

Oyama looked at Akitada, who said, "Perhaps in a day or so."

Without another word, Imagawa left.

Oyama waited until the door had closed, then he said, "That was a very strange way to show one's grief. It's almost as if he expected it."

Akitada was equally shocked but said nothing. "Please finish your examination and report to me."

Back in his office, Akitada sent for Saburo. He came quickly, giving Akitada a searching glance. "Did he know her?"

"He's her father."

"Oh, poor man. I had a look at her earlier. She was lovely and so young. Oyama was also moved."

Akitada recalled the length of cotton and nodded. There was something about this girl that moved men. He had felt it, too. It was not the first time a murdered girl had touched his emotions like this. There had also been the very young prostitute they found in the Yodo River. The helplessness of young women in the face of violence always moved men, who all too often were the purveyors of that violence. But her father had seemed so cold. Cold and possibly angry.

He mentioned this to Saburo, who shook his head. "Grief touches people in different ways. It may not

mean anything. And he may feel anger toward her killer."

"Yes. You're right. Do you know him at all?"

"Imagawa? I know of him. He owns a lot of land in
the province. I expect you were introduced to him early
on?"

"Yes, but I don't remember when. I asked him
where we met. He wouldn't tell me. I was embarrassed.
But surely I'm not expected to remember everyone I
meet, and he hasn't done anything in the meantime to
bring himself to my attention."

"He has a large house here in the city and a country
estate in the Shitara district. They're wealthy."

Akitada sighed. "I suppose I shall have to go see
him. Courtesy demands I speak to him myself. And he
may be able to answer some questions. Perhaps tomorrow, to allow him time." He wanted to say "to grieve,"
but he really hoped that Imagawa would be less angry
the next time he saw him.

7

The Island of the Gods

After snatching a few hours sleep and a cuddle with Hanae, Tora got up with the dawn, dressed again in old clothes, and set out for the place where they had found the dead man.

On the way, he stopped for a rice cake from a vendor, then marched on at a good pace along the waterfront. The sun was up and there was a pleasantly cool breeze from the bay. The bay was beautiful as always; blue and silver under a blue sky. Eventually, the town receded and marshes alternated with stretches of rocky or sandy shoreline. Here and there, a fisherman had built a hut on higher ground, pulling his boats up on the shore at night and pushing them back in the water the next morning for another day's fishing.

Many of these boats were already out in the bay by now. They would return soon with their catch, which the fishermen would carry to the market and sell to housewives and cooks for the day's meals. Fish and shrimp were plentiful here, and Mikawa's food was good and nourishing. Even a failed rice crop did not put too much of a crimp into people's meals with the help of fishermen and the abundance of the bay.

Tora liked fishermen, thought them luckier than farmers, and very smart about the treacherous currents in the bay. Today he was looking for someone to take him to Takeshima.

The green island floated ahead on a deceptively calm sea. The first rays of the sun gilded its dome-shaped top. "Island of the Gods" the people hereabouts called it. Tora thought it was very small. It was said to have a shrine at its top, visited by fishermen praying for their safety at sea and for good catches. Nobody else ever went there, primarily because you needed a boat to get to it, and there was not much else to see there.

But Tora suspected there was some other sort of building there. When he reached a point almost exactly opposite, he stopped and gauged the distance. There was nothing to suggest the body had come from there, but it was possible. Of course, it could also have come from one of the many boats that navigated these waters. But the body had been fresh and had been brought in by the tide. It had not come from very far away.

As Tora stood there looking across the water, a girl's voice asked, "What are you doing?"

Tora turned. She was small, almost childlike, but her bare legs looked strong and her bare arms were well muscled. She wore a sleeveless old shirt too large for her and short pants, a costume identical to what the fishermen wore around here, and her hair was braided into a long tail that hung down her back. Her face was rather pretty.

Tora smiled. "Looking."

She came closer and peered also. "What're you looking at?"

"Nothing much. Just the island. Do you always ask strange men nosy questions?"

She grinned.

Nice teeth, thought Tora, who prided himself on his own, flashing them liberally at pretty young women. This one was a little rough and too young, he thought, having acquired more refined tastes with age, but she was pretty enough if she would take better care of herself.

"What's your name?" she asked.

"They call me Tora," he said. "And yours?"

"Michiko. So you're a tiger?"

Tora smiled. "Have you ever been to the island, Michiko?"

"Many times."

"What's it like?"

"You want to see for yourself?"

"Sure," Tora said. "But I suppose you don't swim."

She giggled. "I could, but I take the rowboat usually."

Tora gauged the distance again. "Can you really swim that far?"

"Sure. I can swim for hours."

"I'd like to see that," Tora said with a laugh.

To his surprise, she stripped off her shirt, then untied her pants, letting them drop to her ankles. She stood there stark naked.

"Wait," Tora said, mildly scandalized, but looking his fill nevertheless. She was a beauty without her clothes: slender but well developed in places where he liked some curves: round firm breasts, a shapely bottom, and inviting thighs. Her skin was tanned all over, proving that she spent a good deal of her time outside naked. He gulped and grew hot at the thought.

She grinned knowingly. "You want to make the clouds and the rain with me now or after we've been swimming?"

Tora gulped again. He was old enough to be her father, more than that. There was gray in his trim mustache these days and some gray at his temples. For that matter, he had a son who was thirteen. He swallowed and asked, "How old are you?"

Her eyes narrowed. "What do you care? Do you like your women old?"

Hanae would not have liked that. "How old?" he persisted.

"I'll be fourteen soon."

"I have a son your age."

"If he's as good looking as you are, you can bring him next time." She postured a bit, smiling, running her hands over her breasts and down her sides.

Tora thundered, "Are you mad? Don't you have any sense? You're a child. You shouldn't be offering your body to any man who walks by. Do you have any idea what some men will do to a young girl like you? Where are your parents?"

She looked startled and dropped her hands. "My mother's dead. It's just my pa and me." She frowned. Looking down at herself, she said, "I'm not a child. I'm old enough to lie with men and they like me." She cupped her breasts. "Come here and touch them. I'm as much a woman as your wife or girlfriend. My breasts are large. Men like them."

"You're disgusting," he snapped and turned his back.

When he heard a sob, he turned back. She was picking up her clothes and putting them back on. When she was dressed, she looked at him. "I liked you," she said in a small voice, her eyes filled with tears that spilled over.

Tora felt ashamed. She was, after all, just a confused, neglected child that other men had taken advantage of. "Michiko?" he said. "Don't cry. I'm flattered that you like me, but I worry about you."

She stood with hanging head. "I'm sorry you don't like me." It sounded sad and somehow accusing.

Tora sighed. "I like you. Too much! You're a very pretty girl, but you'll be ruined if you behave like that. I don't want that to happen. Does your father know you sleep with men?"

She turned away. "My father beats me. I'm trying to earn some money so I can run away."

"You don't earn it that way!" Tora snapped. It struck him suddenly that he had never disapproved of the way prostitutes made their living. Quite the contrary. He used to enjoy their company in his younger years. What had come over him to be lecturing this young girl?

He touched his mustache, thinking of the gray hairs in it and wondered what the girl had seen in him. Surely he was her father's age. Perhaps she had just thought him good for a few coppers. What business was it of his what she decided to make of her life? Clearly, her home life was terrible. Maybe prostitution *was* a better option.

Glancing across at the island, he asked, "Could you row me over there? I'd pay a piece of silver for that."

She swung around and looked at him with wide eyes. "A whole piece of silver? For such a little thing?"

He smiled and nodded, taking the coin from his sash and holding it up. "Can you get a boat?"

She nodded eagerly. "We have a boat. Come!"

She ran ahead, her shirt fluttering and her brown legs flying. Tora shook his head, smiled a little sadly, and followed.

In the next cove was a fisherman's shack, a poor, leaning affair of wood that the sun and sea air had bleached a silvery gray. Some torn nets hung over the railing of a small porch, and an assortment of other fishing tools, oars, and baskets lay about.

"Is your father home?" Tora called after her, thinking that he might cause some problems.

"No," she shouted back and ran to where a small row boat had been pulled up on shore.

The boat was very small and, on closer inspection, as old and scarred as everything else around here. Tora regarded it doubtfully. He was not a good swimmer, especially not in the rough waters of this bay. But Michiko was already pushing it into the water and jumping in.

"Come on," she cried, steadying the bobbing craft with an oar.

Tora sighed and stepped into the water and thence into the boat. He lost his balance immediately and sat down hard in the bottom.

Michiko laughed. "Clumsy!" she cried. "Hold on. Here we go." She grasped the oars and took the boat out with skillful, strong pulls. Tora sat, clutching the sides of the boat and wondering if he should have entrusted his life to such a very small and very young girl. The boat bobbed but it made headway.

Nausea rose and the fear of disgracing himself before this slip of a girl. Snapping a few breaths of air, Tora offered to do the rowing.

She laughed.

Oh, well. She seemed to know what she was doing, it was not very far, and it was her boat. Besides, he was paying for the trip.

This practical view of the situation did not prevent Tora from feeling depressed. Not only had he failed to respond with the usual leap of enthusiasm to Michiko's naked body and her generous offer, but here he sat, a full grown man, being rowed by this slip of a girl while he was in a panic that the boat would overturn and he would find himself in the water.

He was old.

He was past it.

He was useless to his master. In fact, he was probably going to make a mess of things.

While he was thinking these glum thoughts, Michiko had taken them close enough that he could see a small landing stage on shore, red-painted *torii,* and a steep path leading upward from there. He decided this might prove interesting after all, and seeing that she had got them here, maybe she would also get them back safely.

His optimism was short-lived. When the boat touched the shore, the girl jumped out and cried, "Help me push it closer!"

Tora rose, overbalanced when the boat slipped beneath his feet, and toppled head first into the water.

When he emerged sputtering, he heard her laughter. He had lost his sandals which floated out to sea. Since the water was shallow, he scrambled after them, cursing, and managed to fish them out, stuffing them into his shirt.

Michiko had tied up the boat without his help. Thoroughly demoralized, he waded ashore.

"Come on!" she cried and ran light-footed up the path.

Tora wrung as much water out of his clothes as he could and squeezed more out of the straw sandals. Then he followed her, much more slowly, because his wet clothes hindered his stride and the sandals squished and chafed at every step.

The path was steep and steps had been cut into it here and there. It passed through a dense forest of broad-leafed trees, laurels and cleyera. This sort of vegetation was not common in Mikawa, and Tora got a feeling of being in another world, one where he was not welcome. Somewhere a monkey chattered, and he jumped. Except for the animals, they seemed completely alone, but he felt as though a thousand eyes were watching him. The ubiquitous black-headed gulls circled above the trees with their raucous cries, no doubt giving warning to the watchers. Michiko was too far ahead for conversation, so Tora kept climbing nervously and miserably. There might have been more painful, or more dangerous, experiences in his adventurous past, but this was one of the most embarrassing.

Eventually the trees thinned and the sky showed overhead. The path leveled. He had reached the top and a very small shrine. Michiko waited with a proud smile. Thoroughly disappointed by the smallness of the shrine, Tora asked, "Is that all there is?"

The girl's smile faded. "What did you expect?"

"I don't know. Some house perhaps, and a small harbor."

She cocked her head. "Why?"

He did not want to tell her about the tortured man. This island had seemed so promising a place for murder, being close to where the body had washed up. "Is the shrine really all there is?"

"The shrine belongs to Sujin and Susanoo kami. They're the gods of fishermen. It's very important to us." Waving a hand at the many folded pieces of paper affixed to the wooden frame that supported the shrine's thatched roof, Michiko added, "We come here for protection and bring special requests and offerings. The gods understand."

"I'm sorry, Michiko. I honor your gods, but I was on the track of villains. This turned out to be the wrong place, I think. And I got wet for nothing." On second thought, he walked over to a simple stone basin that held some water. Rinsing his hands and his lips, he approached the shrine and made a deep bow before it. On the stone at its foot were some simple offerings, presented on leaves or in a shell: a rice cake, a piece of tofu, some seaweed, the sort of food a fisherman might carry with him on a fishing trip.

Michiko pulled the straw rope and rang the bell. The sound startled Tora for a moment, but then he murmured his prayer for the dead man: "Honored Kami, please help me find who hurt and murdered the man with the tattoo." He bowed again and stepped back.

She took his place and also addressed the gods. He could not hear what she whispered, so he asked her afterward.

She blushed. "I cannot tell you. It would spoil the prayer."

He was silent and walked past the shrine to peer through the trees at the sea below. "Is there really nothing else here?" he asked. "What about the side facing away from land?"

"There's just this shrine. Come, I've got to get back or my pa'll beat me."

Tora sighed. He would have liked to explore the place some more, but he had no right to get Michiko in trouble.

They descended the path quickly, climbed back into the little boat, and returned to solid land.

8

A Haughty Man

When Akitada entered his office, both Tora and Saburo awaited him. He searched their faces to see if they had any news and was disappointed.

Saburo said, "Good Morning, sir. I trust all is well with the children?"

"Yes, thank you, Saburo."

He had left them bent over their books. Yasuko was a very good student, better than her brother. She wrote and read very well indeed and spent her free time reading romantic tales that probably were not very good for the imagination of a twelve-year-old. Akitada thought of the murdered daughter of Imagawa. Had she had a chance at romance?

Yoshitada, who, except for some distant cousins, would most likely remain the only one to carry on the Sugawara name, showed little inclination for study. He wrote an execrable hand and had trouble deciphering even simple texts. His comprehension of Chinese was nonexistent.

Perhaps it had been a mistake to leave Yoshi's entertainment to Tora and Tora's son Yuki. Their interests lay with weapons and horseback riding. There, Yoshi excelled. He was said to be particularly adept at using the bow and arrow while on a galloping horse. This was a useful skill for a future warrior, but a Sugawara heir would become an official like his father someday.

This morning, Akitada felt particularly inadequate as a father, but that was neither here nor there. He asked, "Well, what news do you bring?"

They looked at each other, and Saburo decided to go first. "About the case of the farmer Gonjuro: I've searched the archives for past complaints about money lenders. It seems Gonjuro is by no means the first to have had dealings with this Tojo Muneyasu. As it turns out, the other cases—there were six altogether over the past two years—involved Tojo paying fines to the district prefect for lending money to local farmers. The prefect noted that the plaintiffs seemed confused about the transaction and had no proof that they ever paid back the money owed."

"In other words, the same sort of thing happened before," Akitada commented, "and it sounds as though the prefect suppressed court action in return for money. Why is it that word didn't get around and people kept going to this Tojo for loans?"

Saburo pursed his lips. "Not all loans ended up in dispute. Just the ones where the farmer had lost his receipt or never got one. As for the prefect, collecting a fine from Tojo for not reporting such business transactions is quite proper."

Akitada said, "I don't like it. But you may be right that it is a small matter. Still someone will need to warn people. Make a note to direct the prefect to post such warnings in his district. What are the chances of getting Gonjuro's complaint resolved?"

Saburo looked thoughtful. "In my experience, sir, a man who will cheat people now and then is habitually engaged in an illegal business. Tora or I ought to pay this Tojo a visit."

"Perhaps, Saburo, but there are more urgent matters. Tora, what did you find out?"

Tora reported on the interview with Rabbit. "When I mentioned the tattoo and asked about it, Rabbit panicked and tried to run. I insisted and he said there'd been a man asking questions. When I made an attempt to find out more, he said, 'Takeshima,' and ran as if for his life."

"Takeshima?" Saburo looked puzzled. "Which Takeshima? There must be dozens of them."

"There's only one close to the beach where we found the dead man. It's a tiny island. I had high hopes to make something of that and paid a girl to row me across." He shook his head. "Hate to say it but it came to nothing."

Akitada frowned. "How so? It sounds like a reasonable deduction."

Tora glowered. "Stupid girl! She took a piece of silver to take me across. There's nothing there but a small shrine at the very top. It's a poor sort of thing, just some bamboo poles holding up a roof. Only fishermen go there. Later, when I pressed her, the girl said there used to be an old duck hunter's cabin on the other side of the island, but it's not there anymore. Useless twit."

"Why the animosity?" Akitada asked, raising his brows.

Tora blushed. "It's nothing. Nothing to do with anything, I mean."

"Come, now you have me curious."

Tora glanced at Saburo and back at Akitada. "She made me mad, sir. That girl was a young slut. Stripped off her clothes and proposed doing it right there on the beach."

Saburo grinned. "You've still got it, Tora. Congratulations!"

Tora scowled back. "That's the point. I haven't got it anymore."

Akitada wished he had not asked. "Spare me your reprehensible encounters," he said to discourage further revelations.

Tora was hurt. "There was no reprehensible encounter, sir. I told her to put her clothes back on and then I lectured her."

Saburo laughed.

Akitada's lip twitched. "Oh. Well, I suppose you've finally reached a certain level of maturity. Hanae must be congratulated."

Tora said nothing. He regarded his master with sudden understanding and sympathy. So that was why her ladyship had refused to return with him. He sighed deeply.

A brief silence fell, then Saburo said, "It could be another island."

Tora nodded. "But we can't be checking them all. I'll have to try to catch Rabbit again and find out what he meant."

"Perhaps you'd better wait," Akitada said. "He may already have told people what you wanted. I doubt you'll get any additional information, and asking more questions may be dangerous. We'll have to pursue the matter another way."

"So what do we do meanwhile?" Tora asked.

"I think perhaps Saburo could go see the Aomi prefect. While he's there, he can ask some questions of the people and get a better idea what sort of man this Prefect Ikeda is. The business with the fines troubles me even if they are legal. As for you, we shall have plenty of work with the murder of the Imagawa daughter. We'll pay Imagawa a visit this afternoon. You can tell me what you think of him."

∞

Akitada felt a little guilty for knowing next to nothing about Lord Imagawa. He had been preoccupied with pirates in Mikawa and the case of the assassin's daughter in the capital. The latter had gone a long way toward destroying his marriage. The result was that he had not made an effort to get to know the local notables socially. Besides, it appeared that these notables had also been rather unsociable, making no effort to welcome the new governor or to introduce themselves to him. More than three years had passed without Akitada taking notice of them, although he had probably met them at some of the larger gatherings.

Now he wondered what sort of man this Imagawa was. His reaction to seeing his daughter dead had been strange and seemed unnatural, even if one made allowances for shock. It had raised suspicions in Akitada's mind. He was determined to find out more about the man's relationship with his daughter.

As in most cities and towns, the tribunal of Komachi was at its northernmost edge, with the open country lying just beyond. Since the Imagawa mansion was not far from the tribunal, as were most of the homes of the well-to-do and powerful in Mikawa, he and Tora walked. It was of a good size, surrounded by a tall fence with a roofed gate, and stood in a garden with large trees. Several pavilions adjoined the main hall toward the back. Saburo had told Akitada that Imagawa had another home in the country, spending most of the year there, looking after his crops and hunting.

They were admitted readily enough by a servant who took them across the entry courtyard into the main house. Like the house itself, the reception room was well appointed and substantial. The usual silk cushions rested on the raised dais and several very good scrolls of birds and deer hung on the wall behind it. The servant left to announce them, then reappeared quickly with wine and refreshments, assuring them that Lord Imagawa would see them right away. He withdrew again, leaving them alone.

"A substantial property," Akitada remarked, looking around.

Tora sniffed the wine and poured some. Akitada was not interested, but Tora drank, smacked his lips, and poured himself another. "The wine's not bad either," he said with a grin. "You have no idea what I had to drink in that place near the harbor. My stomach's not what it used to be. Glad we're dealing with a better class of people today."

It was quite improper to speak this way in the home of a family who had lost a daughter, but Akitada had long since given up correcting Tora's irreverent tongue. Tora was no respecter of rank or wealth, but his heart was in the right place and so Akitada merely smiled.

The door opened again and admitted Imagawa, dressed in black silk and looking, if anything, even more forbidding.

"Governor?" he said after a quick bow, "what gives me the pleasure?"

Tora rose and bowed. Imagawa ignored him. Akitada remained seated but he returned the greeting politely. "It's very good of you to see us. Allow me to repeat my sincere condolences. I also speak for Captain Sashima here. We came to assure you that everything possible will be done to find your daughter's murderer."

Imagawa sat down and stared at Akitada. "Thank you, but there was no need. I expected the police to show up. So far that lazy lieutenant has not made an appearance. Really, conditions in Mikawa are rapidly deteriorating."

This comment was an open reproof for Mikawa's governor. Akitada bit his lip. There was no point in snapping back at the man. He said, "Lieutenant Akechi and his men are talking to everyone who may have seen or heard something the night your daughter's body was left in the rice paddy. Were you aware that she was not at home?"

"Of course not. The women's quarters are quite separate from mine."

"In that case, I assume you have meanwhile spoken to your ladies and to the maids?"

Imagawa shifted irritably. "Naturally I informed them yesterday. They are distraught, as you might expect, and have no explanations to offer."

Akitada raised his brows. "Are you telling me that your daughter left her home without telling anyone? Did she take a maid? If so, where is the maid?"

Imagawa snapped, "Of course she has a maid. The maid hasn't come back. I assume she feared punishment. The others have no explanation for what happened. I have expressed my displeasure at such carelessness."

Akitada was bereft of words. How could this man be so uninformed and care so little? Apparently he was more upset by the fact that his women had been careless about keeping track of his daughter than by her violent death.

Tora cleared his throat. "Since you haven't been able to get many answers, sir," he said, "we'll need to speak to the ladies and their maids."

Imagawa fixed him with a glare. "Surely you are joking."

Akitada said quickly, "I'm afraid it's not a joke, sir. I assume you want your daughter's killer found. That means we must know when she left, and where she went."

"I forbid it. It's quite improper for unrelated males to speak to the women in a decent household."

Akitada sighed. "You have no choice in the matter. This is a criminal investigation and that overrules your objections. Not only do we need to speak to the ladies, but we must do so face to face. The circumstances overrule the usual arrangements/"

Imagawa compressed his lips. "Normally such things are handled by constables."

"Would you prefer to have a constable questioning your ladies?"

"Of course not. I just meant that it should be enough if I ask the questions and relay the information to the authorities."

"But you clearly have no idea what's been happening in your household," Akitada said pointedly, having lost all patience with this man.

"How dare you speak to me in this manner?" snapped Imagawa.

"What are you hiding?" returned Akitada, glaring back.

Imagawa gasped. Then he jumped up and stormed out of the room.

"Now what?" said Tora, looking at the door he had slammed behind him. "Maybe we'd better look for the ladies ourselves."

"Give it a moment, Tora. I'm afraid Lord Imagawa has had things his own way far too long. He's not used to cooperating with authority. I'm willing to bet he'll come to his senses."

9

The Ladies

It was longer than a moment, but then the door opened again and a tall woman in a dark green silk robe and a black Chinese jacket entered. Two other women, also in dark clothing followed. Two maids accompanied them. Imagawa did not return.

The ladies approached, bowed, and waited. They ranged in ages from their thirties to the mid-forties. The tall woman in green was the oldest. She had been weeping and clutched a tissue in one hand. All of them looked at the floor.

It was the woman beside the lady in green who spoke up first and made the introductions. "I am Hideko, my lord's second lady." She gestured to the woman in green beside her. "The first lady, Kazuko, is

Hiroko's mother. She is very distraught and begs not to be asked anything. The other lady is Lady Kumoi."

Akitada nodded. "Thank you, Lady Hideko. Lord Imagawa will have told you that I am the governor. The officer beside me is Captain Sashima, commander of the provincial guard." He looked at Imagawa's senior wife and said, "We are both very sorry for this tragedy, but we must ask questions if we are to find your daughter's murderer. Please bear with us."

Lady Imagawa raised tearful eyes to him. "I understand," she murmured.

"Your husband informs me that he knows nothing about what goes on in the women's quarters. Is that so?"

They all looked at him now. He thought one of the maids suppressed a snort. Lady Imagawa compressed her lips and said, "My lord is a very busy man. We try not to trouble him with women's aff . . . with trivial matters."

Akitada noted the correction and thought it interesting. "Very well. Then will you tell me when your daughter left the house?"

There was a brief silence, then her mother said tonelessly, "I'm told she went to visit her friend. It was about the hour of the snake. Two days ago."

Akitada looked at her in surprise. If her daughter had not returned from a visit, why had she not thought it necessary to take any action? "You did not inform your husband when she failed to return?"

She lowered her head and shook it.

"Why not? Weren't you worried?"

"I . . . we thought she'd been detained."

"Detained? Apparently she was," Akitada said dryly and saw Lady Imagawa flinch. "Did any of you do anything?"

No answer. They stood silently with lowered heads.

"And no one was worried? Had she been gone from the house for that length of time before?"

"Oh, no," cried Lady Hideko. "Never. Not that long"

Akitada lost his temper. "What kind of household is this? A young woman leaves the house and doesn't return, and nobody reports it or starts looking for her? Your inactivity may well have been responsible for her death."

Lady Imagawa burst into tears. The others looked at him with frightened eyes. Lady Hideko said softly, "We were afraid her father would find out."

"This is not a matter that can be concealed any longer. I assume she took a maid. What happened to her?"

No answer.

"I take it the maid didn't return either. Did you send to the friend to ask where she was?"

Again no answer.

"Who exactly is this friend and where does she live?"

Lady Imagawa raised her head and wiped tears from her face. "She is Matsudaira Tomiko. She lives only a few houses away."

Akitada raised his brows. He had not expected this. Matsudaira was a grand name in Mikawa. The

Matsudaira clan had resided here for a century or more and owned huge tracts of land.

And he already suspected them of being connected with another murder.

He asked, "So you sent to the Matsudaira home to ask if she was there?"

"No." Lady Hideko hesitated, then said, "We were embarrassed." After a moment, she added, "We thought Hiroko had gone to buy some silk in town. She knew I needed the silk because I was going to sew a new robe for my lord."

Akitada sighed. "But you weren't sure about this?"

They all shook their heads.

"And at no time did you mention your concern to Lord Imagawa?"

They all shook their heads again.

"Were all these efforts of concealing the facts due to fears of what your husband would do?"

They nodded in unison.

Dear heaven, thought Akitada, what kind of man is this husband and father? And the niggling suspicions were back. Imagawa was not just without any love for his daughter, he was also feared by his wives.

He sighed. "Very well. You may go. I shall have to inform Lord Imagawa, of course, so there is no longer any reason to hide matters. If you can think of anything else that would help us find out what happened to Hiroko, you must speak up."

They left, a quiet, subdued line of women led by the still weeping mother of the dead girl.

"Can you believe it?" Tora said. "What kind of people are they? The mother wept, but for all we know she was only upset because her husband would find out."

"I rather think he's already aware of the conspiracy of silence. Please go tell a servant to call him."

Lord Imagawa returned with a face like thunder. "Are you done?" he demanded.

Akitada restrained himself. "Except for having a word with the servants of the women's quarters. We must trace your daughter's activities prior to her death. Your ladies are not sure where she might have gone, except for a visit to her friend in the Matsudaira family. The police or Captain Sashima will also speak to your other servants. Your daughter's maid may have some answers."

"The maid is also gone."

"Yes, but she will surely be found."

"Clearly, my daughter was abducted, and the maid has probably run away. I want the monster who took my daughter found."

"Where would her maid have gone if she's run away?"

"How should I know? I expect she ran home, afraid to face her punishment."

"You punish your servants?" Akitada asked.

"I will not tolerate disobedience. Surely my daughter's death is proof of how important proper discipline is."

Akitada thought otherwise but he merely asked, "And where is the maid's home?"

"My majordomo has that information."
Akitada nodded. "Be so good as to send for him."
Imagawa looked affronted but left.

10

The Servants

The majordomo was an elderly man, thin and pale, with frightened eyes. He came in reluctantly and, putting his hands into his sleeves, bowed quite deeply.

"You're the majordomo?" Akitada asked.

Another bow and in a low voice,"Yes, your Excellency. I'm Yoshimine."

"You've been told what happened, I assume?"

The majordomo bowed again. "A very sad day for all of us."

"Lady Hiroko's maid hasn't been found. Your master assumes she has run away. What is your opinion?"

Yoshimine looked down at the floor. "Otoki is a good girl but still very young. She is only fourteen. She may have gone home. I do hope she is all right."

The majordomo seemed to be a decent man. It occurred to Akitada that a decent man would have a hard life serving a man like Imagawa. He asked, "Where do Otoki's parents live?"

"They are farmers in a small village called Shinohara in the Ama district. It's a long way from here. I do hope she's all right. If you find out something, Your Excellency, would you let me know? I worry about so young a girl being alone on the road."

"I will. Now can you tell me what you know about Lady Hiroko's tragic excursion?"

"I only know what I have heard from the others. The maids will chatter, and I doubt they can be relied upon. I understand Lady Hiroko meant to do some shopping, something about a length of silk to make a robe for her father. Her mother is supposed to have sent her."

"Lady Imagawa seems to know nothing about such an errand. She offered that Lady Hiroko might have called on the daughter of Lord Matsudaira."

"Then I suppose the maids were mistaken."

Akitada frowned. "Was she in the habit of visiting there?"

"Yes, sir. Especially lately. The young ladies are the same age and have known each other for a long time."

"I see. It seems to me that neither Lord Imagawa nor you are very well informed about the comings and goings in the house."

76

The majordomo flushed. "I think that may be so. The women's quarters are not really within my purview and Lord Imagawa keeps busy with his affairs."

"Very well. I'd like to speak to the maids now. I suppose you know which ones serve the ladies directly?"

Yoshimine bowed again. "I think so, Excellency." He departed, and Tora chuckled.

"A dry old stick, that one," he said. "No wonder the maids keep their secrets from him."

"He seems to be a kind man. More likely they manipulate him for their own interests."

Tora grinned. "That, too. I'm looking forward to meeting those sly females."

They trooped in, in twos and threes, all ages. There were twelve of them. Imagawa's ladies were well supplied with servants. Yoshimine followed them in and introduced them, not by name, but by their function. Several were nursemaids, two were seamstresses, and two dealt with laundry. In the end, only three were actually serving the senior ladies and sleeping in their rooms.

Akitada looked them over, marveling at so many members of a household and the attendant cost. He addressed them first as a group, asking if any of them had seen Lady Hiroko leave. Two raised their hands hesitantly.

He next asked if any of the women had any idea where she had gone. This time, nobody raised a hand.

"I thought some of you said she went shopping for silk," he said, frowning at them.

An older woman in front stepped forward. "There's been some talk in my lady's room about a new robe she was making for the master. My lady is Lady Hideko. She said Lady Hiroko might go to purchase some dark blue silk as she was going anyway."

"I see, but you don't know if she really went to buy the silk?"

"No, sir."

"Very well, you may all leave except the maid who attended Lady Hiroko's mother."

The woman who remained behind was well past thirty, thin and reserved. Akitada asked, "What is your name?"

"I am called Omon, sir."

"Well, Omon, what can you tell me about Lady Hiroko."

She looked surprised. "I didn't serve Lady Hiroko. Her maid is Otoki."

"I know, but Otoki has disappeared and I cannot ask her. I expect Lady Hiroko spent most of her time with her mother?"

Omon hesitated, then said, "She used to. But lately she kept more to herself."

"Any idea why?"

Again the hesitation. "No,sir."

Akitada thought she probably had any number of ideas but would not gossip about the family. It did her credit but made things more difficult. "What about this errand to buy silk? It was to be for Lord Imagawa?"

She nodded.

"And whose idea was it?"

78

She turned down the corners of her mouth a little. "The second lady's, I believe. She said as Lady Hiroko was going out, she might as well buy it."

Clearly there was no love lost between Omon and the second lady. "Did Lady Imagawa approve of the errand?"

The face before him closed. "I don't know. All I know is that Lady Hiroko left and didn't come back."

"Yes, that brings me to my next question. When did you and the ladies realize that all was not well?"

"The second lady came to my lady to complain when she didn't get her silk. She wanted to sew the robe before dark and Lady Hiroko had not come back yet."

"So this was late in the afternoon?"

"The sun was setting, sir. My lady got worried."

"But nobody thought to notify Lord Imagawa?"

She shrank into herself a little. "We knew the master would be very angry. And the second lady argued against it because it would spoil her surprise gift."

"Why would he be angry at the maids or his ladies? They had done nothing wrong."

She looked down at the ground. "I don't know, sir," she muttered.

"Very well. Thank you. You may go back now. If you or any of the others recall anything else, no matter how trivial, please let me know."

She nodded, bowed, and scurried out.

"Fat chance," Tora said. "He must beat them all."

"They're certainly afraid of him," Akitada said. "But there are still secrets here. So much was left unsaid. It seems not even the death of a daughter of the house will bring it to light." He sighed. "Come, we have done all we can here. Let's pay a visit to the Matsudaira family. Since the two girls were close friends, the Matsudaira daughter may know what happened to Hiroko."

Tora grinned. "One arrow; two birds."

11

The Matsudaira Family

The Matsudaira mansion was a short walk from the Imagawas. It was clear at first glance that it was both larger and more elegant. Tall white-washed walls enclosed a large area. The roofed gate was wide and tall and, like the walls, was tiled. The roofs of the halls inside this enclosure were also tiled with the same blue-green tiles. Flags with the Matsudaira clan emblem flew above the gate.

"A very proud lord," said Akitada dryly. "I dimly remember meeting him at a dinner right after my arrival. I'm afraid I don't recall either my host or any details, except that there were the usual speeches and raised wine cups. Since then, Lord Matsudaira has kept a low profile. I understand he maintains a garrison of warriors in the country."

Tora nodded. "That's what I hear. Perhaps he has his reasons. Can't say I trust those rich bastards when they keep their own armies."

Tora pounded on the gate with the hilt of his sword. A window opened in the gatehouse, and someone peered out at them.

Tora called out. "His Excellency, the governor. Open up and make it quick!"

The gates swung wide obediently. Inside waited several armed men and servants in white uniforms.

They walked their horses past them and dismounted. Servants ran to announce them, and other servants rushed from the main house to receive them.

"At least it's a well-run household," Tora said approvingly.

Akitada glanced around. The gravel surface of the courtyard was immaculate. Tubs with small trees stood about, and more white-washed walls with smaller gates hid service quarters and other buildings. The soldiers had remained near the gate, watching.

They ascended a staircase with a red-lacquered railing. On the wide veranda, they removed their boots, handing them and their swords to a waiting servant, then walked into the reception hall.

It was larger than the one in the Imagawa house, and its ceiling beams were painted with colorful designs. Akitada thought it looked a little barbaric, but clearly his host had money and cared to show it off.

Lord Matsudaira himself awaited them. He wore a fine robe and court hat. With so little warning of the governor's surprise visit, he had clearly made an effort.

Akitada's first impression was that he was a giant of a man. He was both tall and wide. Even his face was broad, resting on shoulders made even wider by the stiffened fabric of his purplish brocade robe.

He came toward Akitada immediately with outstretched hands and a broad smile on his face. "What an honor, Governor!" he said in a booming voice. "Your visit gives me the greatest pleasure. I'd rather thought you cared nothing for me at all." He laughed and his belly shook.

Akitada ignored the hands but bowed politely, thanking Matsudaira for his welcome and introducing Tora.

Matsudaira murmured, "Welcome, Captain," and turned back to Akitada. "Well here you are, Governor, and very welcome indeed. Come and be seated!"

He clapped his hands and one of a group of servants standing by, dashed forward and knelt. "Go see to refreshments! Matsudaira told him. "The rest of you can wait outside."

Yes, thought Akitada, Matsudaira was a very wealthy man with a large, well-trained staff. He wondered if such household arrangements were needed in Mikawa, which, for all its being near the Tokaido and only a few days' travel from the capital, hardly boasted much of a social life. Indeed, Yukiko had found it deadly dull.

The hint that he had snubbed Matsudaira stung a little. He was guilty of avoiding most of the socializing and restricting himself to attending only official and public functions. On the other hand, neither Matsudaira nor Imagawa, nor anyone else had made much of an effort to befriend him. The reception he had just been favored with was somewhat surprising.

As they seated themselves, Akitada said, "You are very kind. My duties have kept me from the pleasure of accepting invitations from the local dignitaries. I'm afraid my visit today is also of an official nature."

Before Matsudaira could do much more than bow and murmur his gratification, a stream of servants entered with trays of refreshments which they positioned next to Lord Matsudaira and his guests. Bowing deeply, they dashed away again.

Akitada looked with astonishment at the array of dishes of pickled plums and pickled cabbage, of six different kinds of nuts, of small pyramids of fragrant oranges, of rice crackers and seaweed cakes, and several flasks of wine.

His host waved a hand. "Please help yourselves. The sake flasks contain different varieties of wine. You may wish to taste them all before deciding." He poured himself a cup and raised it. "To this auspicious day! May your Excellency and His Majesty prosper for a thousand years!"

Akitada resented these formalities, given his current errand, but he forced himself to pour a small amount of wine and raise his cup, saying, "A thousand years to our August Emperor, and may the house of Matsudaira prosper equally!" It was a little lame, but he was becoming impatient. He sipped, nodded his appreciation, then said, "I'm afraid I'm on a rather tragic errand to-day."

Matsudaira grimaced. "Not one of my servants again?"

"No." Akitada paused a fraction. "At least not to my knowledge. Lord Imagawa's daughter has been murdered."

"What?" Matsudaira's eyes popped open with shocked surprise. "Not Hiroko?"

Akitada thought the reaction was genuine. "Yes, Lady Hiroko. It seems she left her home two days ago with her young maid but did not return. Yesterday, a farmer found her body in his rice paddy. The maid seems to have disappeared."

"Horrible! Have they arrested anyone?"

"We must find the murderer first."

"Poor young girl." Matsudaira bethought himself. "But why come to me?"

"Apart from the fact that she was found on your land—which may not mean anything—Lady Hiroko is thought to have paid a visit to your daughter that day. We came because your daughter may know what happened."

Matsudaira shook his head. "I assure you, she knows nothing. This cannot have anything to do with my daughter. Or with anyone in my employ."

"Perhaps not, but your daughter may know what her plans were. I'm very much afraid that I would like to hear for myself what she has to say." Matsudaira looked as if he were going to balk, and Akitada added, "A murder has been committed and the authorities are by law entitled to full cooperation from everyone regardless of position or rank. So will you please send for your daughter? If you wish, you may remain while we speak to her, but you may not interfere."

Matsudaira flushed. "I must say, Governor, I'm a little shocked by your tone. However, the Matsudaira have always supported the law. I ask that you be considerate. My daughter Tomiko will be very upset by the news."

Akitada said, "I understand and regret this, but you must see that we need to ask her what she knows."

Matsudaira nodded and walked out rather majestically.

When they were alone, Tora muttered, "Very high and mighty, these Matsudaira. Remember that island? It also belongs to them along with most of Mikawa."

"I remember. But they are a large clan. It may not mean anything."

The door opened again and Matsudaira came back, followed by a young woman.

Lady Tomiko of was surprisingly small. She had a softness of face and figure that almost made her appear fat. Her very pretty robe combined fall colors and her gleaming hair trailed down her back. Since her eyes were downcast, it was difficult to see her face.

Her father said, "This is my daughter. I told her that her friend has been found murdered. She will answer your questions." He put a hand on her shoulder. "Come, Tomiko, be brave. You're a Matsudaira, remember!"

She nodded and raised her eyes to Akitada and Tora. She had not wept, but Akitada saw that she was very pale. In as gentle a voice as he could manage, he said, "Lady Tomiko, we are very sorry that your friend has died. We were hoping that you can tell us where she went after she left you."

She swallowed and glanced up at her father, who nodded encouragement. Her voice was a mere whisper. "Hiroko went home."

"Was she with her maid?"

She hesitated and glanced at her father again—who nodded encouragement—then said softly, "Yes."

"Are you sure that she didn't mention some other errand?"

"She said she must hurry because it was late. She was afraid of her father."

"Thank you, Lady Tomiko. That was all we needed to know."

Her relief was enormous. With another glance at her father, she turned and hurried out.

Matsudaira became affable again. "Come, have another cup of wine. I'm sure this is thirsty work. I cannot tell you how shocked I am. That poor child. In confidence I will tell you that there was a time we'd hoped she and my oldest son would make a match of it." He sighed deeply and shook his head. "What a tragedy! I must see Imagawa and express my condolences."

Akitada murmured his sympathy, then asked, "By the way, there has been a curious incident recently. A man washed up on shore. He had a small tattoo on his shoulder. It appeared to be the Matsudaira crest. Can you throw any light on this?"

Matsudaira smiled. "There are many men like that, and some women, too. My family once owned slaves, prisoners from the northern wars. But all of them have by now been released and left our service. Many of them were fishermen."

"Ah. That explains it. I think we have troubled you and yours enough. Thank you for your hospitality, but we must continue searching for someone who saw her after she left here. I assume your gate guards saw her leave?"

Matsudaira shook his head regretfully. "No. The family—and young Hiroko was almost a part of it—use a small gate in the garden. She would have walked from the women's pavilion through the garden and out onto Takakura Street. Takakura Street leads directly to her house. It's a very short walk. My daughter used to go this way when she went to see Hiroko."

"Could we possibly have a look at this gate?"

"Of course. I'll call a servant." He clapped, the servant appeared, received instructions, and Lord Matsudaira excused himself, saying, "I think I should go check on my daughter. This has been very difficult for her."

"Of course. Your concern does you credit, sir," said Akitada with a smile. "I'm afraid I got the impression Lord Imagawa is something of a disciplinarian as a father."

Matsudaira sighed. "He's a hard man, but I'm sure he loves his children." With a bow, he walked out, and

Akitada and Tora followed the servant. They reclaimed their boots and swords, then went into the garden, a very extensive one. The servant took them to a small gate in the back wall. It was unlocked and they stepped through, finding themselves in a narrow street between tall walls and fences. There was no one about.

The gate could be opened from the outside with a metal hook. The servant explained that anyone who used this gate would carry such a hook or return by the main gate. It was clear that Lady Hiroko left after her visit with no one being the wiser.

They were still standing there, gauging distances, when a young man suddenly appeared. He was of impressive size, wore the colorful clothes of a rich dandy, and stared at them angrily.

"What are you doing there?" he called out to the servant. "Who are these people? Why are they here?"

The servant, taken aback, stammered, "Your father's orders, master. His Excellency and the captain wanted to see the gate to the back street."

The young man was not quite an adult yet, but he was already as tall as his father and showed the signs of adding weight to his frame. The resemblance was there, but unlike the jovial senior Matsudaira, this one scowled. Though he looked less than twenty, he wasted no time with politeness and demanded, "What's going on?"

Akitada spared the servant an answer and said, "We are investigating the murder of Lady Hiroko. She was here the day she died and left by this gate. And you are?"

The young lord flushed and then paled. "Matsudaira Kinto. If she left, this has nothing to do with us. You have no business here. Best look among the scum that roams the streets these days." With that, he turned and walked away quickly.

Tora said angrily, "Well, so much for good manners! That one must be a great trial to his father."

The servant said nothing, but his lip twitched.

Akitada thanked him and said, "We'll leave this way."

Once they stood in the narrow street and the gate had closed behind them, Akitada looked back thoughtfully. "I wonder how many warriors Matsudaira keeps."

Tora studied the narrow, blind side street. It remained empty. "He owns a lot of land and many farms," he said. "That means he probably keeps servants and retainers both here and in the country."

"Yes. I'm aware of it. What did you think about his comment on the tattoo?"

Tora frowned. "I'd say he lied. I bet that man was one of his people."

They walked along the narrow alleyway, no more than a short cut between the mansions. None of the small back gates in the walls and fences of the houses could be opened from the outside unless someone had the right sort of key for the lock. The area looked clean and swept, and they found nothing to prove or disprove that it had been the site of an abduction or murder.

12

The Inspector

The following morning, Akitada again found Tora and Saburo waiting for him in his tribunal office. Both looked worried.

"Good morning," he said. "Saburo, I see you got my message. I don't think I can spare you, so the matter of Tojo Muneyasu and Prefect Ikeda will have to wait. Has Tora told you what happened yesterday?"

Saburo nodded. "I spent some time in the archives and among the tax registers last night. Shall I tell you what I found?"

"Yes. Go ahead."

"Imagawa Toshiyasu, the father of the dead girl, owns thirty-three farms in Mikawa, and some additional, but smaller properties in Totomi Province. His father served as Recorder of the Right in the capital and reached the sixth rank, upper grade. It appears that he was instrumental in getting tax-free status for most of the Mikawa lands." Saburo frowned and added, "He contributes a mere one hundred koku of rice, sir."

Akitada nodded. "He's not the only one. The government is scraping by on smaller and smaller tax payments almost every year as the private landowners collect their tax privileges. Go on!"

"He's married. Three wives, and one concubine. He has two sons, but three others died young. Of the two sons, one took vows, and the other serves in the imperial guard in the capital. He has three daughters; two are married to officials in the capital. Lady Hiroko was as yet unmarried, but there had been negotiations with Matsudaira for a marriage with the Matsudaira heir. A very impressive dowry is mentioned, so I assume both parties reached an agreement."

Akitada sat up. "Now I wonder! Might that have been that very rude young man we encountered in the garden?"

"I don't think so, sir. The oldest Matsudaira son serves as Junior Recorder in the ministry of taxation."

"No doubt with an eye to doing his own family some good," commented Akitada.

Tora snorted. "Of course. They're all bastards."

Saburo shot him a glance and said primly, "May I continue, sir?"

Akitada nodded.

"Well, then. The Matsudaira family is particularly interesting. It's a large clan with branches in many of the

92

provinces along the Tokaido. Our local lord, Kinsada, is the clan chief. You asked about any slaves and I checked. He and his father seem to have released all of them. His mother, by the way, was Imagawa's great-aunt. There is a good deal of intermarriage between the provincial nobility. But this is neither here nor there. Matsudaira controls enormous holdings here in Mikawa and across the border in Owari Province, though some of them are in the hands of a younger brother, Kinnori. Matsudaira Kinsada is fifty years old. He has four wives by whom he has eight living children. The boys are Kintsune, the oldest, and Kinto. Kinto is still at home, having been expelled from the university. The rest are girls. Tomiko, the one you met, is seventeen The two oldest are married to provincial lords. The other three are younger than Tomiko." He paused, then said, "Matsudaira is thought to rule Mikawa like its emperor."

Akitada raised his brows. "You don't say? Any signs of disobedience or open rebellion in his background?"

"Not at all, sir. He's well liked here and in the capital."

"Hmm."

Tora opined, "Doesn't mean much. They're all bastards. They cheat the emperor and the poor people and keep all the rice for themselves. Then they hire armies to grab more power." He paused, frowned, and added, "We've got a problem. The whole garrison has only forty able soldiers."

Akitada nodded. "I'm well aware of it, Tora. Hence my question. Saburo, how many men can Matsudaira raise?"

Saburo looked aghast. "I don't know. Surely you don't expect an uprising, sir? There's nothing in his history to suggest anything but loyalty to the emperor. Remember, he has a son serving in the Daidairi."

"I have no doubt you're right, Saburo, but I like to be prepared. This murder may cause some disaffections."

Tora was puzzled. "How do you mean, sir? Surely everybody wants the killer found."

"Perhaps, but frankly I wonder. Both families were excessively secretive."

Tora objected, "I thought Matsudaira cooperated."

"Yes. But his daughter took her clues from him. I worry about the missing maid. She has to have the answers."

"Then she's dead already," Tora said glumly. "The killer wouldn't leave a witness alive. And you won't find her till they cut all that rice in that field. Too bad we can't search it."

They pondered this. The rice harvest was sacrosanct. Not even a governor could order a field destroyed unless he had very good reason for it.

Tora was impatient. "So what can we do?" he asked. "I hate just sitting here, doing nothing. For one thing it looks bad."

Akitada said, "You can check the information we were given. Go to the silk merchant. Fortunately there's just one, or we would have to tackle Imagawa again.

Find out if she was there before her visit to the Matsudaira house and if she did indeed buy the silk, I wonder what happened to that, by the way. But my concerns have rather more to do with the fact that both Imagawa and Matsudaira have raised some suspicions in my mind."

Saburo asked, "How did you come to suspect them, sir? One's the dead girl's father, and the other didn't seem to have anything to hide."

Akitada looked at his assistants with a slight smile. "I know, but Matsudaira was a little too cooperative, and Imagawa appears to be a brute who is feared by all his womenfolk. Besides, there is the body with the tattoo. For all we know he still worked for the Matsudaira, even if he was no longer their slave." He looked regretfully at the stacks of documents on his desk. "Well, we'd better get busy. Saburo, send Prefect Ikeda an invitation. It's time he reported. And then help me get the archives straightened out."

∞

A few hours later, Saburo burst into Akitada's office. Startled, Akitada looked up from his paperwork.

"An official has just arrived from the capital, sir. Someone important. He has a retinue."

Akitada's heart sank. "It must be the inspector," he said. "That's all we need at this juncture."

Saburo was clearly nervous, but he said, "Don't worry, sir. Everything's in order."

Akitada gave him a bleak smile. "Thank you, Saburo. I have no doubts of it, but this inspector is more interested in finding things amiss than in approving my work here."

Since he had had no warning—clearly intentional, because the man could have sent a message from his last stop—Akitada merely tied on his black hat and hurried out to the courtyard to receive the important personage.

The inspector had come by horse; apparently he had been in a hurry to get here. With him were four armed men and two minor officials. The armed men had stayed on their horses, but the inspector and his minions had dismounted with the aid of tribunal servants.

Akitada, followed by Saburo, walked up to the inspector, trying to guess at his identity and failing. Though high-ranking—the rank ribbons put him at the fourth tank, upper grade—this man was younger than expected. He glanced around at the buildings and tribunal staff, then eyed Akitada coldly.

"You're the governor?"

"Yes. I am Sugawara Akitada. I'm afraid I don't recall meeting you before."

"Ono Takenura. I'm a junior censor and currently charged with investigating provincial officials. Can we go inside?"

"Yes, of course. This is my secretary, Kuruda Saburo." Saburo bowed and received a flick of a glance. Akitada said, "Saburo, please see to his Excellency's companions and then join us."

Akitada led the way to his office, where he sent a servant for wine and the scribes to other duties. All this time, the censor, who was at least ten years younger than Akitada, had said nothing and looked disapproving. Thoroughly irritated by now, Akitada gestured to a cushion near his desk and said, "I'm afraid you find us unprepared for your company. We had no warning of your coming."

Ono raised his brows. "You surprise me. I know the prime minister dispatched a letter announcing my visit."

Akitada flushed. "Yes, of course, but we had no idea you would arrive today. Still, we'll do our best. I hope you'll be my guest in my residence?"

"Your house? Aren't you occupying the quarters belonging to this tribunal?"

More embarrassment. The man made a practice of being unpleasant. Akitada bit his lip. "That is what I meant. It occurred to me that you might prefer making your own arrangements."

"Why? The governor's residence is said to be quite commodious. Has anything changed?"

"No. Nothing changed, but I have my family here. I hope the children will not be a nuisance."

"I don't expect to see them. I'm here to work."

So much for basic courtesy to ease the unpleasantness of the coming examination of his conduct! So be it. Akitada decided to make no further efforts for this man. Let him do his worst, as he was clearly determined to do.

He said bluntly, "In that case, I shall inform my servants to get a room ready for you and otherwise stay out of your way. You may speak to Secretary Kuruda if you have need of anything."

For the first time, Ono looked taken aback. He said, "This Kuruda, is he your personal secretary or does he serve the tribunal?"

"Both. He will be able to answer your questions."

"Under the circumstances, I would prefer to work with someone who is not connected to you. For obvious reasons. However, I brought my own man and we must do our best. I will need to commandeer this office."

"I'm very sorry, but the business of Mikawa Province continues and I am still its governor. Another office will be found for you. Excuse me." Akitada did not wait for objections, but went to the door to call for Saburo.

Saburo hovered near the threshold, looking anxious.

Akitada gave him a wink. "Saburo, will you please arrange the large room next to the archives as Inspector Ono's office? He has his own staff but may from time to time consult you."

Saburo said loudly, "Immediately, sir."

Akitada closed the door again and returned to his desk.

Ono said peevishly, "I had expected more courtesy. After all you are the one whose conduct is in question."

Akitada smiled. "Some wine, Inspector?" and held up the flask. He watched the expression on the other's face. After the journey he was, no doubt, dry, but he would not give Akitada the satisfaction. He shook his head. "I shall inspect the room you are offering me and then retire to the governor's residence for a bath and a brief rest."

Akitada nodded. "That sounds like an excellent plan. Please tell the servants if you intend to dine in your room or prefer to sample the many good restaurants in town." There, that should let the oaf know that Akitada had no intention of sharing a meal with him.

Ono glowered and silence fell. Akitada debated whether he should carry his own rudeness forward a little and take up his work again. He decided against it, and after a while said, "The weather has been very pleasant lately. Mikawa has many lovely sights and the bay is always near. The seafood is excellent here. There are also hot springs that you may enjoy visiting. Alas, the town does not have a willow quarter, but there are always people who can arrange matters."

The inspector snapped, "I shall have no time for frivolities, though you, no doubt, know a good deal about such matters."

Such rudeness was too much! Akitada reached for a document. "In that case, allow me not to waste any more time." He started reading, then rubbed some fresh ink. Ono harrumphed.

It would be war!

Saburo returned before new hostilities could break out and offered to take Ono to his assigned office. The inspector rose and followed him out without another word to Akitada.

Akitada regarded the closed door with a smile. Perhaps he had been foolish, but the satisfaction he felt at not allowing himself to be intimidated by this yokel and the men who had sent him outweighed such considerations. In any case, there was no hope that he could come out of this with a favorable report. No, he had done the right thing and would henceforth ignore the man while going on with his work.

Saburo returned. "He's not a very nice man," he said.

"No. He's rude and intends to do his best to ruin me. Knowing this at least absolves us from catering to his wishes. I've let him know that I shall not be sharing meals with him nor will I entertain him in town." Akitada grinned.

After a moment's surprise, Saburo also smiled. "Yes, but I'm afraid he may order me about."

Akitada's face fell. "I'm sorry, Saburo. Do the best you can. I'm very glad I didn't send you off to the Aomi district. I have no idea how I would have managed without you."

"Never mind, sir. I have my ways of dealing with such people. By the way, there's been a reply from Owari in regard to this Tojo Muneyasu."

"Yes?"

Saburo made a face. "Apparently he's a man of admirable virtue who serves His Majesty tirelessly as master of Akasaka post station and also supplies horses to travelers."

"Ah! Amazing how a man of relatively low station can amass so much good will from the authorities."

Saburo smiled. "I thought so, too."

"Well, nothing we can do about it at the moment."

13

Michiko

Tora changed into an ordinary blue robe and black trousers before heading into town. His first objective was the silk merchant. His shop was in the business quarter surrounding the market in Komachi. Both the market and the business area were quite small compared to those in the capital. Tora passed through the market, stopping only long enough to purchase a bowl of fish soup from a woman he knew and whose cooking skills he valued. Bestowing the usual compliments and receiving the usual toothless grin, he made his way to the silk shop.

This was a rather modest affair. Lady Yukiko had rarely bought anything here. The owner, a corpulent man, greeted Tora with smiles and bows.

"How may I serve?" he fluted in a high voice. "Perhaps something for a lady? We have some lovely red figured stuff, fresh from the capital."

"No, thanks," said Tora, who saw no reason to put himself out. "Someone from the Imagawa family was here a couple of days ago. Picking up some silk."

"Yes, indeed. They're good customers." The merchant became nervous. "Is anything wrong with the silk? I made certain the piece was flawless. If there is a problem, I'll be glad to replace it."

"No problem that I know of. Just wondering. Thanks." Tora turned to go.

The merchant cried, "Wait! You must tell me what's wrong. The lady herself inspected it, paid what was owed, and handed the silk to her maid."

"Ah!" Tora nodded and departed, leaving a confused merchant behind.

Outside the shop he paused. What next? Had Lady Hiroko set out on the errand to buy the silk and then gone to visit her friend before going home? Or had it been the other way around? It seemed to him there had been some confusion about that, as there had been confusion about whether she had really planned to buy the silk. Whatever she had done, she had never reached home. She and her maid and the silk had disappeared into thin air. It had either happened on that short stretch of road between the two mansions or somewhere in town.

How had she got into the rice paddy?

And almost more puzzling: What had happened to the maid and the silk?

The Island of the Gods

Someone cleared her throat behind him. Tora turned. A rather large woman, who was leaning on the strong arms of two sturdy maids, eyed him resentfully. "Have you grown roots, fellow? Move aside."

"Oh, sorry," muttered Tora.

"Why are you just standing there?" she grumbled. "People can't get past. Seems to me you should have better things to do."

"My apologies, madam," Tora said with one of his big smiles.

She scowled back and waddled painfully past him. But one of the maids, the younger, very pretty one, returned his smile and winked.

Greatly cheered by this proof that he had not lost his appeal to women altogether, Tora remembered the girl Michiko. On an impulse, he turned his steps toward the harbor.

Pausing only to ask some questions of men working near the boats, he started walking along the beach toward the fisherman's house.

His questions had been about any boat traffic people might have observed between the shore and the island of the gods. The answers had all been negative, but he came away with a sense that he was not being told the truth. His interest in the island had been reawakened by this.

When he reached the fisherman's hut, he saw no one on the shore. Only the small row boat lay on the beach as it had last time. The fisherman must be out fishing. Tora shouted, "Michiko! Hey, Michiko!"

Nothing.

He was about to turn away and go back, when the door of the shack opened. Out stumbled a middle-aged man with bowed legs and a belly. He glanced at Tora, grinned, and stumbled off.

Tora was still looking after him in surprise, when Michiko appeared in the doorway. She clutched something that looked like money. When she saw Tora, her face lit up. She danced down the steps and ran to him.

"Tora! You've come back. Sorry about that man. If I'd known you were coming, I'd have turned him away." Her shirt hung loose and open, giving Tora a good look at her breasts. "I'm so glad to see you," she said. "Come inside."

Tora glared and shook his head. "No, my girl! I'll not lie with you in another man's filth. Have you no shame?" Then he saw her swollen eye. He knew it was going to turn black. "What, did the swine beat you, too?"

She touched her eye. "My pa did it. He caught me. I've got to get away, Tora. I almost have enough for a room in town. He beats me all the time, and not just because I've had a man. That's when he takes the money and then beats me. He'll kill me, if I don't get away."

"Why don't you earn your living by working?"

"I tried. Nobody'll hire me. Besides, he'd know where I was and he'd come after me again."

Tora sighed. "Are you sure you want to be a whore? It's not a very good life."

"It's better than what I have. And I like lying with men."

Tora sighed again. With a body like hers and a bit of cleaning up, she was a tempting morsel. "Tell you what, come with me and we'll see if a friend of mine will take you on. At least you'll be looked after."

She shrieked with joy and threw her arms around him, dropping a handful of coppers in the process. Tora freed himself and bent to pick up the coins. "You slept with that disgusting specimen for ten coppers?" he asked, handing them to her.

"Well," she said with a grin, "I didn't lie down for him. I just got on my knees."

Tora muttered a curse. "Let's go," he said gruffly.

"Wait. I'll get my money." She dashed back into the hut and returned with a small clinking bag that she added the ten coppers to. "Ready," she said.

They walked back into town, stopping at a bath house, where Tora paid for her to have a bath and get her hair washed. Meanwhile, he bought her a simple blue and white cotton dress with a white sash and a pair of cheap straw sandals.

Michiko looked almost beautiful when she showed herself off in her new clothes, her long hair loose and shining, and her face all smiles. Only her eye looked a bit odd.

He said gruffly, "You'll do. Come along!"

"Tora, I'm so grateful. I wish you'd let me show you how much."

"Look here!" he said, stopping to glower down at her, "From now on you sell your body. And you sell it at the highest price. You don't give it away!" Remembering her most recent activity, he added, "You give nothing away, do you understand?"

She nodded with shining eyes. "Yes, Tora."

"But if you really want to thank me, you can tell me about the island. I know there's something going on there."

She lost her smile. "Yes, Tora. People go there at night. They don't go to pray. I asked my father about it and he said it was none of my business and never to talk about what I'd seen, and never to do it again unless I wanted them to cut my throat."

"I thought so. But what are they doing there?"

"I don't know, but there are caves on the island. The caves are sacred to the gods and no one goes there. If they do, they die."

He looked at her and decided she had said enough. "All right! Now forget it. Your father was right."

The rest was simple enough. He took Michiko to Auntie Haru, a motherly sort of madam. Auntie Haru looked Michiko over, asked her age, checked her teeth, took her to another room to check her body, and returned to tell Tora that she would do. Michiko did not return.

"Look after her, Haru," Tora said, feeling a little guilty for having arranged another person's life this way.

"Like my own," Haru said, grinning. "You can have her gratis, Tora."

"Thanks, but I'm a married man now."

She giggled at that and pinched him. "Come, Tora," she said, "you're still a good-looking fellow, and that little one made eyes at you."

The Island of the Gods

He grinned and left, feeling rather saintly.

14

The Fan

Michiko being settled, he turned his mind again to Lady Hiroko's murder. It seemed to him that there was no explanation why both the maid and the silk had disappeared. He wondered if they were also in the field, hidden in all those rice plants. He had hoped the little maid, only fifteen, would turn up safe and sound. Now he faced the fact that whoever had killed her mistress would scarcely have spared her.

He had an awful feeling about it. She was a mere child, and not a streetwise child like Michiko. The majordomo had felt protective of her. Surely she could not have been part of a plot to abduct her mistress. And that meant she must also be dead.

His good mood evaporated. Reluctantly, he decided it was time to search that field.

But when he reached it, he saw that the harvest was in progress. The peasant and his family were in the field, cutting the rice stalks and gathering them into large bags slung across their bodies. Most of the field was already mere stubbles.

A large shaggy dog came to greet him, wagging his tail, and carrying something in his mouth. This must be the peasant's dog, the one who had been confined until harvest time and was now free again. He seemed inordinately proud of his toy, but when Tora tried to take a closer look at it, he backed away.

"Suit yourself," said Tora, scratching the dog's shaggy head. Whatever he was slavering over looked extremely unappetizing, perhaps the skeleton of some small creature, a lot of yellow bones held together by something.

Tora had been seen, and the peasant, having deposited his load, came to speak to him.

"You're the one was here before. The captain, right?"

Tora greeted him. "Yes, that's me. A good harvest? I wondered when you'd cut it."

The peasant wiped sweat from his face with his sleeve. "It's well enough." He gestured at the sky in the west where clouds were building. "It'll rain tomorrow and then we won't get another chance for a while. But his lordship will be happy enough, I think."

"That would be Lord Matsudaira?"

"Yes. We've worked his land for as long as there've been Matsudaira."

"That's a long time. He's a good master, then?"

The peasant nodded. "He's fair. His father was kinder."

Tora looked across the stubbled field to where two women were picking up the last sheaves. "The young lady's maid's still missing," he said. "I wondered."

The peasant gave him a look. "Amida! Sorry. We didn't find her."

"Or some silk?"

"No. Nothing."

Tora sighed. "Well, at least then maybe she's still alive."

"I hope so. You haven't found the villain who did it yet?"

"No."

They stood contemplating the empty field, while the two women made their way toward the house behind the trees.

Tora's eye fell on the dog. "Looks like he found something," he observed.

The peasant snorted. "Some old chicken bones maybe."

"I don't know. Doesn't look like chicken bones. Any chance you can get them away from him?"

The peasant reached down and gently pried the animal's jaws open. "Now what could that be?" he said looking at a tangle of yellowish-brown sticks in his hand.

Tora took a look. "You know, I think it was a fan. They make them from cypress wood in the capital. Maybe it belonged to the young lady."

The peasant pushed the sticky mess toward him. "Here! Take it! I wish I hadn't touched it."

Tora relieved him of the brown sticks and what looked like remnants of red silk thread, and the man wiped his hands on his trousers. He cast a look toward the women who were getting close to the grove of trees. "I'd better go. We need to get the threshing done before dark."

"I'm sorry I kept you." Tora was trying to separate the thin sticks.

The peasant hurried off.

The sticks were indeed wood. The nobles in the capital carried such fans wherever they went. Before the dog had got hold of them, they had been a fan, but not a lady's fan. Women used paper fans painted with colorful pictures. This was a man's fan, though it had been painted at one time.

It might not mean anything, of course. The dog could have found it anywhere, and it might have been dropped a long time ago by someone riding along the road, but Tora tucked the sticks inside his robe and turned homeward.

∞

If Akitada had hoped to escape the inspector by staying out of his way, he was disabused of this illusion. As soon as Inspector Ono had inspected his private quarters, he had returned to his new office, conveniently located next to the archives. There he had summoned his people and Saburo. The files and documents of Mikawa province for the past three and a half years were soon gathered and ready to be subjected to a search for omissions, neglect, errors, oversights, and suggestions of more serious infractions.

It was the latter that Ono hoped for and when the documents did not reveal much of the sort, he took his questions, or rather interrogations, directly to Akitada.

Thus it was still only afternoon when he walked into Akitada's study unannounced and without the customary scratching at the door or clearing of the throat, waving a document in his hand.

"What is this business with this Kitagawa?" he demanded. "A local landowner who seems to have been accused of piracy? I see no results of any investigation."

Akitada's heart had plunged on hearing the name. The Kitagawa case had taken place while he had been absent. It had been handled—perhaps mishandled—by Tora and Saburo, and by the time he had returned from Ise, a typhoon had devastated the coastal areas of Mikawa, including its provincial capital. When he sent Tora to arrest Kitagawa, the man had escaped, presumably back to Mutsu where his master, the governor of Mutsu, had given him protection. The case had never been resolved, and the land, which belonged to a member of the Mutsu governor's family, had simply been given a new betto.

Akitada attempted to explain about the conditions after the storm, but Ono waved this aside.

"It's the investigation I'm interested in. There's nothing here. No accounts of the matter, of the charges, of the prosecution. Nothing, except this very short notation by you to the effect that Kitagawa, accused of piracy, fled the province with his cronies. This is totally inadequate and makes me wonder what happened to the goods you must have confiscated."

"We sold them and used the proceeds to rebuild the town after the devastation from the storm."

Ono's eyes boggled. "You were not authorized to do this. And you did not list the details anywhere. There is no account entry for the moneys gained from the sale and neither do I see anywhere the expenditures for rebuilding the city. Rebuilding what? You could possibly use such funds only for public buildings. Was the tribunal damaged?"

Akitada controlled his temper. "The damage to the tribunal was minor, but the roads had to be cleared, bridges had to be rebuilt, and the harbor had suffered a lot of damage from the storm surge. Then there were the shrines and temples. I'm obligated to make sure they are kept in good repair. I assure you, Kitagawa's treasure was quite inadequate for all of it." He did not mention that he had also helped the citizens clean up debris so they could rebuild. Ono would immediately want him to repay those costs from his private salary.

As it was, Ono looked quite pleased, much too pleased. "Yes, yes. And that should all be covered in the provincial documents. I can see that you have been incredibly slack in your duties. I suppose you'll claim the disaster as an excuse."

Akitada said nothing.

"Very well," said Ono, getting to his feet and taking his document. "We have made a start, but clearly we shall have a great deal of work to do here." With this ominous prediction, he departed.

An hour later, Saburo slipped in. He looked exhausted. "I only have a moment, sir. Has the inspector come to ask about Kitagawa?"

"Yes, Saburo. And I'm afraid my explanations probably made things worse. He left looking very satisfied with himself."

Saburo sat down with a sigh and wiped his brow with a tissue, tucking it away again in his sash. "I explained about the storm, but he got suspicious about the time before. He wanted to know what we had been doing about Kitagawa. I gave him a general idea without mentioning your absence."

"He didn't ask me about that. He wanted to know what happened to Kitagawa's ill-gotten gains. He didn't like my explanation that they had been used to rebuild Mikawa. He said there was no evidence of any of this."

Saburo said, "That's my fault. I should've kept notes and later made entries for the archives. But we were all so busy."

"It's certainly not your fault. We all did the best we could under the circumstances. I was very pleased with you and Tora during those terrible weeks. Don't worry about it. Ono came here to find proof of my wrongdoing, and he will do so one way or another. There's nothing any of us can do about it."

I. J. Parker

"That is unjust. To think that you were absent to rescue the Ise Virgin and now you're made to suffer for it! Can't you get the emperor to intercede?"

"No, Saburo. What happened at Ise must forever remain a secret."

"What if Ono discovers you were gone?"

"Oh, I expect he will."

"What will you say?"

"That I went to Ise on a personal pilgrimage."

"He'll blame you for leaving your post. Just as they did when you went to the capital to help her ladyship's brother."

"Yes. I expect that's what brought Ono here in the first place. We must hope he doesn't know anything about the Ise affair."

Saburo shook his head. "It's not right."

A short silence fell, then Saburo got up. "I've got to get back," he said and left, shaking his head again.

Tora arrived at sunset, looking excited and puzzled at the same time.

"Somebody's come?" he asked, sitting down on the other side of Akitada's desk.

"An inspector from the Censors' Office."

"Really? Why?"

"He's trying to find something to prove that I'm incompetent and lazy. I'm afraid he's already succeeded and he's only been here some eight hours."

Tora gaped at this. "What's to find? Is he making it up?"

Akitada smiled bitterly. "He didn't have to, though I have no doubt he was prepared to do so. The Kitagawa

116

affair and my absence in Ise have provided him with proof that I'm incompetent in handling criminal cases, negligent in record keeping, and most likely engaged in stealing from the government and the people."

"That's utterly ridiculous! What did you say?"

"Oh, I mentioned the storm, but to people who were safe in their houses in the capital that meant nothing. He will soon know that I was absent from my post when I was in Ise."

"But you went there on orders from the emperor himself."

"Unfortunately I cannot explain this because no one must know of the sacrilege."

Tora nodded glumly. "I expect they'd blame that horrible storm on that."

"Oh, yes. And any other unpleasant occurrence since."

"What will you do?" Tora asked.

"Nothing. What can I do? Besides, the man is a very unpleasant person. He's Lord Ono of the fourth rank and has brought his secretary and some armed men, who are quartered with your guards. I refuse to share meals with him and shall stay out of his way as much as I can. Alas, Saburo's not as fortunate. Now, what brings you?"

This startled Tora out of his anger. "Oh. Almost forgot. This!" He reached into his robe and placed a bundle of pale brown sticks held together with a tangle of dirty red thread on Akitada's desk.

Akitada recoiled. "What is it? It looks disgusting."

"Well, the dog had it. So it's been chewed over some. The beast thought he'd found some chicken bones, I think."

"Dog? Oh." Suddenly interested, Akitada peered more closely. "That peasant's dog? The one that barked the night of the murder?"

Tora grinned. "The very same. I went back there to look for the maid, but they've cut the rice and she wasn't there. Neither was the silk."

Akitada used one of his brushes to poke at the tangle of sticks. "A sensu," he said. "A folding cypress fan before the dog got hold of it."

"A man's fan, I think," Tora added.

"Hmm. Where did the animal find this?"

"Well, you can't be sure, but the peasant mentioned that he'd kept the dog tied up or inside until after the harvest. When I got there, the field was all stubble, and the dog was running loose with that in his mouth. I figure the most likely place he found it was the field."

Akitada was turning the sticks over. "You think the killer dropped it?"

"It's likely, don't you think?"

Akitada looked at Tora. "It's possible, but that is hardly proof. Still there are some traces of paint and writing under the dirt on this. Maybe we can decipher the writing. The blades seem to be all there. To judge by the number, it belonged to someone of rank."

Tora frowned. "Didn't notice that. The black stuff looked like more dirt to me. Can you read any of it?"

"A few words. It needs to be cleaned up and reassembled."

Tora brightened. "There may be his name on it."

"Oh, I doubt that very much. But it may become useful once we know a little more. Did you find out anything else?"

"Not really, sir. I stopped by that silk merchant's shop. He confirmed that Lady Hiroko had bought the silk and that her maid had carried it when they left."

Akitada sighed. "What can have happened to that maid? It doesn't make sense. "If she's also dead, she should have turned up by now. And if she's not dead, where did she go? Did they have any reason to separate? They were still together at Matsudaira's place, and they left together. The distance between the houses is only about sixty yards. Too bad no one saw them walking home."

"Well, there's something else I found out. Remember the girl Michiko?"

Akitada looked blank. "What girl?"

"The girl that took me across to the island of the gods."

Akitada frowned. "You have renewed the acquaintance?"

Tora blushed. "Not that way, sir. Will you ever trust me?"

Akitada chuckled. "Sorry. What about her?"

"Well, I managed to get a bit more information out of her. There are caves on that island, and boats go there after dark. She was afraid to talk about it, and apparently so is everybody else."

Akitada sat up. "Pirates! I knew it. Maybe it explains that dead man who was no local fisherman but washed up on our shore. Now I wonder." He sat staring at Tora as he turned thoughts over in his mind. He made up his mind suddenly.

"There's something else. I forgot to tell you. We got a response from the governor's office in Owari. Remember that Tojo Muneyasu who is a moneylender and cheats Mikawa farmers? They gave him a report of glowing praise."

"What does he have to do with any of this?"

"That corpse showed evidence of having worked with horses according to the coroner and Tojo is a horse dealer and station master on the Tokaido."

Tora pondered this a while, then shook his head. "You think this Tojo is involved with the murder of that man?"

"Not necessarily. But I'm curious. I'm curious because we have information that Tojo is a crook, and Tojo is eminently well-placed as a station master to know what shipments of value or wealthy travelers are passing through. Such men have been known to work with pirates."

Tora's face lit up. "By the gods," he cried, "That's right." Then he paused. "But wouldn't the authorities in Owari have some notion of his character?"

"Not necessarily. Or someone is protecting him."

That made Tora stare. "Surely not. That would mean the governor's conspiring with highway men."

"And pirates. Part of the Tokaido traffic also moves by water, and both Owari and Mikawa are located conveniently for post stations that keep track of shipping and of overland transportation. But the governor may not be involved himself."

"We have no proof that that's what's going on," Tora protested weakly.

"Oh, yes, we do. Mikawa has been notorious in the past for piracy. Kitagawa was just a small sample. And now we have a corpse and an island where pirates may be meeting and Tojo Muneyasu, station master on the Tokaido."

"What will you do?"

"No point in wasting any more time here. Tell Akechi what we've found out about Lady Hiroko and then take this to the fan maker in town. The man is skillful and should be able to clean and assemble this. Tomorrow you and I will make a short trip to Aomi to speak to the prefect there. I need to get away from Ono for a while anyway, and I've become very curious about this Tojo."

Tora laughed. "I see your point! It will be just like old times! To tell the truth, sir, the missing maid has started depressing me. It'll be good to get some exercise and clear our heads for a bit."

15

Tokaido Bound

That night the rain started. In spite of the fact that it stayed dark very late, Akitada and Tora were up and ready to leave before first light. Tora wore his armor and Akitada his hunting robe and sword. Both wore straw raincoats and straw hats.

They planned to visit the Mikawa post station on the Tokaido. Akitada was by law obligated to wear his official clothes, but he carried them in his saddle bag. Tora had the option of ordinary clothes, but he wore his armor. You never knew when you might get attacked. The roads were not safe.

The rain kept on, falling steadily, sometimes driven by gusts of wind. The roads were not only unsafe but also muddy, which hampered progress since the horses slipped and had to be kept to a slow pace. There was little chance for conversation.

Akitada contemplated using corvee labor to improve the roads with gravel and stone but rejected the idea. It was harvest time and the peasants could not be spared by their families. Perhaps some of the great lords could be reminded of their corvee duties, people like Matsudaira and Imagawa, neither of whom paid rice taxes. They would probably make trouble and complain to the ministers in the capital, but Akitada's tour of duty was almost over, and with Inspector Ono busily gathering proof of Akitada's incompetence, he had nothing to lose.

The grayness of the day turned the golden hues of ripening rice into a dismal shade of ochre resembling some monks' clothing, and the pines lining the raised road were black instead of green. Mikawa Bay, whenever they approached the coastline, was as gray as the skies. The entire atmosphere spoke of failure and coming disaster.

Akitada was additionally made to feel guilty because any pedestrians on the road were forced to jump aside and kneel with their backs bowed. In these conditions the rules of the road were particularly irksome to people. His rank or the fact that he was the governor was not immediately apparent in rain coat and hat, but they were both mounted and Tora wore his armor. The peasants knew when to bow.

As they rode along the coastline, Mikawa's mountains rose toward the east. Between them and the coast was good rice land, and the crops looked healthy. This cheered Akitada until he remembered that his days in a rich province with very little crime, except for the ongoing concerns about piracy, were almost over and that he would leave his post under a cloud. He had gained the people's trust and was widely respected, but his enemies cared nothing for that.

Or perhaps it made him even more suspect.

Behind him, Tora cursed. Akitada looked back over his shoulder. Tora's horse had slipped and almost unseated him. "Damned animal walks like it's wearing geta," he grumbled, then grinned. "The road's climbing a bit up ahead. We should be able to find more solid ground crossing those hills. Maybe we'll get there before dark."

The road improved and so did their speed, though they got wetter and wetter. Once they left the higher ground again they crossed a broad plain. There was more rice land and farms scattered here and there, each house surrounded by its stand of trees. Watering trenches crisscrossed the land, making a checkered expanse of fields, some bare, some still unharvested.

In spite of the rain, they encountered more travelers now, lines of bearers bent forward, weighted down by heavy loads but forging ahead through the heavy drizzle.

Several river crossings meant getting even wetter. There were ferry boats, but since they were on horseback, they could make better time by fording the shallows themselves.

It was getting dark when they finally reached Toyohashi, a huddle of thatched houses. The land was mostly watery around here; they were on the coast and close to a river delta. Toyohashi was port town on Mikawa Bay, and the mouth of the Toyokawa River was an immensely wide area of sandbanks and narrow river arms. On the opposite side was Owari province. The Tokaido highway passed here. Its Mikawa post station was Yoshida. Akasaka, the other post station across the river belonged to Owari Province. It was there that the notorious Tojo carried on his lucrative multiple businesses as post station master, horse dealer, and money lender.

But it was too late to pay him a visit, and both Akitada and Tora were weary, hungry, and wet. They made for Prefect Ikeda's house.

It was a substantial place just outside the small town. Ikeda was a successful landowner, though not a nobleman. His people had long served as lower level administrators in the province. Akitada knew him from the regular visits he made to report to Akitada in the provincial capital. He knew nothing against him and had thought him to be a good and trustworthy official until now.

They rode in through the open gate and dismounted. Grooms hurried up and when Tora had identified Akitada, a good deal of excitement ensued. Visits from governors never happened without warning. Neither did such officials arrive without retinue.

Ikeda came running out into the rain in his house robe and bare feet, goggling at his guests.

Akitada greeted him with a nod. "We are in need of shelter, Prefect," he said and then introduced Tora. "Terrible weather you're having."

126

Ikeda chuckled weakly at this and ushered them inside. "Get rooms ready," he shouted to a maid servant. "And heat the bath."

Shivering, Akitada said gratefully. "You read my mind. We are deeply obliged to you."

A short while later, they joined Ikeda in his reception room, wearing cotton robes provided by their host and feeling warm and refreshed by a soaking in a hot bath.

A maid servant brought in a number of dishes. Ikeda apologized for the poor food, not having expected such important guests, but the rice and a simple hot fish soup were very welcome. And the wine was also quite decent. Akitada was inclined to give Ikeda the benefit of the doubt on the matter of Gonjuro and the money lender.

He raised the subject of their visit. "While I'm very glad to pay you a visit, Ikeda, I must confess that I've come for another purpose. I've had to deal with a case I couldn't resolve. Since it involves one of your people, I decided to come and take a look for myself."

Ikeda bowed. "I'll do my best to be of assistance, Excellency."

"It concerns a peasant by the name of Gonjuro. It seems he borrowed some money from a man across the border, paid it back, but did not get a receipt. Now the moneylender, a man named Tojo, demands more payments. Are you aware of the case?"

Ikeda nodded. "Yes, Excellency. And I can assure you that the man has no case. I'm very sorry he troubled you with his foolishness. Gonjuro isn't very bright.

He came to me also. He's just confused about the matter. He got drunk with the money and fell asleep somewhere. When he woke up, the money was gone and he decided he must have paid it back. Tojo Muneyasu is a very respectable man who generously lends money to farmers for rice seed. I think you can put the matter from your mind."

Akitada's suspicions returned with these assurances, but he said, "Ah, very good. That means we can just look around a bit here, maybe visit the temple, and then return."

Ikeda was all for it and offered himself as a guide to the local sights the next day. Akitada and Tora withdrew to their rooms, where bedding had been spread.

As they parted, Tora yawned. "Well, after a good night's sleep, I'll be ready to take on any villains that might reside here."

Akitada said in a low voice, "You may have to. I think Ikeda lied. And that means he's in someone's pay. Tomorrow we'll visit Gonjuro and ask him a few more questions."

Akitada was suddenly exhausted. He ignored the pile of wet clothes on the floor and crept under the quilt to fall asleep instantly.

∞

The next morning the rain had stopped, the sun was out, and Akitada found that someone had cleaned and dried his clothes overnight. The maidservant arrived with them and hung them on a clothes rack. She then brought hot water and offered to shave him. Ikeda treated his guests well.

Akitada submitted to her ministrations, asking, "Do you know a farmer called Gonjuro?"

She paused scraping his chin and looked sad. "Yes, you honor. Poor man!"

Akitada assumed she referred to his having lost all his money and said, "We'll pay him a visit today and see if he can be helped somehow."

"Oh!" She paused again and stared at him. "Is the other gentleman a healer?"

Since Tora looked every bit the warrior and had worn his armor, this puzzled Akitada. "No. Why do you ask?"

"Gonjuro's been hurt. They say he's very bad. I thought that's what you meant?"

"Hurt? How was he hurt?"

She finished shaving him and mopped his face with a hot towel. "People say he was attacked. He didn't come home and his wife found him by the side of the road when she went looking for him. There was blood everywhere and he was near death."

"I didn't know." Akitada ran a hand around his chin, complimented her, and gave her a piece of silver. She bowed many times, then left, carrying her razor, towels, and water bowl with her.

Akitada was slipping into his robe, when Tora came in.

"I like that maid," he said, grinning. "Are you sure our host isn't to be trusted?"

Akitada looked grim. "Sssh. The maid just told me that Gonjuro was beaten up so badly he may not live. We'd better see him right away. I don't like this at all.

Gonjuro comes to me to complain, and as soon as he gets back, someone teaches him a brutal lesson about making trouble."

Tora's eyes widened. "The bastards. Let's go then."

16

Gonjuro

Ikeda waylaid them as they were asking for their horses. "Your Excellency!" he cried, coming from the house, "Are you leaving already? I'd hoped to show you something of the area."

Akitada said, "Forgive me, Ikeda. No, we aren't leaving. We'll just look in on Gonjuro, since I hear he's near death. Then we'll return and accept your invitation."

"But . . ." Ikeda was momentarily at a loss for words. "Let me get my boots and I'll join you," he offered.

"No," Akitada said firmly. "It will upset his family to see so many people arriving suddenly. I'll just pay my respects. That's all."

Ikeda desisted. They got on their horses and, having been given directions, set off.

Gonjuro's home was tiny and in urgent need of repairs. Outside several small, half-naked children played in the muddy water. The farmer's wife came out to see who had come and stood barefoot, staring up at them, clearly in awe of their appearance.

Akitada smiled down at her. "We came to see Gonjuro," he said. "Is he inside?"

She shook her head, then nodded, then just stepped aside, gesturing at the door.

They dismounted. Akitada told her, "I'm the governor. Are you Gonjuro's wife."

She was still speechless, but nodded.

"How is he?"

He was not sure whether she fell to her knees because she had suddenly comprehended who had come to her home or because the question reminded her of her fear and grief. She knelt, her head bowed and her body racked with sobs.

Akitada decided to go see for himself, and ducked under the low lintel. Inside everything spoke of abject poverty. The rain had come through the roof, and water stood in puddles on the dirt floor. In a drier corner her husband lay on a pile of dirty bedding. His breathing was labored.

There was very little light, and Akitada walked over cautiously. What he saw shocked and nauseated him.

Gonjuro was unrecognizable. His face was grossly swollen, both eyes were sightless, his nose had been broken, and so had his jaw. Blood still trickled from his nostrils and mouth and, ominously, from his ears. His arms lay outside the cover. One was also swollen and looked broken; the other was bruised badly and that hand was bloodied.

"Dear gods!" muttered Akitada.

Tora joined him and cursed. "Animals!"

The wife had come in behind them. She had stopped crying and now just stood there, wringing her hands. "He hasn't moved or talked today," she said. "The day before he moaned. Is he dying?"

Akitada bent closer. "Gonjuro?" he asked.

The wounded man gave no sign that he had heard.

Akitada straightened and looked at the man's wife. "I don't know," he said. "He's badly hurt. What does the doctor say?"

"No doctor. We have no money."

Tora was quicker than Akitada and pushed a couple of pieces of silver at the woman. "Run, get one!" he said.

She gave him a grateful look and bent down to touch her husband gently. "Just you wait," she said, "the governor himself is come. He'll make you better." Then she ran out.

Gonjuro said nothing and probably had not heard or understood. Her promise that Akitada would make her husband better added to the guilt he already felt because this man had suffered this because he had come for his help. As there was no place to sit and nothing they could do for the wounded man, they went outside.

Gonjuro's wife returned quickly, pulling along an aged, white-bearded man in a fusty black gown. "It's

Doctor Ito," she told Akitada, barely slowing down before dragging the doctor inside.

They waited.

"I hope he knows what he's doing," Akitada said, frowning. "Gonjuro looked very bad."

Tora was dubious. "Since when do they have doctors in small towns like this?"

"He's probably the pharmacist. That is, unless he simply passes himself off as a doctor. Maybe I should go in again."

But there was no need. The doctor emerged, followed by the weeping wife. He approached Akitada, bowed deeply, and said, "She says you're the governor. Could that be true?"

Tora snapped. "It's true and where are your manners?"

The old man looked from one to the other and prepared to kneel awkwardly. Akitada stopped him. "No. A man of your venerable age need not observe all the courtesies. You are a doctor?"

"A pharmacist, Excellency, though I live retired now, but still people come to me. Gonjuro's dying, I think. I'm sorry for it. If his wife had come to me when she first found him there might've been a chance. He's got a fever and probably won't last the day. Silly woman asked a monk to have a look at him. The holy man sat and prayed over him but did nothing else." He gave a little snort. "No miracle, I'm afraid. I gave him some medicine for the pain. He took very little of it."

Akitada decided he liked the doctor, though the news was very bad. He asked if he had been paid. The doctor said, money had been offered but rejected. He gestured to the house and the muddy children. "They need whatever they have more than I do." Bowing deeply again, he walked away.

"A decent man!" Sometimes Akitada needed to be reminded that they existed.

He went to speak to the weeping woman. "I'm very sorry that the news was bad. How will you manage?"

She shook her head. "Don't know," she sobbed. "The kids, they'll want food. But the funeral . . ."

Akitada and Tora exchanged glances and both collected a nice sum to tide the family over and pay for a simple funeral.

Akitada said, "We'll find those who did this and punish them."

She just shook her head.

"The doctor said you sent for a monk to pray for him?"

"The Reverend Shinyo," she muttered, staring at the money that filled both her hands. "From the Juraku-in."

There was only one temple in town, a poor affair with a two-story pagoda and two or three halls.

With a sigh, Akitada turned away from the peasant's house. "Come, Tora," he said. "There's nothing else we can do here. I want to ask the Reverend Shinyo a few questions."

At the Juroku-in they also caused some excitement. Clearly the temple was in need of donations. Their request to speak to Shinyo made some hopeful faces fall.

"Is someone ill?" asked an older monk.

"It's about Gonjuro," Tora told him.

"Oh! What a pity!" The monk shook his head and led them to a hall where Shinyo was patching up the scraped knee of a sniveling youngster. With a smile, he patted the boy's head and sent him running back to whatever game had caused the mishap.

Shinyo was so thin that it seemed a gust of wind would blow him away. Unless he practiced some strange ascetic regimen, Akitada thought, he was far from well himself. But he asked his question, and Shinyo's face fell.

"The poor man," he said. "He suffered terribly. I told the wife to have his arm set. It was broken, and so was his knee. They beat him with cudgels and staves. She said she had no money. I cleaned him up a bit and gave him some medicine for the pain. I left some more for the wife to give him. How is he?"

According to the doctor, he's dying. He was senseless when we saw him a short while ago."

"Oh. I must go see them. Poor woman. All alone with three small children. They lost the farm and they'll be evicted."

Tora muttered a curse and apologized.

Shinyo glanced at him, smiled a little and said, "Yes. It's a cruel world. Poor Gonjuro will be in a much better place where he'll be given justice and the good will be rewarded."

Akitada, who stood for justice in this world, at least in Mikawa, was painfully aware of his failure. He had wanted to help but had come too late. All he could do now was to bring the evil men who had beaten Gonjuro to justice. He said as much, but Shinyo shook his head.

"He talked a little, a very little, but he didn't know who his attackers were."

"Did he say anything?" Akitada pressed.

"Nothing that made any sense. I thought he said it happened in Akasaka, but he was found here, in Toyohashi, not far from his house. He had crawled, but he couldn't have come from Akasaka in his condition."

"Perhaps he meant the men who attacked him came from Akasaka," Tora suggested.

Shinyo thought, frowning with concentration. "Maybe. I can't be sure. I didn't want to press him. He was in such pain."

"We understand," Akitada said. "It's something at least. Thank you."

"But," objected Shinyo, "if they were indeed from Akasaka, that's in Owari. Nothing can be done. It's up to the authorities there, and they don't investigate crimes committed here."

"Just as they don't investigate people cheating poor farmers from Mikawa," Tora said angrily.

"Was it about that then?" asked Shinyo. "Yes, that man who runs the post station has a bad reputation around here. I've been warning people against borrowing from him, but they get desperate, and he has the funds."

They thanked the monk again and headed back out into the sunshine. It was such a blue and golden day that it seemed impossible the world could hold so much violence and suffering.

17

Akasaka

When they returned to Prefect Ikeda's house, they found the prefect pacing outside. He rushed to meet them.

"Your Excellency! There you are. I wondered what had happened. I thought we would visit some of the more interesting places while you are here. I'm quite ready."

Akitada dismounted. "No need, Ikeda. We've decided to have a look at the post station and then cross over into Owari."

Ikeda wrung his hands. "But why. Excellency? It's a fine day for visiting the temple."

"Thank you, but we are just coming from there. We're grateful for your hospitality, but we'll push on. I might pay a visit to Owari's governor while I'm there."

The idea had come to Akitada as he spoke. Fujiwara Michinori was one of Kosehira's cousins and so, in a sense now also related to Akitada. He hoped that his ties to Yukiko, frayed though they were, might stand him in good stead.

Ikeda had paled. "But your Excellency, you have no retinue. It's much too dangerous on the Tokaido for two unattended travelers."

"Ah! You have a lot of trouble with highwaymen, do you?"

The prefect flushed. "Well, sometimes. Especially in Owari. There's no security there whatsoever."

"I'm glad you told me. I must warn my cousin."

"C-cousin?"

"Yes. Didn't you know? I'm married to one of the Fujiwara ladies." Akitada smiled.

"Oh." Ikeda bowed deeply. "You are to be congratulated, Excellency. A fine family! Very fine indeed. Can I send some local constables with you? They aren't much good, but they have swords and can run alongside."

Tora laughed out loud at the suggestion. "Prefect," he said. "Both the governor and I are quite used to fighting, and we're armed. Your constables would just slow us down and attract attention."

Ikeda gave in with a poor grace. Tora and Akitada went to their rooms to fetch their saddle bags. Since it was not raining and they would pass government post stations, Akitada put on his official hat but tucked away the rank ribbons.

Tora asked, "Were you serious about seeing your cousin?"

Akitada chuckled. "Yes, though I doubt he considers himself related to me. I owe him a visit and decided that we might need some support in case we run into trouble with Tojo."

The world had dried out somewhat, which was just as well as they now rode across a wide plain within sight of the bay. Yoshida, the last post station in Mikawa if you traveled the Tokaido from the east toward the capital, was small and primarily busy with seeing travelers and supply trains across the wide delta of the Toyokawa River.

The few houses belonged mostly to people who worked on the Tokaido and did some farming. The Tokaido, a major link between the capital and the eastern provinces served not only ordinary travelers, but also government personnel, and the endless numbers of supply trains of goods that were produced in the provinces and bound for the capital. The workers were employed by the post station, some to look after the horses, stationed there for government use, some as ferrymen, some as bearers or messengers. Already small groups of travelers had arrived and waited for service of one kind or another.

Much of the river mouth was silted up badly, and the river had split into five or six arms before it reached the bay. In between lay wide sandbanks. The sandbanks could be walked across but two of the river arms were too deep and the current too rapid to wade across. Here ferrymen plied flat-bottomed boats and carried passengers across. Government personnel carried wooden permits and traveled free. If they traveled far, they were also allowed horses and free food. Neither Akitada nor Tora qualified. Mikawa was thought to be close enough to the capital to make its officials pay their own way.

Yoshida offered little beyond a small office, a guest house, and a small stable. Akitada paused only long enough to watch if people carried out their duties properly. Satisfied, he and Tora walked inside the small office to pay for the crossing. Akitada asked the post-master whether the highway ahead was safe.

He adjusted his bow to their presumed status and said, "Two incidents only, your lordships. And both attacks were made on big pack trains. One happened between here and Totomi Province, the other in Owari. They don't seem to bother with ordinary travelers. You should be safe enough. Where are you going?"

Akitada said they were bound for the capital. The stationmaster bowed deeply again and wished them a safe trip all the way.

Akitada was frowning as they turned away. "How do they get the news of valuable goods coming through?"

"Maybe they have watchers up and down the high-way," offered Tora.

Akitada nodded glumly as he thought about the situation.

They set out across the sandbanks and crossed two smaller arms of the river on horseback, passing some nuns and some more well-to-do travelers in kago. The nuns were slow, but the kago-bearers were running at a good pace, considering the burden of their passengers who were suspended between them from the thick pole that rested on their shoulders.

Above them stretched a blue sky, and geese flew northward, calling out to each other.

At the deepest part of the river, groups of travelers had already gathered, waiting for the ferry.

Tora and Akitada dismounted, showed their permits and climbed into a boat. Two agile and half-naked youngsters swung themselves into their saddles and took the horses across. Tora watched them anxiously to make sure they did not mistreat or injure the horses.

This form of travel was repeated once more before they reached solid land again and found themselves in a sizable town.

Akasaka.

This post station was much larger than the previous one and included several types of lodging, horse stables with pastures, and restaurants.

They had been listening to the travelers who had come on the same boat. Apparently Akasaka had a reputation for good food and willing women. The town supposedly housed the most beautiful prostitutes on the entire Tokaido. Tora decided they must check out the town.

Akasaka's restaurants, wine shops, and lodging houses crowded together on both sides of the road. Maids and waitresses were outside, beckoning in the travelers, promising all sorts of delights, thus promoting not only the business of their employers, but also their own.

Tora was in a very good mood, pointing out comical encounters and laughing at the determined attempts of the women to pull men inside and the weakening reluctance of several travelers. Hearing Tora laugh, Akitada's heart lifted as well. He had missed that hearty laughter and worried frequently about his old friend's health. But here and now the old Tora had emerged again.

They had left their horses at the post station to be fed and watered and now decided to eat in a restaurant not blessed with aggressive waitresses. They found the food good and the wine passable. Tora smacked his lips over some fried abalone. When they were done, he stretched, belched, and said, "The trouble with a good meal is that it makes you sleepy."

"No time for rest!" Akitada waved over the waiter to pay for their food. Giving the man a generous tip, he asked, "What's the road to Nagoya like?"

The waiter was pleased and assured them, "Excellent. You should make good time."

"Is it safe? Any bandits?"

The waiter grinned. "It happens, but they attack only the rich transports. Besides you two gentlemen are well armed. They wouldn't dare."

"That's reassuring. About how many bandits are there when they make an attack?"

"Maybe six or seven. Maybe ten. It depends. They're quick and gone before the bearers can do anything." The waiter smiled almost proudly. "They're good, those guys." He bowed again and was gone.

Tora glowered after him. "I suppose he's got a cousin or two among them. What a place! Now will we go take a look at that villain Tojo?"

"Very well! Lead the way."

With his rank ribbons out of sight, Akitada could be presumed to be of lower rank than the handsomely armed Tora. This amused him and he walked a step or so behind. Tora clearly enjoyed the role reversal, shooting an occasional glance over his shoulder to see how Akitada was taking it. Akitada laughed.

Both knew this was not a game.

The Akasaka post station encompassed an entire compound of buildings. At first glance, the activities looked merely typical of any important post station with a pack train passing through. The courtyard was filled with travelers and bearers. The bearers squatted on the ground next to their burdens, awaiting orders from their overseer. It was too early for them to stop for the night, so they enjoyed a brief rest. Their load appeared to be mainly rice. As pack trains went, this one was not large, a mere twenty men or so. Akitada did not see any armed guards and wondered. This lack of protection made them vulnerable to attacks by bandits.

But just then a very fat man emerged from the door of the station. He was with another man of ordinary appearance. They looked over the bearers and their goods. The fat man seemed to count them. A brief discussion ensued and the ordinary man, presumably the overseer of the pack train reached into his sash to pay the fat man. The fat man counted the money, then waved over two big men who had been leaning against the wall of the building, looking bored. They lumbered over, received instructions, and joined the pack train.

"He's hired protection," Akitada said.

"Those two ugly brutes are supposed to keep that pack train safe?"

Tora had a point. The two looked more like bandits than respectable hired swordsmen. One had an ugly scar across his face, evidence of some past fight. Both were armed with swords but looked unkempt.

Akitada said, "The fat man must be Tojo. Given his character, he may be working with the robbers. He's well-placed for it, seeing exactly what passes through here and what its value may be."

"Amida! That's terrible. Those bearers won't put up a fight."

"Of course not. I think we should follow them until Nagoya. Just in case."

Tora glanced at Akitada. "I'd like a good fight myself, sir, but you've got a family to consider. And besides, won't that be very slow?"

Akitada said dryly, "You have a family, too. This has never stopped you before. Besides, I don't see what choice we have. If there is an attack, perhaps we can scare them off."

It was likely to be dangerous and he felt a small thrill. He thought about the children. Kosehira would look after them if something were to happen to him, and he would leave them well provided for. And there was something else. This journey had finally given him a chance to get away from all the dreary formalities and repetitive duties of his life. For a little while, he would try to forget them and trust in his ability to defend himself.

Better the uncertainty of action than the safety of inaction.

But the pack train was not ready to leave just yet. Tora and Akitada watched and wandered about among the other travelers who had come for information or to rent horses or engage kago bearers. Among the latter was a neatly-dressed man who traveled with his carefully veiled wife.

Akitada said, "The monk said Gonjuro was talking about Akasaka. Since he was in no condition to have come from there, I think he blamed the attack on someone from Akasaka."

"They'll hardly own up to beating a man to death."

Akitada sighed. "No. You're right. But why don't you chat with those grooms over there. Ask them if they're missing any of their men."

Tora raised his brow. "You're thinking of the dead man on the beach?"

"Yes. The coroner said he had been working with horses."

Tora walked away.

Akitada looked into the post station. The main office of the station contained two clerks who dealt with requests for horses or bearers. He saw that Tojo worked in a separate room behind the office. He was talking to some people he could not see.

Akitada watched the clerks. The man with the veiled woman had come in and was negotiating for the service of kago-bearers and the rental of a horse.

Tora returned a short while later. "You were right. They're missing one man who hasn't come back from a trip to Mikawa. His name's Tomezo. They're complaining that he left them with too much work. You think he's the dead man?"

"I don't know, but now that we have a name, we can check."

At that moment, three thugs came out of Tojo's office. They had the faces and the manner of men used to the lowest forms of crime. Like the two who had been assigned to guard the pack train, their hair was unkempt, they were scarred, and they wore the flashy clothes favored by low-class but successful crooks. All three were armed. One had a sword slung over his shoulder; the other two had pushed long knives through their belts.

As they passed, Tora stumbled clumsily, bumping into the man with the sword. The thug erupted in curses.

Tora glowered back. "Watch where you're going, oaf!" he snapped.

The man reached for his sword, then took in Tora's armor and Akitada's formal attire. Grunting something unpleasant, he turned away and the three men left.

"What was that all about?" Akitada asked, puzzled.

Tora grinned. "I wanted a good look at his tattoo?"

"His tattoo?" Light dawned. "Oh. Well? Did you get a good look at it?"

"On his arm. It says 'dog'."

"Really? I think that's a type of tattoo given to convicts. Come on, let's see what they're up to."

18

The Attack

Outside, the three thugs were climbing on horses and riding off through the gates.

Tora asked, "Do you think the Matsudaira are involved in this?"

"I don't know." Akitada rubbed his ear. "There's not enough to go on. It's very easy to make mistakes when you don't know who your enemy is." He had felt once again the ground shifting under his feet. The decision to travel on and pay a visit to Owari's governor in hopes of learning something about Tojo and about piracy activities between the provinces had just become a good deal more dubious. He had no idea if he could trust Fujiwara Michinori. After all, Kitagawa had worked for a Fujiwara, even though that one belonged to the northern branch of the large family. He also did not know if this governor extended his protection to the Matsudaira clan, who had large holdings in Owari.

But the governor was well in the future. At the moment, they had reason to think there would be an attack on the pack train, probably on the next stretch of the Tokaido. They could not let the pack train be robbed without at least making an attempt to scare the bandits away.

But it was another hour before the pack train was ready to depart. By then, the sun was already setting, and the bearers grumbled. They had hoped to stay the night in Akasaka.

Tora and Akitada watched them load the rice bales on their backs, line up and, on a command from their mounted overseer, start off at a fast trot, singing "hussa, hussa, hussa" to keep in rhythm. Somewhat to Akitada's surprise, the man with the veiled female had decided to join the pack train. He now also had a horse and his lady traveled in the kago between two bearers, who joined in the sing-song of the others. The end of the procession was made up by the two armed men, now mounted. Evidently the young couple had decided to benefit from their presence.

Tora went to get their horses and brought them back, saddled and rested. They mounted and started after the pack train.

At this late hour the traffic on the Tokaido had thinned a great deal. A government messenger passed them at a gallop. A farmer headed homeward from the market. A pair of monks walked along, chatting and leaning on their long staffs. The pack train had disappeared.

Akitada and Tora passed the monks, who were walking at a leisurely pace. The road was level and very good. The raised roadway was partially paved and lined with pine trees. All about them were rice fields and farms, and to their left the bay sparkled in the last rays of the setting sun.

Dusk came quickly. By the time they had left the plain behind and the road was climbing into a small mountain range, the sun had disappeared.

Tora looked ahead to where forest hid the road. "I don't like this," he said. "Let's try to catch up with that pack train."

"It's still fairly light, and we must be close to the next post station," Akitada said, but he spurred on his horse.

"Those bearers have been moving faster than I'd have thought possible," he shouted across to Tora when they had covered a mile without seeing the pack train. They were riding abreast now that there was no one else on the road.

"Eager for bed, no doubt." Tora grinned.

"You want to stop at the next station or go on to Nagoya?" Akitada called back.

"I'm for going on, but it will be dark."

Akitada gestured at the sky. "We'll have the moon."

Before Tora could answer, they heard noise up ahead somewhere. They were by now in the forest, though some light still remained in patches. Akitada reined in his horse.

"Listen!"

Tora stopped also. Then they both heard it. Shouts. A woman's screams. Whinnying horses."

Tora cursed and spurred his horse forward, his hand already drawing his sword. Akitada followed suit.

In this mountainous area, the road had become uneven and they could not go very fast.

As he rode, a sudden memory rushed through Akitada's mind: the street in front of their house, the overturned palanquin, and Yukiko with the madman's knife at her throat. He had also been on horseback and with his sword drawn, and he had come too late. His life had fallen apart as a result.

They gained a high point and saw below them in the semi-darkness the bearers and their loads scattered along the side of the road, the overturned kago, and among them strange men, men with knives and swords, and farther along horses and more men loading rice bales on them.

Tora roared something and kicked his horse into a neck-breaking gallop down the uneven roadway.

There were warning shouts, and the bandits paused to stare.

Akitada followed a little more cautiously. If Tora had hoped that his shouting and sudden appearance would send the bandits scampering, he had been wrong. Those with weapons stood their ground. The rest started loading the horses again in a hurry. The situation had just turned dangerous.

Tora was already among some bandits, perhaps two or three, slashing down right and left with his sword, his horse rearing, and men jumping aside. Akitada flung his own animal into the fray and collided with a bandit. The long Sugawara blade bit down at the man, as he tumbled. But another bandit came from the side, his long knife raised and slashed at the horse. The animal screamed, reared and threw Akitada. He came down hard on his sword arm, momentarily leaving him help-less. As he was trying to raise himself, he saw the man with the scar. He was coming for him, teeth bared and gleaming in the moonlight, his sword raised. Akitada thought himself lost, shamefully killed by a mere bandit on a highway. But Scarface did not reach him. With an animal snarl, Tora ran him down and slid out of the saddle.

Akitada's horse had taken off wildly. Tora's followed it. The man with the scar was cursing and trying to get to his feet. Tora cut his head off with a single swipe of his sword. The blood that spurted from the wound was blacker than the night.

Strangely, there had been relatively little noise ex-cept the sound of metal striking metal when swords met knives, the heavy breathing of the horses, an occasional moan from a wounded bearer, and the grunts and growls of the fighting men. But suddenly it was almost silent.

Akitada thought it was over, but then he saw that the bandits, four of five of them, had decided to defend their take. Akitada, still winded and off balance, only managed to bash the hilt of his sword into the snarling face of one man and swung around just in time to avoid a slashing cudgel. Behind him, Tora shouted, "Kill the bastards!" and someone screamed.

Akitada swung his long sword in a wide arc to make himself some room, then turned to look for Tora. He was barely in time to strike at a man who was jumping on Tora's unprotected back, his knife raised high.

After that it was over. The remaining bandits were running. There was no point in following, so they stood and watched them escape. The roadway was littered with rice bales, bearers, and bodies. Their attackers had even discarded those bales that they had already managed to load, swung themselves into the saddles, and a moment later they were gone.

Akitada wiped sweat from his face. Beside him, Tora staggered to the side of the road and sat down abruptly. Akitada, who had been scanning the pack train bearers looking for wounded and wondering about their horses, glanced over at him.

Tora was covered with blood as black as ink!

Akitada was beside him in a few large strides. "You're bleeding. Where are you wounded?" he asked, his heart in his throat

Tora looked up at him, then down at himself. He did a quick check, then shook his head. "Not mine. What about you?"

"I'm all right." But suddenly Akitada's knees buckled and he sat down beside Tora. "Thank heaven," he muttered, having forgotten totally his previous bravado. "Thank heaven, you're all right, Brother. You frightened me."

Tora gave him a crooked smile. "Good for another battle, eh?"

They smiled at each other. Tora had tears in his eyes, and Akitada felt a strange kind of joy. He put a hand on Tora's knee. "I thank heaven for you. Fate gave me the brother I never had. I don't want to lose you."

Tora briefly touched Akitada's hand, then cleared his throat. "How're we going to manage without horses?" he asked, looking away, embarrassed.

The bearers had started moving about chattering with excited voices, tending to two of their own who seemed to have minor wounds. Their overseer came to speak to them. He had a bloody rag tied around one hand.

Stopping before them, he bowed. "We thank you for your help, honored sirs," he said.

Akitada rose. "You're welcome, but you can help us find our horses."

The man turned and shouted an order to the bearers. Then he said, "It was very lucky that you came along just then."

Tora also got to his feet. He chuckled. "Don't be silly, man. We've been following you from Akasaka. That villain of a post station master set you up. Those two guards he gave you were part of that gang."

The overseer turned to look around. "They're gone," he said blankly.

"One's still here." Tora walked over to one of the bodies and turned him over on his back. It was the man with the scar.

The master shuddered. "Horrible. What shall we do about the gentleman?" He nodded toward the kago. Beside it, the man lay on the ground. The veiled woman, no longer veiled, was bent over him.

Akitada walked over. "Is your husband wounded, madam?" he asked.

She raised a tear-stained face to him. "They wanted to take me with them. He argued with them. One of them stabbed him."

"Where?"

She gestured to her husband's chest. Akitada saw that her veil now stopped the bleeding from a wound in his side. It was just below his rib cage.

Tora had joined them. He took in the situation quickly, checked the wound, and said. "It's stopped bleeding, but it looks deep. He'll have to ride in the kago."

She said, "He cannot travel like this. We must stay here and wait for a doctor."

Akitada shook his head. "You cannot stay here. They may come back."

She shuddered. "Very well. I'll ride his horse." She turned to the two bearers who stood beside the kago. "You must take him very gently. Please. I'll pay you extra."

They nodded eagerly enough. With their help and Tora's, they lifted the wounded man into the kago. He muttered something and passed out again."

Akitada turned back to the pack train's overseer and pointed to the bodies. "Drag them off to the side, then load up your men. We'll go on to the next post station.

There you make a report and leave it to them to clean up."

The man looked frightened. "Do you think they'll come back?"

Akitada saw that someone had found their horses. "Don't worry. We'll follow you. After that you're on your own."

19

Nagoya

Just before they reached the next post station, they passed a temple and monastery. Akitada sent the pack train ahead with Tora, while he took the young woman and her wounded husband to the temple.

There they found a monk in residence who had some medical skill and would look after the wounded man. The young woman was allowed to shelter there as well and stay with her husband.

To Akitada's surprise and admiration, she was quite calm and businesslike. She paid off their bearers and thanked Akitada for his assistance.

By the light of the candle burning in the room where he was taking his leave of her, he saw that she was both older and more beautiful than he had thought her earlier. On an impulse, he told her he was traveling on to Nagoya but would return this way in a day or two. He would look in on her and her husband then.

She blushed a little at this and gave him her hand. "You are most kind," she said. "I don't want to trouble you, but the fact is that we are quite alone and far from help. If you do stop by, you might carry a message for me and post it."

He agreed readily. Her eyes were quite lovely. She reminded him of someone from his past, but he could not search his memory while he held her warm hand. Embarrassed, he let it go and said, "I'm Sugawara Akitada. Currently I serve as governor of Mikawa." He saw her eyes widen at this and went on quickly, "May I know your husband's name and yours?"

She blushed again and bowed very quickly and deeply. "Forgive me, Your Excellency," she said softly. "My manners . . . but I had no idea." She was still blushing when she looked him in the eyes again. "My husband is Iseya Heishiro. He's the schoolmaster of the provincial school in Totomi Province. I'm called Sadako."

"I hope all will soon be well with him," he said, bowed, and left.

∞

They did not reach Nagoya and the Owari tribunal until late at night. Not only did they have another thirty miles to cover from the site of the attack, but reporting what

160

had happened took additional time. At least Akitada's horse proved to be only slightly wounded in the hindquarter from the knife attack.

When Akitada had rejoined Tora, the latter had asked about the wounded man.

"I don't know," Akitada had said. "It had seemed a deep wound, but it was dark and I didn't look closely. What did you think?"

"I didn't think he'd survive the trip to the temple."

"That bad? Poor woman! I told her we'd check on them on the way back."

Tora looked surprised at this. "Well, she's very pretty," he commented, with a smile.

Akitada snapped, "Only you would think of that under the circumstances."

Tora laughed.

The tribunal was locked up for the night, but they roused a sleepy-looking guard by determined pounding at the gate. The guard was ill-pleased and had a good mind to turn them away—especially when he took in the blood stains on their clothes.

Tora, tired and frustrated, barked, "Pull yourself together, you bag of useless garbage! This is His Excellency, Lord Sugawara, Governor of Mikawa."

Akitada smiled and reattached the rank ribbon to his hat. The guard gaped, bowed, and opened the gate wide.

The tribunal resembled the one in Mikawa, though perhaps it was somewhat larger. The governor's private residence was part of the tribunal compound and that was where they were taken.

Fujiwara Michinori joined them, sleepy-eyed and irritated, but also curious.

"Sugawara? Can it be? And covered with blood. What in heaven happened to you?" He glanced at Tora.

Akitada made the introductions, apologized for their late arrival, and explained about the bandit attack.

Michinori shook his head. "Foolish thing, to travel with only one companion. You should've known better."

"Yes." Akitada was quite ready to agree, since Michinori had a point. "But things escalated. We had set out to look into a complaint about an Owari post station master and found it necessary to accompany a pack train. There were rather strong indications it would be attacked. Paying you a visit was an afterthought since we were already halfway."

It was not the most flattering speech to make under the circumstances, but Michinori took it quite well. "I see," he said, "Well, I suppose what you need most right now is a bite to eat and bed. We can talk in the morning about your adventure." He gave a chuckle. "I see you're up to your usual exploits, Akitada."

A practical man! Akitada was inclined to like him.

They were shown to rooms, told the bathwater was still hot, and found a light supper and the bedding spread when they returned from their bath. Akitada ate very little and slipped under the covers. Yes, he thought, it had been like old times. An adventure. And he fell asleep smiling.

∞

The Fujiwara Michinori they encountered the next
morning was a far more cheerful, jovial man. He came
to embrace Akitada and called him "cousin." Tora he
made welcome also. They shared their morning meal
with another person, this one Tora's equal at the Owari
tribunal, a Captain Kawamura. Tora relaxed immediately and they chatted quite amiably with each other about
their staff and the quality of the new recruits and new
methods of drilling them.

The meal was excellent. In addition to a flavorful
gruel, there was rice, dried bonito, cooked shrimp, and
platters of fresh fruit.

"How's your lady?" Michinori asked after he had
enquired about Akitada's rest.

"She serves at court," Akitada said, adding with
some embarrassment, "I haven't seen her since this past
spring, but she is quite well. Thank you."

"Yukiko always was a remarkable girl," said
Michinori with a chuckle. "Very smart for her age.
Kosehira dotes on her. I must say it surprised me that
he married her to you."

Akitada, who had been rather surprised himself, was
not offended. "Kosehira is my best friend," he said with
a smile. "I had lost my wife the previous year, and I
think he pitied me."

His host laughed at this. "You should know
Kosehira better. No, he always thought you were the
most brilliant, the bravest, and the most loyal of men.
Nothing but the best for his Yukiko, you see."

Akitada thought that Kosehira's exaggerated opinion
of him was surely partly responsible for the fact that

Yukiko had eventually found him a great disappointment. But he only said, "Thank you. You're very kind, but I'm none of those things and not exactly in favor at court at the moment. As a matter of fact, an imperial investigator, a man called Ono, is in Mikawa at this very moment, doing his best to find enough evidence of malfeasance to get me recalled."

Michinori's eyes grew round. "You mean you left him there?"

Akitada nodded. "He's a very unpleasant man."

Michinori gave a laugh and slapped his knees, causing Tora and the Owari captain to look at them curiously. The governor said, "You're certainly a brave man, Akitada. Not that it needed proving. Tell us about your meeting with the bandits."

Akitada obliged and Tora filled in any details he might have missed. The faces of their listeners grew longer and longer. When they were done, Michinori looked at Captain Kawamura. "I want something done immediately," he said. "Send your men to arrest this Tojo and those of his people who appear to be involved. They'll be witnesses against him. And so will the pack train people. You should be able to catch up with them if you're quick." He paused, frowning. "And stop at Narumi station. They may have more information."

Narumi was the station where Akitada and Tora had parted from the pack train.

Tora said quickly, "If you permit, sir, I'd like to accompany the captain. I may be of some use."

His request was well received, and he and his new friend departed.

Akitada was very pleased with the speed and determination with which his colleague dealt with the situation. He expressed his admiration.

Michinori said, "I'm angry that this should have happened behind my back. Your story has shamed me, cousin. Also, I'd like to get this sorted out while you're here."

Akitada gulped. He had not planned on staying more than a day. In fact, he had told Mrs. Iseya he would be back by then. "Do you really need me?" he asked in mild protest.

Michinori grinned. "Cousin, we'll have an excellent time. I can use your experience in dealing with this and you can settle most of the affair as it affects your province at the same time." He paused, then added the clincher: "And besides, you and I will make reports to the prime minister. That should avert any repercussions in case your investigator tries to make trouble."

It was a brilliant suggestion and clearly his best option. Again, Akitada expressed his appreciation to Michinori, who merely laughed. "Come," he said, "we have a free morning before work begins. What would you like to do?"

∞

They spent the morning sight-seeing. Michinori was newly appointed and, unlike Akitada, he did not venture forth without retinue. The result was that they saw a lot of bent backs as they passed. But the people seemed content and the children waved.

They visited the local shrine, where they were received by the shrine priest and his attendants and then worshipped. They next went to the harbor, a more important one than the one in Komachi. Near the harbor was a large restaurant with a private room upstairs which afforded a fine view of the ships docked below and Mikawa Bay beyond. Michinori praised their food and wanted to know if Mikawa had any better to offer. By this time, they had become friends and Akitada had invited Michinori for a return visit.

Over a truly delicious meal of assorted delicacies from the sea, Akitada mentioned the body with the Matsudaira tattoo and possible piracy connections.

Michinori listened with interest. "Oh, piracy," he said. "You cannot stop it and should forget about it. Every fisherman on the coast of our country helps the pirates. And the pirates operate everywhere, especially here where so many transports of tax goods take to the water to avoid the expensive and time-consuming overland journey. From what I've seen, it's not all that serious."

Akitada digested this. "I thought we were expected to put a stop to it," he said.

Michinori wiped his mouth with a moist towel provided by a pretty waitress, and smiled. "My dear cousin," he said, "the people in the capital only care if they lose a big tax transport. And in that case, they're likely to dispatch some assistance. A mere governor cannot police the sea the way he polices his province. Impossible!"

It was true, of course, and their success in uprooting Kitagawa had got them little praise from their superiors.

Kitagawa's had been a small business as piracy went. This thought depressed him.

"Come," said Michinori, "don't let it get you down. Have some more of this excellent pickled fish and another cup of wine. We need sustenance for this afternoon's work."

Akitada obeyed. "But do you think Matsudaira could have a hand in this? I still have a murder victim on my hands. Two, in fact."

His colleague cocked his head. "So you still solve murders? I thought maybe the paperwork and all the other duties as a governor would curtail your interest in crime."

Akitada had long since got over being embarrassed by his personal involvement in murder investigations. But Michinori had a point. There was very little time for it these days, and he left most cases to the police lieutenant Akechi. He smiled a little therefore and told Michinori about the dead man with the tattoo, a tattoo that was the same as the Matsudaira crest. Then he told him about the murdered daughter of Imagawa and how the Matsudaira name had cropped up there again.

"And you think they are connected? But how? It sounds utterly farfetched, if you'll forgive me."

"Nothing to forgive. I agree with you. It must be a coincidence. I met Matsudaira on the occasion." Akitada shook his head. "To tell you the truth, I don't see how he could be connected with either murder."

"I know nothing against the Matsudaira. They are a couple of brothers, by the way, and there are some cousins, too. In fact, I met Matsudaira's eldest in the capital. He's started to make his way up the rank ladder in the government. He seemed a very nice, well-behaved young man."

"I'm told that the murdered girl was to be his wife. Strangely, neither father stressed this fact very much."

"No doubt Matsudaira has already considered new connections. That can cool off a previously friendly relationship rather quickly."

"You're quite right, I think. Oh, well, we may never find out who killed Tojo's man, any more than we can prove that he sent his thugs to beat up the farmer who complained about him."

"Well, Tojo will be stopped at any rate. I promise you that. Then you can concentrate on the murdered bride."

They concluded their enjoyable meal and returned to the tribunal on the friendliest terms. There, Michinori set in motion a major investigation into gang activity along his stretch of the Tokaido. Messengers were dispatched to alert prefects of districts along the way. Orders were issued to arrest anyone known to be connected with bandit activity. Requests were sent out to landowners for troops to make a sweep of the area near Akasaka and to patrol the highway until sufficient arrests had been made.

Akitada was impressed. He decided that he had been much too easy-going. In particular, he had never thought of conscripting troops from landowners, and the tribunal guard, though well-trained by Tora, was completely inadequate to dealing with a criminal organization like Tojo's.

20

The Widow

Akitada and Tora spent four days in Nagoya. During this time, Tojo was arrested, along with some of his people. So were a number of the bandits, rounded up by the soldiers Michinori had dispatched to search the area around the attack site.

Both Akitada and Tora attended the interrogations. Indeed, Tora had participated in the capture of the bandits. The interrogations were accompanied by floggings with bamboo rods. These sessions were ugly, and Akitada was often nauseated, but they produced information. More importantly, they served as encouragement to others to speak freely.

Somewhat to Akitada's surprise, one of Tojo's men volunteered that he and two others had gone on Tojo's

169

orders into Mikawa to teach a peasant a lesson. The peasant had been Gonjuro. On the strength of this, Akitada recommended that Tojo be assessed blood money to be paid to Gonjuro's widow.

In between the arrests and hearings, Michinori insisted on taking Akitada around the sights during the day, and in the evenings, they lingered over their evening rice, reviewing the day's events and chatting.

But time had stretched and seeing that Michinori had matters very well in hand, Akitada knew it was high time he returned to his own duties. This was not in deference to Ono, the inspector, but because the unsolved murder of Hiroko weighed on his conscience. So, on the fifth day of their stay, Akitada and Tora took leave of their genial host. Akitada repeated again his invitation to his new friend, and they set out for home to fine autumn weather and dry and safe roads.

Tora chatted quite happily about the efficiency with which the Tojo case had been dispatched, but Akitada listened with only half an ear. He noticed that the leaves were beginning to turn. Autumn always made him sad. He dated this melancholy feeling back to his journey to Naniwa. He had traveled on a boat when they had found the nameless girl, still in her teens and even in death of a transcendent beauty.

Or at least that was the way he remembered her now, recalling the feeling of pity that such youth and beauty had been discarded to death. He had also lost Seimei that autumn. And yet, the season and the scenery along the Yodo River had been beautiful.

Once they reached Narumi station, the mountains approached the shore. They would soon pass the temple and monastery where they had left the wounded man and his wife. Akitada had promised her to come back, but they had stayed longer in Nagoya, and the couple might well have traveled on.

Tora, who had been back and forth between the site of the attack and Nagoya several times with Michinori's search parties, had fallen silent and seemed to doze. Akitada glanced at him and wondered if his friend had driven himself too hard in the past days. Tora was no longer young. The gray in his hair outweighed the black, and his face was deeply lined.

When they reached the turn-off to the temple, Akitada said, "You don't mind if we call in here to see how the lady and her husband have fared?"

Tora looked confused for a moment, but then agreed readily.

They greeted the gatekeeper, who recognized him. Akitada asked, "Are your guests still here?"

The gatekeeper looked sad. "The gentleman died as soon as you left, sir. But the lady is still here. I think she was waiting for you."

Akitada felt guilty to have abandoned the couple and then have delayed his return until now. They turned their horses over to the monk and walked to a small building he pointed out to them. It was quite primitive, a simple wooden structure often found in mountain temples to accommodate visitors.

Akitada stopped outside and called out, "Mrs. Iseya?"

She appeared so instantly in the doorway that it seemed she had been waiting there. "My lord," she said eagerly, her face momentarily bright with relief. She faltered. "I didn't think you'd come any more."

He had forgotten what she looked like—if he ever knew, for it had been night—but he saw now that she was quite tall and slender. She was plainly dressed in a dark brown cotton gown with a black sash around her waist. Her hair had been long the last time he saw her, but she had twisted it up at her neck. She was quite pale but seemed serene. He guessed she must be well into her thirties.

"He died," she said simply, her voice forlorn and tears glistening in her eyes. "Heishiro died when you left."

Akitada said awkwardly, "I'm very sorry," and Tora added in a soothing voice, "He was badly hurt."

She looked at Tora as if she had only now noticed him. "He died because of me," she said, her voice sounding almost angry.

"No!" Akitada said quickly. "He did what any man would have done. The blame falls on those who would kill a man in order to rape his wife."

She flinched and looked down. "It wouldn't have mattered. I wish he hadn't tried to protect something of so little value."

Tora stared at her, shook his head, and stalked off.

Akitada glanced after him, then asked her, "Might we sit down?"

She hesitated, then came down the steps to perch on the low ledge outside the building. Akitada sat down near her. He could see her profile now. It was quite charming because he could not see the lines of grief and the swollen eyes like this. She must have been a beauty once.

"Why do you say you're of no value?" he asked, genuinely curious.

She did not look at him. "I was the wrong wife for him," she said.

"The wrong wife?"

She still would not look at him. Raising her hands and letting them fall again in a gesture of helplessness, she said, "His family didn't approve. His first wife and his children hated me. But I was a widow and had hoped . . ." She sighed. "I was going to leave him, but he applied for the position in Totomi, away from his family, and begged me to come with him. So I did. We were on our way back for a visit because he missed his children so." She hung her head and buried it in her hands. "I first caused his unhappiness and then his death," she said in a muffled voice.

Akitada did not know what to say. Grief is a terrible thing. You encounter it wherever your thoughts carry you and always you blame yourself, even when there was no choice and you had no hand in what happened. He knew it all too well. After a while, he said, "He loved you. All his actions prove it. So you were of great value to him. He chose you over his family, and he chose to protect you against the attackers. Never again say that you are of no value."

She curled up in tears, her head touching her knees. Akitada let her weep. She wept for him also. He longed with all his heart for Tamako. He even longed for Yukiko who had so clearly found no value in him.

Across the way, two young monks walked together. One was gesticulating as the other listened. The scent of pine hung in the clear air, and somewhere a bell rang. They had been sitting so still that two sparrows arrived, pecking around in the dirt and shooting them occasional glances from their bright black eyes.

After a while, her weeping abated and she sat up, dabbing at her face with her sleeve. "Forgive me," she said thickly. "I didn't mean to do this. Your kindness . . ." She broke off.

"What are your plans?" he asked, more out of embarrassment than anything else. "Can I still take a message?"

"No, thank you. I shall travel back to Totomi to settle his affairs, such as they are. His family will want his things. After that . . . I don't know."

Shocked, he asked, "You will not join his family?"

"No." She straightened her shoulders and added fiercely, "I'd rather die."

"Then what about your own family?"

"I have no family."

"No one at all?"

She just shook her head.

He was embarrassed that he had been prying into her life, her affairs. "What about funds? Will you manage? And your husband's funeral?"

"The monks were very kind. He was cremated here. I have his ashes and will send them to his family with his things. I have enough to see me home." Her voice broke a little on that last word and she added quickly, "Thank you for caring, but I will be perfectly all right." She finally turned her head to look at him. "You must be a very good man. You stopped those bandits and you tried to help Heishiro and me even though we were complete strangers. Thank you and may Amida bless you."

Her eyes were swollen from weeping and her face was splotched, but Akitada felt unaccountably moved and protective. It was with a great effort that he reminded himself that he had no right to meddle any more in her life. He said, "I hope his blessings will also see you safe. If I can ever be of service . . ." He hesitated. "My provincial headquarters are in Komachi. I shall be there until the end of the year. After that I shall be in the capital."

She looked astonished but rose to make him a deep bow. "Thank you, my lord, for such kindness, but I shall do very well."

Akitada rose as well and returned the bow, then went in search of Tora.

∞

At Akasaka, they found little change, except that Tojo was gone and another man was now master of the station. They did not linger but took the ferry rides across the Toyokawa River and arrived in Yoshida at sunset.

Their first stop was at Gonjuro's farm. As it had not rained again, the mud puddles had disappeared, but Gonjuro's children seemed quite as dirty as last time. They paused in their games to stare, and their mother came out. When she recognized them, she hurried over and knelt, bowing deeply.

"Please get up," Akitada said. "We came to see how you're doing."

She stood, wrapping her hands into the skirt of a stained dress. "We're well, your honor," she said. "We had a fine funeral for Gonjuro and everybody came. He must be very proud."

"I'm sure of it," said Akitada. "We came to tell you that they found the man who cheated Gonjuro. You'll be getting some money for the grief he has caused you."

She brightened a little and looked at her children. "Gonjuro will like that. Thank you, your honor."

It was little enough for the loss of her husband. Akitada had not wanted to call the remuneration blood money. He looked down at her and sighed. He should have come sooner. Another example of his lack of foresight. "Tell the prefect if you're in need. He'll get a message to me."

She smiled then and thanked him, and they rode away.

"What will you do about the prefect?" Tora asked.

Good question.

There was little doubt in Akitada's mind that Ikeda had been in Tojo's pay, but he had no idea how deeply the prefect was involved. "What do you think we should do?"

"Nothing tonight. I'm tired and hungry, and Ikeda keeps a very comfortable house."

21

The Return

Seeing Tora's exhaustion, Akitada left dealing with Ikeda until the morning. Ikeda greeted them with many questions—news of the arrest of Tojo and his crew had reached him—but Akitada fended these off, asking instead for rooms and a light meal.

Neither he nor Tora felt like talking. He ate little though the food was quite appetizing, and then went to sleep.

The next day he bathed and had himself shaved again. The maid reported that Tora still slept and Akitada told her to let him rest. What he must do did not require Tora.

Dressed formally, he went to speak to Ikeda. Ikeda received him nervously, smiling too much, chattering too cheerfully, urging rice gruel and assorted side dishes on him until Akitada said quite harshly, "Enough, Ikeda! Sit down and listen."

Ikeda sat. He was turning pale and beginning to sweat a little.

"You have heard about Tojo's arrest."

Ikeda nodded. "I couldn't believe it, Excellency. What a horrible thing. I had no idea—."

Akitada cut him off. "Don't lie to me. I know well enough that you worked with Tojo. Remember, Tojo has confessed."

Ikeda's jaw dropped. He made an inarticulate sound, then fell to his knees and knocked his head on the floor. "He lied, Excellency! He lied if he said I was involved. I had nothing to do with the bandits. Never! I swear it."

Akitada looked down at the cowering figure. "Hmm. What about Gonjuro?"

"All I did was let Tojo know that Gonjuro was going to complain to you. I had no idea that monster would send his men to beat him up."

"Even if I believed this, you would still have caused the man's death."

Ikeda wailed, "I'm sorry! I didn't know. You must believe me."

"I do not believe you; however, even the small part you admit makes you culpable. You are herewith dismissed. You will also pay Gonjuro's widow fifty pieces of silver. After that, you'll await the outcome of an investigation into your actions. Do you understand?"

Ikeda nodded several times and pleaded in a choking voice, "Please allow me to defend myself, your Excellency."

Akitada said vaguely. "We shall see. I'm returning to Komachi today. You will hear more when the investigation is completed."

With that, Akitada walked outside to wait for Tora. He was thoroughly disgusted with Ikeda but knew well enough that he could do no more than dismiss him. He doubted that much more could be proved than that Ikeda had been Tojo's informant.

Tora joined him soon after. He looked more rested and asked, "Are we going to take Ikeda apart now?"

Akitada smiled at him. "Already done. If you're ready, we'll leave. I've had enough of Ikeda's hospitality."

Tora looked a little disappointed. "That maid of his would be a fine addition to your staff, sir."

∞

After another day's ride, they reached Komachi. The weather had been dry and pleasant on the return trip, but both Akitada and Tora were glad to be home. Tora immediately headed for his own quarters and the arms of his family.

Akitada looked in on his children. He found them well and eager to hear about his journey. He told them what had happened, leaving out the violent and gruesome sights. The result was that Yoshi dashed off to get the full version from Tora.

Akitada looked after him, a little saddened that Yo-shi's affection for Tora seemed often to outweigh his closeness to his own father. He sighed then looked at Yasuko. She was twelve and would be thirteen with the new year. She was very pretty. At least he thought so. Every time he saw her she reminded him more of her mother. But Yasuko had become quiet and withdrawn since Yukiko had left. It was understandable. Yukiko's youth had made her more of a companion to his daughter than a wife to himself.

"Are you happy, Yasuko?" he asked.

"Yes, Father."

A short silence fell. He was about to get up to see Saburo, when she said, "What happened to the couple?"

He knew instantly whom she meant. He said, "I'm afraid the husband died. I'm sorry. I didn't mean to distress you."

She looked at him with her clear eyes. "I'm not distressed. I just wondered. What did his wife do?"

"The monastery took care of the funeral and she will travel home."

"To her children?"

From what he had gathered, she was returning to a bleak future, but how could he explain this to his daughter. Time enough for her to discover that fate often treated women harshly. He would do his very best to protect her, but nothing was certain in life. He said, "I don't think there were children. They had not been married long."

"Oh. Poor lady." She brightened. "I forgot. There's a letter from Yukiko. You'll tell me what she says, won't you?"

He promised and left.

A letter. Finally!

He had hoped for so long. He hurried to his study. There, on his otherwise bare desk, lay the letter, still sealed. Waiting.

But in the end he could not open it. Perhaps the fear that it would bring more pain stopped him. In any case, he left it untouched and went across to the tribunal.

There he found Saburo but also an irate Ono.

Ono jumped up. "So there you are! I thought you had fled to the Ezo. How dare you absent yourself like this when you're under investigation?"

Like a criminal, thought Akitada. With an accusation of treason thrown in for good measure. He regarded Ono coldly. "I have been in Yoshida, Akasaka, and Nagoya," he said. "No doubt you'll be disappointed to hear that I was engaged in official business for Mikawa province and His Majesty."

"What official business?"

"Investigating banditry on the Tokaido. Now you must excuse me while I check my mail and speak to Saburo."

"What banditry? You're making up this story."

Akitada shook his head. "You'll get a copy of the report that the governor of Owari and I prepared and sent to His Majesty."

Ono's face fell. "I want to go over some questions I have with you."

"Sorry. They'll have to wait until tomorrow."

"You cannot refuse to answer my questions."

"I'm not refusing. I'll answer them tomorrow."

Ono glared but finally departed.

Saburo said, "Sorry, sir."

"I expect he has given you a very bad time, Saburo. Forgive me for leaving you to bear the brunt of his spite."

Saburo grinned lopsidedly. "As I said, I was well prepared to handle him. Did they tell you that a letter from Lady Sugawara has come?"

"Yes. Yasuko told me. I'll read it later. Just now you'd better report on any urgent business. And then, I think I'll get some rest."

"There isn't much, sir. I've been kept too busy by Lord Ono to work on the case. Akechi has come back from Shinohara. The girl's not there."

Akitada drew a blank. "Shinohara?"

"You may recall that we were looking for Otoki, Lady Hiroko's maid? Her family lives in Shinohara, in the Ama district."

"Ah! That's not good. I do hope that young girl is alive."

"Yes, sir. Oh, and the fan maker brought the mended fan."

"Did he really? Where is it?"

Saburo brought him a box that had been on the book rack, resting on top of documents. Akitada opened it and took out the mended fan.

"Beautiful work. The thing was chewed to pieces by that dog. He not only assembled it correctly, but he used the same red silk and I think he must have touched up the painting."

"Yes, very fine work. It's amazing such talented craftsmen live in a province."

They admired the barely damaged image of red maple leaves and deep green pine needles against a pale sky with clouds. The clouds were decorated with silver dust.

"That's a pheasant in that tree," said Saburo, pointing. You can still see its colors. It's a very fine fan. Must've cost a good deal of money."

"Yes, indeed," said Akitada. "Well, it's an autumn fan, so it was dropped recently. But we knew that anyway. Anything this dainty wouldn't have survived many days." He laid the fan down and stretched. "Well, we can ask some questions. A fan this fine would be remembered."

"I doubt its owner will come forward," Saburo said dryly.

Akitada chuckled and wished him a good night.

∞

Back in his own study, Akitada found that the maid had spread his bedding. She had also left him some hot tea, being kept warm on a small brazier, and a covered bowl containing clear soup with vegetables. It was not, perhaps, as luxurious as the service at Ikeda's place, but it showed a certain amount of thoughtfulness, and Akitada hoped he would remember to thank whoever had brought these things.

Now he poured himself some tea and picked up Yukiko's letter. He turned it in his hand as he took a few sips, then laid it back down in order to eat his soup. The soup was only lukewarm, but it was tasty. Another cup of tea later, he finally unfolded the letter.

"My dear husband," she had written. "I wonder sometimes if we ever met. It has all become so unreal, like dewdrops disappearing with the sun. You left the capital in the spring mist, and now the autumn wind blows colored leaves on my veranda. How are the children?" And then there was some empty space before she wrote, "I pray every day that you will come."

He put the letter down and sat staring blindly into space. It was such an odd letter. She had refused to come back with him in the spring, preferring to live with her parents, and later at the imperial palace. Why was she telling him now that she missed him, or that it seemed as though their life together had never been?

She was right about that. Even here, in this house where they had lived together for a number years, where her chrysanthemums still flowered every fall, even here that time seemed to have never been.

And why that final plea to come? A plea that sounded somehow urgent?"

He dared not believe in her love any longer, and yet.

Eventually, he put away the letter, and tried to go to sleep. But thoughts of Yukiko rambled about his head, none of them pleasurable. He was a coward. He did not want to rush back to the capital because he feared another quarrel, another rejection. In his heart he knew it would come. Their worlds were too different and that he was so much older could no longer be ignored. He abhorred the courtly life she craved and would never measure up to the young men of high rank who surrounded her.

He did sleep eventually, exhausted both in body and in spirits, but dismal dreams of blood and violence troubled him.

22

Hiroko's Secret

Akitada was up before dawn, cheerless and bitter. He brewed himself some tea and then took brush in hand and composed an answer to Yukiko.

"My dear wife," he wrote. "You are much missed here. The children ask about you all the time. There have been few letters until now. I shall pass your greetings on to Yasuko and Yoshi. They are both well. I regret that I cannot come to the capital. It appears I am still under investigation as a result of my last unauthorized visit. A Lord Ono has been here for days, busily searching for proof that I'm unfit as a governor." He closed by expressing his hopes that she was well and happy.

It was a very cold and impersonal letter. Not a word of poetry in it. But it was probably rather typical for such missives between absent officials and their wives. The trouble was that it was not typical for him, but rather an expression of his disillusionment.

For a moment, he was tempted to tear it up and write another letter, a passionate one, declaring his love and begging her to return to him. But he resisted, sealed it and took it with him for Saburo to send by messenger with other mail to the capital.

∞

In his office, he told Saburo about Ikeda.

"I have dismissed him," he said. "His assistant will manage for a while, but we must find a new man soon."

Saburo nodded. "I recall there were one or two local men who had applied for the appointment. I'll look into it."

They went through the letters that had arrived in his absence. Akitada dictated answers and would have felt content with their achievements, if the letter to Yukiko had not rested on top of all the new mail that Saburo carried off with him.

Ono arrived before he could brood too much about his marriage. He came armed with questions and accusations. Some of the questions concerned the Tokaido affair. Clearly the man was worried that Akitada would somehow escape his carefully built charges of dereliction of duties. Akitada answered these with some amusement, seeing Ono's dismay at the close collaboration between Akitada and Fujiwara Michinori.

But then the issue of his Ise visit arose again. Ono expressed his doubts that Akitada had merely visited Ise to worship at the shrine. He had somehow found out that Akitada had not gone to Ise openly under his own name and rank. He wanted an explanation that Akitada could not give. It was very unpleasant to be called a liar, even when you were.

Eventually, Ono left with the ominous words that his report was almost ready and that Akitada should be prepared to travel back with him to face the censors.

He could only imagine what effect his arrival in the capital as a discredited official would have on Yukiko.

Tora trailed in soon after, looking better after his rest.

"Saburo says the fan has come back," he said, sitting down across from Akitada. "And Otoki didn't go back home."

Akitada brushed a hand over his face. Ono had managed to put the murder of Hiroko from his mind. He got up to get the box on the book rack.

"A bad morning with Ono?"

"You can say so."

"But at least you had a letter from your lady?"

"Yes. She sends greetings to everyone," Akitada said vaguely.

"That's all?"

Akitada frowned at Tora. "Yes," he said firmly and handed the fan to Tora.

Tora gave him a searching glance, then let it go and studied the fan. "It doesn't seem the same fan. This is almost as good as new. And that's a fine painting. Some lady's?"

"No. It's a man's fan, an expensive one. Its seasonal decoration makes it the sort of thing used by young men who place importance on their attire."

Tora made a face. "Bet we'll get someone to identify it in the Matsudaira household."

"Perhaps, but there is a problem. We cannot produce the fan and imply that someone in the family has killed the girl."

"My money is on them," said Tora. "There's Hiroko's connection to the family. She was practically promised to the oldest son and the daughter was her best friend. And besides, there aren't that many men in Komachi who would carry such a thing."

"Hiroko disappeared after her visit to the Matsudaira house. She was alive before. Besides, it is always possible that she carried the fan herself. It could have been a memento of some sort."

Tora frowned. "Come on, let's go and ask some more questions. You don't want to sit here and be made miserable by that arrogant lordling Ono."

And so they walked into town together, Akitada carrying the fan in his sleeve. They did not visit Matsudaira immediately but called on Hiroko's father first.

Lord Imagawa greeted them with, "There you finally are. Have you got my daughter's killer?"

"I'm afraid not, Imagawa," Akitada said, skipping any titles to make a point about the man's manners.

Imagawa did not even blink. "Then what do you want? I must say your entire administration is incredibly lax, and so I have told Lord Ono."

Akitada suppressed a grimace. Ono had certainly been busy in his absence. He said, "Lieutenant Akechi has been busy interrogating possible witnesses. As you know we would like to find out how a nobleman's daughter ended up in a rice field outside town. However, in the meantime this has turned up." He showed Imagawa the fan, opening it so only the painted side showed. "Have you ever seen this before?"

Imagawa looked, then shook his head. "No. Why?"

"It was found near your daughter's body."

Imagawa snapped, "This belonged to a man. A nobleman, I'd guess. Are you suggesting one of the good people did this to my daughter?"

"Why are you surprised? Surely your daughter associated only with your own kind. However, she may have carried it herself. Perhaps a reminder of someone? She was promised to Matsudaira's oldest son, wasn't she?"

Imagawa hemmed and hawed, then said, "There was some discussion, but Kintsune is in the capital. No, I don't believe this is his."

"Would you take the fan and ask your ladies if they ever saw it before?"

Imagawa grudgingly took the fan with him and left.

Tora grumbled, "He wouldn't say, even if he knew whose it was. They all stick together."

"Not necessarily. I have a feeling that he is no longer very friendly with Matsudaira, but it isn't clear if that is because his daughter was murdered after a visit there,

or if something went sour on the marriage negotiations." Akitada paused. "Or maybe it's something altogether different."

Imagawa returned, handed back the fan and said
none of his ladies or their maids had ever seen it before. He glowered and added, "I expect you to do better than this, governor. Maybe you need to look into the
poor performance of your police lieutenant. Clearly this
was the work of some depraved commoner. Perhaps
that peasant on whose field she was found killed her.
Have you investigated him and his family? Why are you
plaguing us with your insulting questions?"

They left. Outside, Tora said, "He hasn't changed.
Cannot believe one of the "good people" might actually
kill. I think he cares more about his rank than his
child."

"You're probably right," Akitada said, "but I got the
impression we left him just a little uneasy."

Matsudaira received them as courteously as before.
Unlike Imagawa, he did not press them about the progress of the investigation. On the whole, he acted as if
the murder did not concern him or his family any longer.

Akitada mentioned the fan and said it was somewhat
the worse for wear but seemed to have had a very pretty
picture of maples and a pheasant on it.

Matsudaira asked, "What happened to it?"

"A dog found it, most likely near the body. Have
you ever seen such a fan?"

Matsudaira smiled. "No, but they sell such things in
the better shops. I consider painted fans unsuitable for

men. Sorry, I cannot help you. I hear you've been in Owari. May I ask what the occasion was?"

"Some problems with highway robbery on the Tokaido. A gang operated out of Akasaka. They were robbing pack trains passing through. The master of the past station in Akasaka had a hand in warning the gang of any good hauls passing their way."

Matsudaira's eyes grew round. "You don't say! Shocking. But surely Akasaka is in Owari."

"Yes, but I got some information that made me travel up to Yoshida with Captain Sashima. We decided to cross over and check out the opposite station and discovered a pack train with rice on its way to the capital. Since we witnessed some suspicious activities, we decided to follow the pack train and stopped an attack."

Matsudaira glanced at Tora, who grinned back impudently. "You had soldiers with you, I take it," he said. "Surely that means you knew what was happening when you left here."

Tora said, "Oh, no. Complete surprise. No, it was just the two of us."

Akitada added, "Fortunately Governor Fujiwara and I work well together. The gang and its collaborators have been arrested."

Matsudaira stared at him. Words seemed to fail him. Then he said, "Ah, very good work," he said. "Yes, good work." He fell silent again, chewing his lip.

Akitada rose. "Well, we'll be on our way."

Matsudaira, started. "Wait, there's something else. I'm afraid I just found out that my daughter forgot to mention something about her friend. Allow me to get her so she can tell you herself."

He hurried out, and Akitada and Tora looked at each other.

"What could that be all about?" Akitada asked.

"He was shocked to hear about the gang business. Bet he went to send off some letters."

"Perhaps." Akitada sighed. "I wish I knew what's going on. These provincial lords are becoming much too independent and powerful."

They did not have to wait very long. If Matsudaira had been sending off messages, they must have been oral. He came in, leading Lady Tomiko, who looked flushed and nervous.

They exchanged bows, and Matsudaira said, "My daughter mistakenly kept her friend's secret, but since Hiroko is dead and her murderer must be found, I told her she must consider herself released from her promise and tell all."

Akitada looked at the daughter, who would not meet his eyes. "I could wish you had spoken up before, Lady Tomiko, but I do understand about promises. Please tell us what you know."

She glanced up at him quickly and said in a low voice, "Hiroko was meeting a man."

23

The Lover

Akitada was so dumfounded that he asked, "Are you sure?"

"Yes. She told me that the only way she could see him was to say she was with me."

Her father compressed his lips and shook his head.

Akitada asked him, "And you knew nothing about this? Hiroko was promised to your son."

"Not precisely promised. There had been some talk at one point. I must say, I'm very glad it came to nothing."

"Who is this man?"

It was Tora who asked the only really important question, but it came to nothing. Hiroko had never revealed his name to her friend, though she had clearly been in love and excited about seeing him.

"Did she say where they met?" Akitada asked.

"No. Well, once she mentioned a pond. I just thought that it must have been in his garden."

"But how can you be sure that she told you the truth about all this? She might have been making it up." Akitada said.

"I saw one of his letters. It was a love letter with a poem. She said he was a student and wrote the most beautiful verses but that this one made her sad. When I didn't believe her, she showed it to me. It was elegantly written in a man's hand, so I believed her."

"Do you remember what was in the letter?"

She frowned, trying to think. "I remember the poem. At least I think I do."

"Well, what was it?"

She closed her eyes and recited, "The dream of our love is fleeting; but how much more fleeting will it be when we're apart?"

"It sounds like a farewell poem. Did she say that he was going away?"

"She said he might have to go, but she hoped he would stay."

"Now think back to the letter. You say it was well written. Was the letter signed?"

She giggled, covering her mouth. "Oh. Yes, it was very funny. He'd signed it 'The Junior Candidate of the Iris Bower'."

Akitada chuckled also. "When did she show you this letter?"

Suddenly serious again, Tomiko twisted her hands together and shuddered. "A few days before she . . . before the last time she was here."

Akitada said soothingly, "You are doing very well, Lady Tomiko. Now please think of that last visit. Was she going to see him?"

"Yes."

"And did she give you any idea whether it would be a sad farewell or an ordinary meeting?"

"I don't know. She only stopped for a moment and seemed upset, but that might have been because she had very little time. She was always afraid of her father."

"As well she should have been," said her father firmly. "I trust I shall never have to find out such a thing about you."

"Oh, no, Father."

Akitada did not see any point in protracting the questioning, so he thanked her and her father, and they took their leave.

As they were walking away from the Matsudaira mansion, Tora said, "Well, that turns everything upside down. A lover! I guess we have a new suspect."

"The story is intriguing, but let's not jump to conclusions."

"The fan could be his."

"First we need to find this elusive young man. Then we can worry about the fan."

"You know she probably got involved with him because her father was an unfeeling ogre."

"Are you sure the story we just heard is true?"

Tora gave him a glance. "You think Lady Tomiko lied? But why would she do that?"

"I don't know, Tora. All I know is that people have been lying or hiding things all along."

Tora grunted. After a moment, he asked, "How can we find this lover? If he's real, I mean."

"The alleged quality of the writing and the signature both imply that he attended the university in the capital or plans to. A candidate is a student who is taking final examinations."

"If she didn't lie about the letter."

"I think perhaps the letter is real. Though to tell you the truth, what with all the romances the young women are fond of these days, she could have been quoting something she read."

Tora stopped walking. "Look," he said, "either she told the truth or she lied. If she told the truth, we need to find him."

"Yes. Let's consult Saburo."

∞

Saburo listened with interest. "Hmm," he said. "A number of the better families in town may qualify. No-body quite as illustrious as Matsudaira or Imagawa, but well off enough to have sent a son to the university. Shall I find out?"

"Yes!" Tora clapped his hands. "Do it now! Saburo. If we find him, we may have our killer."

"Can't. Lord Ono requires my assistance."

Akitada sighed. "When will the man be done?"

Nobody knew the answer to this. Saburo left and Tora and Akitada remained to ponder the new development. After a while, Tora said, "Isn't taking a secret lover pretty bad behavior among the good people? Especially if she was promised in marriage."

"Yes, very bad, but not unheard of. I wish I knew what sort of young woman Hiroko was. From what we have seen of Imagawa and what Lady Tomiko said, she was afraid of her father. Clearly she had reason to be. Or else, as you said, perhaps her unhappiness at home drove her to this young man."

"Exactly. Her father beat her."

"Well, the Imagawa household didn't strike me as a happy place. And something wasn't quite right about that betrothal. Matsudaira denied it had happened, and Imagawa avoided the subject. It occurred to me that an unhappy young girl might be seduced rather easily and run to this man in hopes of escaping her home."

Tora pondered that. "I don't know much about how the good people live and what their daughters might get up to. All the girls I've known either got married or went into a brothel or into service. Either way, not much fuss was made about secret lovers and such."

"I wish I knew what happened to that maid. Poor young thing. Fifteen years old."

Tora said philosophically, "Well, if she's alive, she found another job."

At this point, Saburo slipped back in. "I think I may have a name for you, sir. The local judge, Ishimura, has a son who has been attending the university. He's been home for a visit for a few months but expects to go back soon. One of the clerks happened to mention it. This might be a place to start."

∞

Since Ono required Akitada again, Tora went alone to call on Judge Ishimura. It was by then late afternoon. He found the judge lived comfortably in a well-built house not too far from the mansions of the wealthy nobles. His knock on the gate was answered promptly by a very proper housemaid who took his boots and admitted him to a large room with thick tatami mats on the floor, many books and scrolls on bamboo racks, and a desk that was larger and more finely made than the one his master used in the study of his residence.

The doors to a small garden were open and a cushion lay ready on the veranda in case the judge should feel inclined to admire the changing leaves on his maple.

Judge Ishimura appeared rather quickly and offered him a seat and some wine. Tora declined the wine.

The judge, a tall middle-aged man with the long beard of one of the ancient wise men, asked if the governor had sent him.

"In a way," said Tora. "I'm working on a murder investigation."

The judge raised his brows. "Really? Isn't that Lieutenant Akechi's job?"

"Akechi is also working on this. But since the case concerns some of the province's most important people, the governor is looking into the matter himself." He paused for effect. "You see, Lord Imagawa's daughter has been murdered."

"Good heavens! I hadn't heard. What can I do for you?"

"Lady Hiroko is said to have been meeting a young man who's a student. I understand your own son is about to return to the university in the capital? By any chance is he here now?"

The judge did not take this well. He turned an alarming red. "What if he is? He has nothing to do with any murders. Do you have any proof that he even knew Lord Imagawa's daughter?"

"No, sir. But he may know the other students in the city and perhaps even be aware of a romance."

"Oh!" The judge chewed his lip, then got up to tell a servant to call his son."

A slender young man with large, soulful eyes and the soft red lips of a girl came in a moment later. Tora had dim views of such youths. They were clearly unfit to do anything but read and write poems. But he moderated his antipathy.

The judge said, "My son Arihito." He frowned at him. "This is about a murder. It seems someone killed Lord Imagawa's daughter."

The effect of this was striking. His son gasped and started shaking.

His father frowned. "What? Are you acquainted with the young woman?"

The son nodded. Tora saw with disgust that he had tears in his eyes. At least this search turned out to be ridiculously easy after all. Here stood his suspect.

The judge bit his lips. "Tell the captain what you know about this deplorable situation."

Since the young man said nothing, Tora asked, "You knew Lady Hiroko?"

The judge's son did not look up. He sniffed and murmured, "Yes."

Evidently blunt speech was in order. Tora asked. "You were lovers?"

The young man gave a shudder and hung his head even more. His father said harshly, "Raise your head and answer the man. If you have engaged in a romance, there's no need to be embarrassed. You're at an age when such things are quite natural."

This surprised Tora. He protested, "Lady Hiroko belonged to an important family and was promised in marriage to the Matsudaira heir."

"Really?" The judge smiled. "How very enterprising of you, Arihito! Was she pretty?"

His son turned on him. "Shut up, Father! She's dead!" He made a soft sound that was almost a sob before turning back to Tora. "Yes, we were lovers, Captain. At least, I loved her. I wanted her to be my wife, but . . ." He glanced at his father.

Judge Ishimura said quickly, "Of course not! You know quite well how important your career is. I'm not a wealthy and powerful man who can provide you with a life of ease. It's necessary for you to study hard and win the sorts of honors that will secure you a position in government. Then you may look about for a wife."

Suppressing a temptation to sneer, Tora looked from father to son. "But wouldn't a marriage to Lord Imagawa's daughter have given your son a life of ease?"

The professor said, "You don't know Imagawa very well if you think that. He'd never have permitted such a marriage. Men like that have no understanding of real ability. All they look to do is keep their money and land in the family."

Arihito said angrily, "I don't care about his money and land. He beat Hiroko and her mother. We couldn't let him find out about us."

Tora took a deep breath. "So you've been in the habit of meeting Lady Hiroko secretly. For how long had this been going on?"

"We met this past spring, but we didn't . . . that is it wasn't serious until last month."

"And how did you manage it?"

"There was a shrine fair. She was there with a friend and the friend's brother. We talked a little. But it wasn't until a month later that I saw her again. She was with the same friend. We walked together a bit and she agreed to meet me."

"And where did you meet?"

"Oh, different places. The shrine once or twice. By a lake. And any time there was some fair or festival."

"But you became lovers. Surely that didn't happen in the open."

Arihito blushed to the roots of his hair. "There's a place near the market, in a side street. It's called The Iris Pavilion. We met in a private room. Nobody saw her come or go."

Judge Ishimura said, "You should have kept your mind on your studies. What were you thinking of?" But he looked rather pleased.

His son did not answer. He clenched his hands and asked, "How did she die? And when?"

"About two weeks ago. The coroner says she was strangled on the ninth day of the month. Where were you that day?"

Arihito blinked. "That was when I went to see my aunt. She's a nun in the Atsuta convent in Nagoya. Hiroko didn't know. I was gone for two days. Oh!" He covered his face. "I wish I were dead instead."

His father said, "Don't be ridiculous! The young woman was careless to be going out and about and engaging in affairs. There are many evil men about, as you should know well enough as the son of a judge. I cannot imagine a household where the daughters are permitted to roam the streets at will." The judge pursed his lips.

His son turned on him. "How dare you, Father? She may have been coming to see me. It was you who made me travel to Nagoya so suddenly I couldn't get a message to her. I'll never forgive you for that." With this, he ran from the room.

The judge heaved a sigh. "The young are so impulsive," he said, rolling his eyes. "Never mind. In another week he'll be back at his studies in the capital, and, as I recall, there are plenty of pretty girls there always ready to console a young man. Did you want anything else?"

Tora opened his mouth, then closed it again. He said, "No," and walked out.

24

The Iris Pavilion

Tora knew the place called the Iris Pavilion. It was a house of assignation. Clearly the un- worldly poet-student had known his way around. This, somewhat surprisingly in view of Tora's own past, angered him. Even given the fact that the two had had no place to meet in private, Arihito should never have taken the daughter of Lord Imagawa to such a place.

Still, as houses of assignation went, the Iris Pavilion was well-run. When Tora arrived there, he was met by a middle-aged woman in a dark silk dress. She looked like a well-to-do merchant's wife and had a nice smile.

"I am Mrs. Ito," she told Tora with a bow. "I'm the owner of this house. How may I be of assistance?"

Tora glanced around the small reception room. It contained some neat cushions, a hanging scroll painting of iris, and a vase of chrysanthemums and autumn leaves. A wine flask and some cups waited on a small stand.

Perhaps misinterpreting Tora's silence as shyness, Mrs. Ito said with a smile, "This is your first visit here, I think. You may put your trust in me. I do not gossip about my guests, and neither do my maids."

"I'm Captain Sashima. From the tribunal," Tora introduced himself.

She waved a small hand. "Names are not required, Captain." She gestured to the cushions. "Please have a seat. May I offer you some wine?"

Tora, being somewhat parched, decided to accept.

She knelt beside him and poured his wine. "As I said," she continued, "we guarantee complete confidentiality. So, if you'll just tell me if you plan to bring a lady? Or if you would prefer me to provide you with a charming companion, I have three lovely young women working here. They are talented in music and dance. I'm certain you'd be well pleased."

Tora drank, smacked his lips, and said, "Good. I can see you do your clients proud, Mrs. Ito."

She laughed a little, a small trill of a laugh as she refilled his cup. "I do my best, Captain."

Seeing that he was about to disappoint her, Tora took only a small sip this time. "Well," he said, "I'm here officially, I'm afraid."

Her smile faltered. "Oh. I assure you, we obey every law, and the girls are all here of their free will. I don't own them. They work for pay."

"Good, but that's not why I'm here. I believe you've been making rooms available to Judge Ishimura's son on occasion?"

Her lips compressed. "No names, Captain. I ask nobody's name. That way, people's secrets remain theirs."

Tora glowered at her. "Not this time! This time, you'll speak. The young woman he brought here is the daughter of Lord Imagawa, and she's been found dead."

Her shock was palpable. She turned white and swayed for a moment as if she were about to faint. Tora reached for the flask and poured a cup of wine. "Here," he said. "Drink this. Then pull yourself together."

She obeyed. Putting the empty cup down, she cried, "I didn't know. I didn't know who she was. I knew him, of course, but he brought her in the back way. We have a secret entrance that people can use if they don't wish to be seen. And the maids just left food and wine outside the door. They stayed in the pond pavilion.

It's separate from the main house for privacy."

"You say you knew him. Was he a frequent visitor?"

"Well, only lately. He told me who he was."

Tora raised his brows at this. "I thought he might have cared about secrecy."

She smiled a little. "He seemed very inexperienced. With women and places like this, I mean. You say she was Lord Imagawa's daughter? What could he have been thinking? When there are so many pretty girls available. Mind you, he's a very nice looking young man." She had become almost voluble in her surprise.

"So you never met her?"

"Not until the last time. That time she came and he wasn't here. And then I didn't really know who she was. She was alone, you see."

Tora stared at her. "That can't be right. She had a maid with her that day. Maybe you just didn't notice."

"No maid. That's why I didn't think she was one of the good people. They don't go about without a maid or companion. And also, it was late. What was she doing out alone on the streets after sunset?"

Tora did not know. He was thunderstruck by the absence of the maid. He began to wonder if this particular young woman was someone altogether different. But the judge's son had identified Hiroko as his lover. What had happened to the maid?

"When was this?"

"Oh, earlier this month."

"Could it have been on the ninth day?"

"Yes. I think so. A moment." She rose and consulted a book. "Yes. It was the ninth. I had kept the pavilion open for them and was disappointed when he didn't come to pay for the evening."

Tora asked, "Can you show me where they met?"

She nodded, eager enough now to be cooperative. "Nobody's using the pavilion tonight. Come with me."

They walked through the house, past a bevy of curious young women dressed in colorful robes for their evening's work, and out into a small garden. There was a pond, though not a very large one. And there were iris plants growing around it. On its far side sat what looked like a garden house. This turned out to be the pond pavilion. It contained a single room of only four tatami mats, a roll of bedding, a lantern, and a brazier for warmth on cold nights. All the doors could be closed against curious eyes, and a back door led to a narrow path and a small back gate in the fence.

Mrs. Ito said, "Clients make the arrangement during the day or a few days ahead and we get the pavilion ready. Then later, the couple may come from the back street. It's very private. The young man always asked for the pavilion."

Tora looked at everything. "I wonder how he knew about it if he was so inexperienced."

She smiled, "No doubt, a friend told him."

"If they arrived the back way, you didn't actually see them together, right?"

"No, that's right."

"Then you don't know if the young woman usually brought a maid."

Mrs. Ito frowned. "I don't know, but this is a small room. Where would she go?"

"Perhaps she waited outside."

She looked dubious. "I suppose it's possible."

And it was equally possible that Hiroko had not come here at all. He looked long and hard at Mrs. Ito. "Think back to the ninth when the young woman came alone. How do you know this if she came in the usual way, from the back?"

"Because she came to the front and asked for him. She said she was to meet him in the pavilion and he wasn't there. I told her he had not come and sent no message. I could see that upset her. She stood for a moment, then she thanked me and left."

"And she had no maid with her?"

"None that I could see."

"What did she look like?"

"A little taller than me. Quite pretty. Her hair was long and loose, just held by a ribbon in back. She had on a very nice silk gown of a pale gold silk with green-shaded undergowns."

It had been Hiroko. The more he learned about Lady Hiroko, the less he understood what had happened. He asked, "She left then? Did you see what direction she went?"

"No. We were too busy for me to watch her."

"What time was it?"

"Later than this. It was almost dark. I was thinking that we needed to send out for some hot dishes for the clients and the girls."

Tora thanked her and departed.

25

The Lake

Tora paused outside the Iris Pavilion and looked around. Where had Hiroko gone when she had not found Arihito for their usual assignation? What had been in her mind? The obvious solution was to return home, but she had not done this. And what had she done with the maid? It all began to look somewhat desperate.

The Iris Pavilion was in a pleasant part of the town. Here there were gardens, a small shrine or two, and some private homes. Right across from Tora was a small lake, and a good restaurant, called unimaginatively Lake Restaurant. Appetizing smells came from it. As he watched, a waitress came out to hang some paper lanterns. When she lit them, the Lake Restaurant instantly looked enchanting and otherworldly in the gathering dusk.

Tora considered the problem faced by Hiroko. Clearly she should have gone home as quickly as possible, but from all they had learned she had dreaded home. She must have been upset when Arihito had not met her. Perhaps she had felt abandoned by him. She knew he would leave soon to return to the university. This might have been their final meeting.

On an impulse—and perhaps also drawn by the tempting smell of food and the pretty lanterns—Tora crossed the street and entered the restaurant.

He had eaten here before and was greeted with a broad smile by the woman who owned it. Bowing deeply, she said, "Welcome, Captain. We've missed you. Have you been away?"

"For a few days." Tora looked from her to the Iris Pavilion across the street. "I'm wondering. Did you by chance notice a young lady come from The Iris Pavilion a few weeks ago? It would have been on the ninth in the early evening."

She laughed. "There are always women coming from the Iris Pavilion. And men, too. Sometimes they come together and eat here. Mrs. Ito doesn't provide first class meals. I wouldn't have noticed anyone in particular. Besides we're very busy here. No time to watch the Iris Pavilion."

"Yes, I know. But this young woman was one of the good people. And she was probably crying. I thought you might have noticed her."

212

"A lady? Coming from the Iris Pavilion? You must be joking."

Tora sighed. "I suppose it was too much to hope for. Well, I'll have a bite to eat."

She took him to the back where large doors stood open to a narrow balcony overlooking the lake. It was a pretty view. The last light gleamed on the water and the willows along its bank were still a faint gold. A few people strolled down there, stopping now and then to watch the ducks. He ordered fried abalone, a shrimp stew, and eggs stuffed with seaweed.

The waiter brought the wine first, and Tora sat, looking out at the lake and thinking about a distraught young woman. He was not sure how a noble lady would act after such a disappointment. If she felt abandoned by a young man who was below her in rank, she might well have thought of some desperate step. A peasant girl would have shrugged it off and gone on to the next man. Hiroko, being in love, could have gone to Arihito's home to ask for him. But the professor had certainly not mentioned such a visit. Would he have lied? It might be a good idea to talk to the man again.

His food arrived and with it the owner. "Captain," she said. "About that lady. We did have a curious thing happen around that time. I'm not sure if it was on the ninth day, though. There was a woman, down by the lake. She was standing there for a very long time, such a long time that one of the waitresses thought she meant to drown herself. Everybody was soon staring out instead of serving the guests. But as it turned out, she had been waiting for a man, because one came, and she went away with him."

Tora considered it, found it interesting, and asked, "What did she look like?"

"Too far to see for my old eyes. But I'll send Midori over. She has sharper eyes and took a great interest."

She bustled off and Tora started on his food. Midori arrived, small, bright-eyed, and flirtatious. Tora warmed to her immediately.

"Ooh! It's you, Captain. I've wanted to meet you forever. And you're investigating a crime? Did that man abduct the pretty lady?"

Tora swallowed a bite of abalone and grinned at her. "Midori, my pretty flower, you've made me a happy man."

She blushed and knelt down beside him. "Allow me," she said softly and refilled his cup raising it to his lips.

Tora reminded himself that he was on duty—and also married—but the temptation was great. This charmer could not be more than eighteen or nineteen and she clearly found him attractive. He sat up straighter, pulling in his stomach, smoothed his mustache with a finger, and flashed his smile at her.

She giggled.

He took the cup and sipped, looking into her eyes. "Thank you, my dear. You spoil me. But tell me, your mistress says you have good eyes and you saw the young woman by the lake and also the man she went with?"

She nodded and busied herself serving him a bowl of rice with broth. "I saw them. There was a bright moon that night. Mind you, I thought someone like her in such very pretty clothes might have done a lot better than some old geezer."

Tora had rarely found his work more pleasurable or rewarding. He chewed his rice and sipped the broth, looking at Midori with warm appreciation as she chattered on about the lady and how long she had waited and about her clothes—it sounded like Hiroko—and how it had not taken the geezer very long to arrive.

"When you say 'geezer'," Tora finally interrupted. "What exactly do you mean? Was he a very old man?"

"Oh, not so very old, but a bit fat. And I recognized him. Definitely not a girl's dream!"

"Ah. Who is he and how do you know him?"

"I've seen him before. He's been to the restaurant and he likes to walk around the lake. He must be fifty and he's very ugly. He was pawing his waitress." She wrinkled her nose. "As if anyone wanted someone like him, and him probably married anyway. He's got a shop on the market, selling combs and fans and such stuff."

Tora almost dropped his bowl. "He sells fans?" he gasped.

"Yes. And a lot of other things. I went in there once, just looking, you know. He came rushing out to show me some combs, but some awful woman called him away and came to wait on me. She could tell I had no money and practically threw me out." Midori glowered.

Tora tsked. "So what happened with the young woman and this guy?"

"They walked away together."

"Which way?"

She pointed. "So what happened to the pretty lady?" she asked.

Tora popped one of the eggs into his mouth and reached for his money. "She's dead," he mumbled, chewing, and counted out a couple of pieces of silver to pay his bill.

Midori squealed and the owner rushed over. Tora apologized for scaring the girl and left.

Outside it was fully dark by now. The fan merchant's shop had been long closed. It would have to wait for another day.

26

The Missing Maid

Akitada had had the unpleasant task of reporting the contents of Yukiko's letter to the children. He had never lied to them, and so he informed them that she was well but had asked him to come for a visit.

Yasuko said quickly, "Will you go, Father?"

"I told her that I wish I could come but am too busy at the moment. In any case, we will soon all return to the capital."

Yasuko's face fell. "But that's months to go!" she wailed.

The impatience of children.

Yoshi did not seem perturbed. He looked at his sister in astonishment. "Why do you want to leave? This is a wonderful place to be. Plenty of room to ride my horse, and Tora takes us hunting. Those things I can't do in the capital. All I ever do there is study with the tutor. You should have some fun things to do."

Yasuko did not answer her brother. She looked at Akitada accusingly, "I miss Yukiko. She spent time with me like Tora spends time with Yoshi. Now I'm all alone. All day long." She was talking herself into tears.

Akitada felt guilty. He never seemed to have enough time for the children. He said soothingly, "It won't be long at all. And maybe I'll dust off my old flute this evening and we'll make music the way we used to."

Yasuko was not consoled. "It won't be the same at all without Yukiko playing her zither."

In the end he had fled to his work.

He found that routine matters had stacked up in his absence, particularly since Saburo had been occupied with supplying Secretary Ono with files he wished to consult. It could not be helped, and he set to work with great determination. He had made some progress when Tora came in.

"You won't believe what I found out yesterday," he said. "Sit down and hold on to your hat." He sat down himself, grinning broadly.

Akitada washed out his brush. "I'm sitting and there is no wind, so go ahead."

Unabashed, Tora cried, "It was Ishimura's son, but he didn't show up for their meeting and she went off with another man. What do you think now?"

Akitada frowned. "What other man?"

"A fat merchant. And guess what he sells in his shop?"

"Tora, I don't want to play guessing games. Besides, you're leaving out a lot, I think. Start at the beginning."

Disappointed that he had failed to make his dramatic revelation, Tora said, "Well, he sells fans."

"Surely he's not the man who mended our fan?"

"No. At least I don't think so. I haven't found him yet." Seeing Akitada's face, he said, "Oh, all right. From the start: Saburo guessed right. It was Judge Ishimura. His son was home all summer from attending the university in the capital and he used his time well. He saw Hiroko at a fair and one other place and propositioned her. She agreed to meet him." Tora paused to shake his head. "They met in a house of assignation. That Iris Pavilion isn't a restaurant. It's a whore house."

Shocked, Akitada said, "You could find a better word surely. And can you have this right? It doesn't sound like Lady Hiroko . . . or a judge's son."

"Well, the owner calls her place a house of assignation, but she provides women in case you don't bring your own. And I've got it right. It all fits. They described her clothes. Yes, people saw her on the day she was killed."

Akitada stared at him. "It's unfathomable! But go on!"

Highly satisfied by the fact that he had finally made an impression, Tora went on to describe the pond pavilion, and the fact that Mrs. Ito had only met Hiroko on that last night, when she had come to report that her lover had not come.

"He says he went away for a couple of days to visit an aunt who's a nun in Nagoya, and he didn't have time to tell Hiroko."

"How did they exchange messages?"

"They didn't. He set up the next meeting during the previous one."

Akitada shook his head. "Go on!"

"Well, having been stood up, Hiroko apparently went across the street to a small lake. That's where she was seen by the owner of the Lake Restaurant and her staff. One of the waitresses took a particular interest. She described Hiroko's clothes and saw the fat merchant pick her up. She'd been watching because she thought Hiroko was going to drown herself in the lake."

"Dear Heaven!"

"Well, knowing what we do, it's possible she intended to do it. Her beloved"—Tora grimaced here—"also said that her father had been beating her. Where was she going to go?"

"So this merchant is now your suspect? Because he sells fans? And where was her maid during all of this."

Tora scowled. "No maid. Mrs. Ito said she didn't bring a maid to their meetings."

"Ah!" Akitada sat up. "Did you report all this to Akechi?"

"Not yet. It was late last night before I got the stories."

"Maybe we'd better have Akechi join us. That maid must be found."

"What about the merchant. I thought I'd go find him today."

"He won't run away. It's high time we did something about the maid. Go get Akechi so we can fill him in and find out exactly what he's been doing."

∞

Tora returned an hour later with Akechi. He had already informed the lieutenant of his news. Akechi looked depressed.

"It seems I've missed most of what's been happening," he said after saluting. "I'm truly sorry, Governor. I've been wasting my time talking to fishermen about the other corpse, since Captain Sashima and you were looking into the Imagawa situation. I didn't expect to get much information at the victim's house or at the Matsudaira place."

"No, that's quite all right. Anything at all on the body with the tattoo?"

"Nothing, sir. Though I got the feeling nobody trusted me much."

Akitada remembered what Fujiwara Michinori had said about fishermen and their close collaboration with pirates. He nodded and said, "For that matter, we didn't do very well there either. Please sit down. Some wine?"

Akechi sat. "Thanks, no. Too early for me." The lieutenant scratched his beard. He was still downcast and looked at Tora for help.

Tora smiled, looking smug. Akitada realized that Tora's fondness for investigating had put him in competition with the police captain and that the latter had not dared to set his wits against Tora's or his governor's. He suspected that Akechi had missed clues, but did not have the heart to point this out.

"Lieutenant," he said, "what do you make of this tale Captain Sashima has brought us."

"It doesn't sound very likely—if you'll forgive me, Captain. Lady Hiroko in a house of assignation? And later going off with some merchant?"

Tora frowned. "Don't be so sure, Akechi. In my experience, the good people do some very strange things."

Akitada suppressed a smile. "This merchant, did Captain Sashima describe him to you?"

Akechi nodded. "The description probably fits several of the tradesmen. I'll look into it today."

"It can wait. We've been wondering about that maid. No body has turned up. Where can she be?"

Akechi threw up his hands. "I've taken my men, and we've searched all the fields and woods outside the city. And we've put up notices on all the notice boards asking people if they've seen Otoki. Nothing. Of course, her body may have been taken out in a boat and thrown overboard. If they tied rocks to her, she would go to the bottom."

"Well," said Akitada, "I prefer to think that she's alive but hiding somewhere."

Both Tora and Akechi looked at him in surprise. Tora asked, "Why would she do that? Surely she would've run home or to the police if she knew what had happened to her mistress."

"I think she either doesn't know or if she knows she's too afraid she'll be punished. Remember Imagawa is known to have beaten his daughter. What do you think he'd do to her maid?"

They considered it and nodded.

Tora asked, "But where would she go? Otoki's only fifteen and a peasant girl. She doesn't know her way around."

"I think she's at home with her family."

Akechi protested, "But I went there and talked to them. They hadn't seen her and knew nothing about her."

Akitada said, "I meant to ask you about that. What was their manner when you asked if she'd come home?"

Akechi thought back, chewing his lip. "They were puzzled. Her mother isn't too bright. She just stood there, looking down the entire time. But her father was very firm. They hadn't seen her for several months."

"Did they seem worried?"

"I didn't think so, but they may be by now. It probably hadn't sunk in when I talked to them."

"Hmm." Akitada smiled. "I think they're hiding her, afraid of what Imagawa will do to her. If she told them about the beatings, they will not want her to go back."

Tora jumped to his feet. "Let's go and find out."

At that moment the door opened and Secretary Ono strolled in. His demeanor was so impressive that Akechi scrambled to his feet and saluted. Neither Tora nor Akitada bothered with the niceties.

Ono snapped, "Couldn't help overhearing the captain. You can't leave. I forbid it."

Akitada burst into laughter. Tora chortled. Akechi looked shocked.

"How dare you?" Ono demanded. "This behavior proves your unfitness to serve in the government in any fashion whatsoever. I outrank you. More to the point, I'm here to investigate assorted offenses you have committed. The fact that you treat me in this shameful manner shall be noted."

Akitada sobered. "By all means make a note of it, Ono. We are actually not far apart rankwise, you know. However, I agree that your current function deserves proper respect. Unfortunately you carry it out in a manner that allows for no respect to you as a person."

Ono gasped and turned white. While he was still trying to find words, Akitada continued, "Since you burst in here during a conference without regard or respect for my office, you are unaware perhaps that we are engaged in solving the murder of Lord Imagawa's daughter. This has priority over any new calumnies against me that you may have thought up. Captain Sashima and I will leave now. Whatever you want has to wait."

Ono turned on his heel and left.

A brief silence fell, then Lieutenant Akechi asked Akitada, "What a very unpleasant man. Can he make trouble for you, sir?"

"He will try, Lieutenant, but that's neither here nor there. We have work to do. I would like you to come with us for another visit to Otoki's parents. I know you've been most diligent in your searches for another body and so we must conclude that the girl is still alive. At her age, I would guess she ran off home. At any rate, let's make sure."

Akechi looked a little unhappy about this, but a short while later all three were riding out of town.

The harvests were almost all done. Akitada had been told that it had been a very good year. He was glad that he would have something satisfactory to report to his superiors, even if he could hardly claim to have had a hand in it.

The fields lay bare. Already the world was taking on the emptiness that always preceded winter. It would be a long time before the colors and scents of spring would lift their spirits again.

Otoki's family was large but owned a small farm. Their house stood some distance from the village and they approached it by a dirt road that ran straight for half a mile. That was how Akechi saw a sudden movement behind the house. His eyes were sharper than those of his companions. He pointed. "Sir, someone just ran into that small grove of trees."

"Go check it out! You, too, Tora," Akitada said.

Both Akechi and Tora spurred their horses and galloped past the farm house and to the grove. Akitada continued to the house and dismounted. Nobody seemed to be at home. A dog was barking somewhere behind the house.

Peasants did not have the privilege to leave their fields with their families. There was too much work and the nation depended on them. Akitada saw that sheaves of rice still awaited threshing in a shed nearby. In fact, it looked as though he had interrupted this activity.

As he waited, the door finally opened. The farmer came out, took a few steps, and asked, "What do you want, sir?" He looked belligerent.

Given Akitada's clothing, his behavior was suspicious. Normally, peasants knelt and bowed. Akitada, far from being angered, smiled at him and asked, "Are you the father of Otoki?"

The man scowled. "I have a daughter called Otoki. She's not here. She works in Komachi."

"I think you know that isn't true."

The man glared. "I haven't seen her. Not for more than a month."

"She served as maid to the daughter of Lord Imagawa?"

"Yes." His scowl deepened.

"Why did she leave her position?"

There was no answer. The peasant clamped his mouth shut. But by now there were voices behind the house, one of them the high frightened one of a girl. The peasant turned and a woman, presumably his wife, came running from the house, followed by a gaggle of frightened-looking children.

Tora and Akechi appeared around the corner. They were on foot, leading their horses. On one of them sat a weeping girl.

Akitada smiled. "Ah! Otoki. Finally. We've looked everywhere for you." He glanced at Tora. "Did you tell her about her mistress?"

Tora said, "She knew already. Akechi told her parents when he asked for her. That's when she really panicked."

Otoki's mother flung herself down on her knees before Akitada. "Please, your honor, don't hurt our

Otoki. She's done nothing. She knows nothing. She ran away because of all the beatings."

"We're not taking Otoki," Akitada said. "Please get up. We just have a few questions and then you may all get on with your lives."

Otoki's father now came closer. "Her lady told her to go home," he said. "She gave her her wages, and Otoki left Komachi after dark so the master wouldn't find out."

That explained why no witnesses had come forward who had seen Otoki. Akitada turned to the girl, who had calmed down somewhat.

"Why did you leave, Otoki?" he asked her.

She gulped and said in low voice, "The master beat me for not telling him where my lady was going."

"And where was she going?"

She hung her head and shook it. "It was a secret."

"Did you go with her?"

She looked up, surprised. "Not the last time."

"But you used to go with her?"

She nodded. "I waited outside. In the garden."

"When exactly did you leave to go home?"

And so the whole story came out. Otoki had left the Imagawa house with Lady Hiroko on the ninth day of the month. They had gone to the Matsudaira house, stayed briefly and then left by the back gate. Lady Hiroko had told her to wait somewhere until dark and then start walking home. That was the last she had seen of her mistress.

27

The Fading Chrysanthemums

They rode back to Komachi contentedly. This was due primarily to the fact that Otoki was alive and not another corpse rotting somewhere in the countryside. They were also pleased that Otoki had confirmed a number of suspicions, namely that Lord Imagawa had been a harsh master and father, that Lady Hiroko had indeed been meeting a lover, that her friend, Lady Tomiko knew all about it and had kept the secret from Hiroko's father, and that Hiroko had gone off to meet Arihito in the Iris Pavilion. While Otoki's story had filled a number of gaps in their investigation, it had not produced the name of her killer or indeed how or where her murder had happened.

They discussed some of these things on the way.

"I think she wasn't going home that last day. That's why she sent Otoki away," Akitada said.

Tora pointed out that they still did not know what had happened to the silk she had bought. Akitada had no answer to this. Privately he wondered if the whole silk story was part of the web of lies they had been told. He told Akechi to speak to the silk merchant again, and asked Tora to find the fan merchant. As for himself, he decided rather grimly to make himself available to the detestable Ono in hopes of concluding his investigation and being rid of him.

But when they reached the tribunal, a surprise awaited them. The courtyard was filled with armed men and their horses, and a fine palanquin stood at the foot of the tribunal stairs. With considerable astonishment, Akitada recognized the Fujiwara insignia on one of the standards carried by the outriders.

Had Michinori come for a visit already?

But then one of the armed men came to him, grinning broadly. "We brought your lady to you, sir," he said, looking up at the stunned Akitada. "Her father sent us with her."

That explained the Fujiwara insignia.

But why had Yukiko come?

Tora clapped his hands and shouted, "Your lady's come home, sir! What joy! Hurry up and greet her! It's high time, too!"

In a daze, Akitada dismounted, thanked his father-in-law's people for looking after his wife and then climbed the steps to the tribunal.

He found Yukiko in his office. She was seated between Saburo and Lord Ono, both wreathed in smiles. When Akitada came in, she rose and came to him quickly with her well-remembered grace. She smiled, bowed formally, and said, "I have returned, my honorable husband."

Akitada remembered very little else that passed, except that Ono seemed surprising pleasant. Akitada led Yukiko to their private residence, wondering why she seemed so jumpy.

"Are you quite well, my dear?" he asked anxiously.

"Of course."

As they passed through the garden, he remembered the attack in Owari and asked, "Have you had a safe journey?"

"Oh, yes. Father insisted I take twenty of his men, armed as if they were headed for battle. I was quite safe. But the trip was much slower than when you and I took horses. Father felt that my current rank did not permit me to ride. I thought it a great pity."

She was chattering nervously and with an awkward formality. And she mentioned her current rank. His wife was no longer just his wife. She was one of the empress's ladies now. But she looked strained and tired. In the end, he said only, "I'm glad you had a good journey." She said nothing.

When they passed the chrysanthemums she had planted so long ago, Yukiko stopped. "Oh," she said, "they're already fading. But they must have been very pretty. Did you admire them?"

Akitada had not noticed the chrysanthemums when they had finally bloomed but he lied and said, "They were beautiful." His mind was full of questions. Had she come home to stay? Or was this just a short visit to inform him of some future plans that did not involve him? He wished with all his heart she would leave the service at court and be his wife again.

But he did not quite allow himself to hope for such thing. It was enough that she had come. So he did not ask and instead took her to see the children.

They were thrilled, especially Yasuko who was full of questions about the emperor and empress, about the clothes they wore, about the things they did. Yoshi's interest focused more on special contests that Yukiko might have attended. He was disappointed to find out that none of these involved manly sports but instead silly games and poems.

It was Yasuko who asked, "Will you stay with us now?"

Akitada held his breath.

Yukiko smiled at his daughter and said, "I have a whole week, then I must return to my duties. But you and your father will soon come back to the capital yourselves."

Yasuko pouted and Akitada suppressed his own disappointment. She had come. That must be enough. It was good to see them all together again and to hear their laughter. Slowly Akitada allowed himself to hope again.

Even pale and much thinner, Yukiko was more beautiful than he had remembered in all his daydreams, though many of them had been during sleepless nights. She had added a striking elegance and grace to her demeanor that he did not recall. How wonderful she would be for Yasuko.

How wonderful she would be for him.

Already he thought of the night, hoping she would welcome him as in the past before their quarrel. He tried to catch her eye, but she was preoccupied with the children. And then he remembered her journey. He must be patient. She needed rest above all.

Reluctantly, he left them together after a while. He talked to the servants, making sure that a fine dinner would be prepared for that night and that Yukiko's room would be ready for her. Then he went to face Ono.

He found him in the archives and said, "I have some time now. What did you want to ask me?"

Ono jumped up and smiled at him. He actually smiled. What he said astonished Akitada even more.

"My dear Akitada, I would certainly never interfere in your welcoming your lady properly when she has only just arrived. What a charming lady she is! She was very gracious in telling us a little about Her Majesty and life in the inner palace. Of course, I have an elderly cousin who is mistress of the wardrobe, but I'm afraid she can have no idea about their Majesties' daily life. No, it is only the younger ladies of the very highest rank who take part in those gatherings. You are to be congratulated on your marriage, Akitada."

Akitada gaped at him and murmured weakly, "Thank you."

"So do not let me interfere in your plans. I have what I need and most things have been explained to my satisfaction either by you or the worthy Saburo."

"Well, if you can spare me . . ."

"Certainly, certainly!" Ono waved him away with a broad smile and a wink.

∞

That evening they ate together like a family again. Akitada had adopted this custom from Kosehira because he had enjoyed the togetherness of parents and children. Before marrying Yukiko he had usually eaten alone, but the cheerfulness of a family meal in Yukiko's family had struck him powerfully.

He was instantly aware again of the strain in his wife's demeanor. She ate little and chatted with too much animation. In the end, he guessed that she dreaded the intimacy of the coming night. So as soon as the children had gone to their rooms, Akitada said, "You'll be tired, my love. I shall leave you to get a good night's sleep. Perhaps we may share our gruel in the morning while sitting on the veranda?"

She blushed and avoided his eyes. "Yes, thank you, Akitada. You're very understanding."

∞

Akitada woke to sunshine and birdsong and a sense of happiness. For a little while, he thought, for these short ten days I shall be a husband and she will be my wife. It is not much and yet it is wonderful. The thing to do was to forget about the past and the future and pretend for a little while.

234

He rose, washed, and shaved. Dressed in a dark blue silk robe she had sewn for him, he walked to the kitchen where he found cook already stirring the morning gruel.

"It's special today," she told him with a smile. "In honor of your lady, sir."

Yukiko's visit had made them all happy. Akitada asked the cook to fill two bowls and then carried them on a neat footed tray to Yukiko's room. He was not used to this duty and concentrated carefully on balancing the tray and not spilling anything. Appetizing smells rose from the bowls.

At Yukiko's door, he paused and cleared his throat.

"Akitada?"

"Yes. I brought some gruel."

She opened the door. She must just have got up. Her face was rosy and she still wore the thin white silk undergown she slept in, though she had thrown a rose-colored robe over it. Her breasts were partially visible under the fine silk. Akitada stared, then let his eyes wander lower.

She reached out and pulled him into the room, shutting the door behind him. He stood, still foolishly holding the tray until she took it from his hands and set it down.

"Have you missed me?" she asked stepping closer.

He made an inarticulate sound and took her into his arms, kissing hungrily her face, her neck, her mouth, her eyes. "Yukiko," he murmured, and "Oh, Yukiko. It's been too long."

She drew him toward the bedding, tugging at his sash, while he pushed back the rose-colored robe and buried his face between her breasts, completely mindless with lust.

They knelt down together. He tore at his clothes in his impatience. She lay on her back, her silk undergown rucked up, revealing one smooth thigh, and looking up at him. Akitada untied his trousers. All these clothes! Why had he not gone to her before dressing?

He was about to get up and step out of his trousers, when Yukiko sat up and cried, "No! Oh, please, don't!"

Akitada paused to look down at her. She had covered her face with her hands and was weeping. Still on his knees, he moved closer and asked, "What's wrong, my love? Are you ill? What can I do?"

She rolled onto her stomach, her back heaving with wrenching sobs.

"Please, Yukiko. Tell me. Whatever it is, we can deal with it. Please talk to me?" He was painfully aware of his own discomfort, having been so suddenly and inexplicably stopped from making love to his wife.

She murmured something he could not understand.

"Yukiko, nothing is so terrible that we cannot talk about it. Please!"

She sat up again but would not look at him. "I meant to seduce you," she said in a broken voice, "but I cannot do it. Dear gods, to what depths I have fallen!"

Akitada said nothing. He just looked at her. So, he thought, our problems are not over after all. Serves me right to believe in my good fortune.

After a while, during which she merely sat with her face turned away and her head bowed, he said, "I think you'd better explain."

She took a deep, shuddering breath and said quite clearly and impatiently, "Oh, for heaven's sake, Akitada! I would have thought it's obvious. I intended to have you make love to me because I'm with child."

Her words struck him like a thunderclap. His mind reeled for a moment before he comprehended fully what she was telling him. Strangely, what pained him first was that he had been so slow to understand and she was irritated with his stupidity. Then he searched his mind, wondering if he should feel anger, grief, or shame.

Not shame, he decided. The offense, if there was an offense, was not his. And while he was shocked and disappointed, he should not have been. The life style at the palace made love affairs almost inescapable. He was angry with himself. He even managed to feel a sliver of pity for her.

After some thought, he got up and put the rest of his clothes back on. When he was done, he sat down again a little distance from her and asked, "What are your plans?"

She turned around then to stare at him from swollen eyes. "What can I do. My fate is in your hands."

"Surely not. Do you wish for a divorce so you can live with the father of your child?"

"I shall never live with him!"

It was said with a sort of explosive emphasis that surprised him. He suddenly wondered just how this had happened. He asked, "Who is he?"

"I'm not going to tell you."

It was probably best, he thought dispassionately. He had no intention of killing the man, but their lives might bring them into contact, and that, Akitada thought, he could not bear.

"Do you love him?"

"No." After a moment, she added, "Not any longer."

"Did you tell him about the child?"

"No! Never!"

Akitada sighed. "Have you told your father?"

"No!" She wailed and flung herself down before him. "Please, don't tell him, Akitada. If you have ever loved me, don't let him know. Promise me!"

"Who else knows about this?"

"Nobody! We were very discreet."

He did not tell her that his sister had known or guessed. In the end, there was really only one option, and Yukiko probably knew it as well as he.

"Akitada?" She knelt, looking at him anxiously.

And still she was so beautiful and desirable, even now. But she was not for him. He sighed again. "Very well," he said. "Then I can see only one way. We shall pretend that the child is mine. Your visit here should account for it. You shall continue as my wife and we shall raise the child as ours."

She murmured, "That's very generous. It will not be a burden. My father and I will see to it that the child's future is secure."

He felt the first anger and rose. "I'm not doing this because I hope for future benefits from you or from my father-in-law, Yukiko. I'm doing it to spare him and you scandal and grief."

She bowed her head. "Yes, Akitada. I know. I'm sorry." She was weeping again.

Ten days with Yukiko!

Surely someone would notice the tension.

"For the sake of the family and my pride, would you at least pretend to find me tolerable?"

She gasped and Akitada turned and left.

28

The Fan Seller

Tora and Hanae had had their own celebration of Yukiko's homecoming. After their evening rice, Hanae had been especially beguiling. She very clearly made an effort to seduce Tora. After all these years, their marriage had settled down to a certain normalcy. Though Tora still relished making love to her and she seemed to enjoy their bouts as well, neither had made any special efforts or bothered to whisper sweet words into each other's ears. So Tora was surprised but gratified, and a mutually satisfactory night ensued.

He slept late and got up in a hurry and guiltily, because duties awaited him and he also wished to see his master's face this morning. The many months of his loneliness had depressed Tora, who felt strongly that all that was needed was a woman in his master's bed.

He found his master in the tribunal office, dictating something to a scribe. There was no sign of any particular contentment that he could see and he decided that his lady must have been too tired the night before.

"Have a seat, Tora," his master said and finished dictating the letter.

Tora caught a few words that puzzled him, and when the scribe had left to make a clean copy, he asked, "You're sending for a companion for Yasuko?"

"Yes. My wife will shortly return to the capital. Her leave doesn't allow a longer visit. Yasuko has been lonely without her and will take this departure hard. I've decided to try to get a suitable woman to join her. She's old enough for a companion instead of a nursemaid."

"Sounds good," Tora said. "But we'd been hoping your lady would stay this time. Aren't you disappointed?"

Foolish question. Tora could see he was. And he did not answer the question. A small muscle in his jaw tightened and he would not meet Tora's eyes.

Instead he said, "There's work to be done. I expect you'll be locating the elusive fan merchant?"

So! There had been another quarrel. Tora felt a surge of anger toward Lady Yukiko. What had come over her? Couldn't she see how much her husband had missed her?

Tora was becoming depressed again, but he said nothing and set out to have a look at the merchants near the market.

Komachi did not boast a very large number of fan merchants. However, apart from the man who had mended the broken fan, there were a number of shops that sold them along with other items. Given that the fan had been a fine one, Tora decided to start with those that sold expensive curios.

These numbered two, and while one of them had some fans, the proprietor did not fit the description of a fat man Tora had been given by Midori; he was skinny old man who moved about with a cane. The second shop belonged to a woman and sold no fans.

Tora visited next the silk merchant who had sold the silk to Lady Hiroko. He reasoned that a shop dealing in fine fabrics might well also sell accessories like fans. Besides, he knew the owner was fat. And Tora thought there was no harm in checking up on Akechi who was supposed to have looked into the disappearance of the silk.

As last time, the oily proprietor rushed to serve him. Yes, Tora thought, he would not mind it if this fellow turned out to be the killer. It made sense. He had met Lady Hiroko earlier the day she died.

"Welcome, Captain," the man cried, bowing several times. "How may I serve you?"

First things first. "Do you sell fans?"

The round face fell almost comically. "Sorry, no. We could perhaps find one for you. Is it for a lady?"

"No. It's for a man. Something with maple leaves."

"A painted fan? I'm afraid there are very few to be had in Mikawa. Most of the nobles buy such things in the capital."

"Ah!" Tora regarded the round figure before him thoughtfully. "Has Lieutenant Akechi been by?"

"Yes. He looked in late yesterday. Asking about the silk for Lady Imagawa. I told him what I told you. The lady came, bought the silk, and gave it to her maid. That's the last I've seen or heard about it."

Tora narrowed his eyes and barked, "That's a lie!"

The man took a step back, his mouth falling open. The women pawing the silks gave little cries of distress and hurried out of the store.

"You're lying," Tora repeated, a little less loud. "We've spoken to the maid. They never came here that day. What do you say now?"

The man's hands began to shake. He retreated a little farther. "Maybe it was another day? I swear it's just like I told you. The lady was very particular that it be the right shade. She was making a robe for her husband."

"What?"

"Yes. She said she was making a robe for her husband. As a surprise. Ask the lady. She'll tell you."

Tora was beginning to see the confusion. He tried to think back to his last visit. Had he made it clear that Lady Hiroko and her servant were involved? Maybe not. He recalled he had been in a hurry and it had merely been a matter of confirming something they had been told at the Imagawa house. And now that also escaped his memory. He was sure they had talked about Lady Hiroko picking up the silk, but had they ever said she did?

"How old was the lady who bought the silk?"

The merchant fluttered his plump hands. "Oh, I don't know. Not old. But not young either."

"And her maid?"

"Her? She must have been at least forty years old. A dry old stick."

There it was. One of the wives had bought the silk.

Tora had the decency to apologize for doubting the merchant. But on his way out, he paused. "By any chance, do you frequent the Lake Restaurant?"

"What lake restaurant? What's it called?"

"Never mind!"

Somewhat cowed by his mistake, Tora began a systematic series of visits to each and every shop that was remotely likely to sell fans. This consumed considerable time and it was already past midday before he stepped into a small shop that sold all sorts of small objects ranging from medicine boxes to carved water containers and tassels for reed screens.

The shop owner's name was on the door curtain. It was Naganori. And Naganori was middle-aged, of average size, and round of figure. He seemed strong and agile enough to strangle a woman. Walking up to Tora with a little bounce, he offered his services. Tora eyed him hopefully. "Do you sell fans?"

"Yes, indeed. If the gentleman would just step this way."

Tora stepped this way and was shown some ten or twelve fans, both the solid round ones that were only a few coppers and those that opened and closed and cost more. None of them was painted, and none resembled in the least the quality of the fan found by the dog.

"I wanted something with some painting on it. I thought perhaps maple leaves and a pheasant since it's fall." He watched the man's face for a sign of recognition and saw none.

The merchant said regretfully, "I'm very sorry. You describe a very fine fan. I have never had anything of that quality."

"Hmm." Disappointed, Tora looked around the shop wondering how to proceed. Once he had cast this bouncy, smug character as the murderer, it would have been very nice if he had also been the one to drop the fan. But you could not have everything. He asked, "Are you familiar with the Lake Restaurant?"

This produced a smile. "Yes indeed, sir. It's a very nice place. A bit too rich for my purse usually, but the food is delicious. Sometimes I just walk past it to catch the smell of their fried shrimp." He chuckled.

Tora remembered the delicious smells. "By any chance, were you there on the ninth day of this month?"

The man blinked. "The ninth?" he asked, looking puzzled.

Before Tora could answer, a very fat woman waddled from the backroom. She stared at Tora with sharp black eyes set into doughy cheeks. Her tiny mouth was pursed. Shifting her gaze from Tora to the merchant, she demanded, "What's this about, Naganori?"

Naganori gave Tora an apologetic look. "My wife, sir."

Tora did not like her and so ignored her. "You were seen," he said to Naganori. "Why were you there?"

246

His wife pushed herself forward again. "Where were you? Answer him, Naganori."

Naganori shot her an anxious look. "I don't know, sir. That's quite a while ago. I may have been taking a stroll. Why do you ask?"

She placed herself between her husband and Tora. "What's this all about?" she asked him in a belligerent tone.

She was too heavy to move aside, so Tora glowered at her and said, "Your husband was seen talking to a young woman near the Lake Restaurant."

She glared at Naganori. "What? You went there again to pick up whores?" Her voice had become shrill and she had turned an unpleasant shade of red.

"No, my dear, I didn't," her husband pleaded. "It was nothing. Quite harmless, I swear."

"Then why does he want to know where you were on the ninth? What have you been up to besides whoring?"

"Nothing, I assure you, dearest. Nothing at all."

"That Lake Restaurant is across the street from one of those houses. That's where you were! With some whore! Spending our hard-earned money on your filthy pleasures."

Her arms were akimbo now and she moved in a threatening manner toward her husband, who backed away with such a look of fear on his face that Tora almost laughed. It was clear that he would not get anything out of the man while the woman was present. He took Naganori firmly by the arm and pulled him outside. There he walked him to the corner. Naganori walked with faltering steps and an occasional moan. When they reached the corner, Tora stopped and glared at him. "Very well, now speak!"

The man looked back to where his wife stood outside their shop, watching. "Oh, dear!" he whimpered. "She'll not give me any peace now."

"You have more to worry about than your wife."

Naganori squeaked. "I did nothing. I swear."

"As I said, you were seen with the young woman. People saw you by the lake talking to a young woman and walking off with her."

Sounding almost relieved, Naganori said, "Oh that! Was that on the ninth?" He paused. "Yes, there was this pretty young woman who looked like she was going to walk into the lake. She was weeping. I stopped and asked her what was wrong. She said she didn't know where to go or what to do. I could see she was upset. It was getting dark and it's not very safe on the streets and she looked and talked like one of the good people, so I offered to take her home. That's all."

"Where did you take her?"

"I don't know. She knew the way, and the moment I could see she was safe, I left."

"Show me the place!"

Naganori cast another glance back at his wife, but he seemed to think it better to postpone returning to her and started out across the town. It became clear after a while that he was headed for the lake. But he went past it and also past the Iris Pavilion before he stopped. He pointed.

"She went that way. That's all I know."

"Did you watch to see where she went exactly?"

"No. It was getting late. What is this about?"

Tora studied him with a frown. "What's that mark on your neck?" he asked suddenly, bending closer.

Naganori scooted back. "Nothing. It's nothing." He looked frightened again.

"It looks like you got scratched. How did that happen?"

The man covered the scratches with his hand and said, "I don't remember."

"You don't remember? They're pretty well healed by now, but they must have been bad."

"Wait! It was my friend's cat. I remember now."

Tora did not believe a word of this.

"What did you do after you left the young lady?"

"I went home."

"Your wife will confirm this?"

Naganori shuffled his feet. "Well, I may have stopped by my friend's house for a little."

"The friend with the cat?"

The merchant nodded. "We play a game of *go* now and then."

"His name?"

"Must you get him involved?"

"Yes."

"His memory's not what it used to be."

"His name?"

"Hankei. He makes *tatami* mats and reed shades. He lives near the Enkan shrine. Please don't mention any of this to my wife. I was just trying to help the young woman."

Tora grunted and looked at the man. He looked frightened. Was it from guilt or because he would have to face his wife? Tora decided to leave him to deal with his problems. Naganori was not going anywhere if his wife had anything to say about it.

29

A Father's Wickedness

There followed a period of such intense soul-searching in Akitada's life that he performed his daily duties almost automatically. It was as if he had retreated from the world around him, seeing it only in snippets as if through the branches of trees or hidden by fog. He was aware that this was part of the struggle to contain the pain Yukiko's betrayal had caused.

It was not very successful.

His dilemma was aggravated by the fact that he must see her daily at family meals, putting on a cheerful face for the sake of the children. He looked forward to her departure but knew that their future lives together would always require an effort, though he hoped that time might make it easier.

Occasionally he reproached himself for not accepting the situation more stoically. Few marriages between men and women were close. Indeed, most men seemed to care more for providing sons than for a loving relationship with their wives. Perhaps in his later years, when the succession was secured and his wives established in their household positions, a man might lose his heart to a beautiful courtesan and spend his remaining life with her.

It was not a tempting image.

He did give Yukiko credit for putting a good face on things before the children, but the pretense was awkward for both of them. The nights were especially difficult.

To prove their happy cohabitation to the household, he slept every night in his wife's room. It was an uncomfortable arrangement, since he would not share her bed and it would have looked strange if he had carried his own bedding to her room. After all, they were supposed to lie in each other's arms.

Neither slept much, nor did they talk much beyond some small courtesies. Akitada dreaded the nights so much that he protracted going to her room until very late, sitting on his veranda and staring out at the night, thoughts of future miseries chasing themselves through his mind.

Once, as they lay awake in the darkness, she asked in a low voice, "Will you ever forgive me?"

He did not answer her question. He said, "I have long been aware that our marriage was a mistake. I bear the responsibility for it."

She was silent after that, but later he thought he could hear her weeping.

A certain amount of progress was made in that outer world. Ono departed, declaring himself quite satisfied and carrying his papers with him. He had not stopped being pleasant since the day he had met Yukiko.

The power of being well-connected would apparently save Akitada's career once again!

Tora and Akechi reported. Since the silk had been bought not by Hiroko but by her stepmother, the confusion had been no more than a series of misunderstandings on their part and that of various servants. It looked as if they were once again left without a clue.

As for Naganori, they really had nothing against him except some scratches. And if they had to absolve Naganori, that only left Hiroko's lover, Arihito, who had been in Nagoya at the time of the murder.

Akitada decided to leave the investigation entirely to Akechi and withdraw into his painful routine of tribunal business and personal life. But in this instance, Tora, who had developed a disconcerting habit of watching him with a puzzled expression, chose to continue searching for the killer on his own.

∞

Tora was troubled. The new closeness that had developed between himself and Akitada during their Tokaido adventure seemed to have evaporated. Since Tora knew his master better than anyone, he was aware that something was very wrong. He guessed it had to do with Lady Yukiko, who also looked pale and strained. It was not a matter he could discuss with Akitada, but he mentioned it to Hanae as they lay beside each other in bed.

"I think it's her service at court," Hanae suggested. "She arrived looking very peaked. If I didn't know better, I'd have said she was with child. But the master spends every night with her, so you are quite wrong if you think they quarreled. Maybe the problem is that neither is getting much sleep." She giggled. "I think you must've forgotten what that's like."

Tora could not ignore such a challenge, especially not when he had been worried about all the gray hairs he seemed to have on his head and in his mustache lately.

As for the murder investigation, Tora was quite pleased that it had been left to him and the police. Since Akechi was nervous about demanding to speak to Lord Imagawa's ladies, Tora made the matter of confirming the silk purchase his first errand the next morning.

To all intents and purposes, Imagawa seemed to have shed no tears over his daughter's death, though he immediately asked if her killer had been arrested.

Tora informed him that the investigation was ongoing and that they were getting close to an arrest.

"Oh, don't waste my time with your lies," Imagawa snapped. "You've done nothing and that police lieutenant is totally useless. He hasn't showed his face here at all. I shall complain to the government in the capital about the incompetence of the people they assign to this province."

Stung to anger by this, Tora snapped, "Sir, given the fact that you have driven your daughter to seek men outside your house, our problem is a little complicated. Apparently, she was accustomed to roaming the streets at night."

Imagawa's mouth fell open. "What? Are you mad? How dare you? Get out!"

Tora stared back at him, unperturbed. "The facts speak for themselves. Firstly, the coroner found that Lady Hiroko was no longer a virgin. Then we have witnesses, including her best friend, Lord Matsudaira's daughter, who knew about her affairs. Several of them also said that you used to beat your daughter and your wives. You also beat her maid. Unfortunately, we do not have the power to interfere in people's private lives, but I think you should be very careful about bringing charges against the police and the governor."

Imagawa had changed color. Controlling himself with an effort, he said, "Lies. Those are all lies. I'm a strict man, but I do not beat my family. I demand to know who has been saying such things."

Tora was getting tired of him. "I need to speak to your ladies."

"Absolutely not! I shall not help you besmirch my character any further."

Perhaps, thought Tora, it would have been better to get the information from the ladies first before accusing their husband to his face. The master would have handled this better. But he had been very angry with this man for a very long time, and hearing Otoki's story had brought his feelings to a boil.

He said, "Shall I report that you refuse to cooperate, sir?"

"Report away!" snarled Imagawa.

"I must warn you that this will mean you are now a suspect in Lady Hiroko's death."

That took the man's breath away. He stood and stared at Tora, the muscles in his jaw working furiously. Eventually, he said through gritted teeth, "You must be mad! I have never been treated with such disrespect. My family is an ancient one. Such insults are not to be borne. You'll be sorry!"

Tora suppressed a smirk. Imagawa was hardly a very martial figure. Beating helpless women was more his style. He said nothing and waited.

After a long silence, Lord Imagawa said grudgingly, "Very well, since I seem to have no choice in the matter. But I insist on being present while you ask your questions."

He left and in due time returned, followed by his three wives. All three looked frightened and brow-beaten. They stood silently, looking at the floor.

Before Tora could address them, their husband said, "This man, who works for the governor, has dared to accuse me of beating my family. He even seems to think I killed by own child. Tell him he's wrong."

Tora looked at them His first lady started shaking. It was his second lady who spoke up. "My lord has always been the kindest of husbands and fathers," she said, her hands folded at her waist. "We are all very happy and take pleasure in serving him. You must have been told lies."

"There you have it!" her husband said.

The third lady did not speak and seemed to shrink into herself. Tora saw that they were all afraid, though the second lady seemed to have found a way of dealing with her situation. Tora felt pity for them. It was an unhappy household, and the recent events had done nothing to fix that. He decided they deserved the truth, at least as much of it as he knew.

He said, "Lady Hiroko has been meeting a lover in town. I expect she told you she was visiting her friend, Lady Tomiko, but she did not stay there. Instead she spent the time with a young man in a house of assignation."

Hiroko's mother bowed her head a little more. The other two ladies stared at him open-mouthed.

Imagawa thundered, "Who is he? I demand to know his name. He's the man who killed her. Why isn't he under arrest?"

Tora gave him an unfriendly look. "He was not in town when the murder happened."

"He probably lied. I want his name. He seduced my daughter. Who is he?" His face changed as a thought occurred to him. "Is it that idiot Kinto? It must be. She was always over there. By the gods, I'll show Matsudaira what I think of his sons treating my daughter like a common slut. They're not above the law."

Tora thought this an interesting reaction. "What makes you think Matsudaira's sons are involved in this?"

"They toyed with my daughter. First Kinsada and then his halfwit of a brother." He started pacing. "I should have put a stop to it, but I thought a marriage with Kinsada might be arranged. I should have known better. No Matsudaira can be trusted! Oh, the insult is not to be borne!" His face dark with helpless fury, he waved clenched fists about to mark his words. His wives showed little reaction.

Tora decided to end this unpleasant scene. Turning to the second lady, he told her, "I came today to ask about some silk Lady Hiroko was supposed to buy in town?"

The second lady said, "Oh, she wouldn't go. I had to go myself. I was making a new robe for my husband so I went later in the day. Why do you ask?"

"It's unimportant. Just a small matter that needed clearing up." He turned back to Imagawa. "We have found your daughter's maid. She ran away because you beat her. She is back with her family. Her father is very angry but will not bring charges."

Imagawa snapped, "The girl was lazy and stole. I only kept her on because her father is one of my peasants. We're well rid of her."

Tora bowed to the ladies and departed with a mere nod to Imagawa.

30

The Storm

Yasuko burst into her father's room in the afternoon, her eyes shining and her demeanor hardly ladylike. Akitada hoped he would soon have an answer to the letter he had sent off. The girl badly needed guidance in her manners. However, seeing her happy face after days of pouting was a relief and he smiled at her.

"You didn't tell me!" she cried, plunking herself down across from him.

"About what?"

"About the child. Yukiko is to have a child after all. She just said so."

I. J. Parker

Akitada wished she had not done so. After all, no one was to know about it yet. So he asked, "Have you told anyone?"

"No. Why?"

"You know Yukiko serves the empress. It would be very improper for anyone to know before she announces it in the palace." This explanation made no sense, but he hoped his thirteen-year-old daughter would accept it."

"Oh," she said gleefully. "It's a secret! I'll tell no one, I promise. Not even Yoshi."

"Good! Besides, speaking of a birth before it is a fact may attract evil spirits. We have been unfortunate before. Let us not tempt fate this time."

"Yes, Father. I'm sorry. It's only that Yukiko mentioned the possibility. I do so want a brother or sister to take care of."

"Very well, then. You may pray at the shrine for a little brother or sister."

"I will. I will!" she cried and was up and dancing out of the room happily.

Akitada sat quite still. He did not know when the child was to be born. Perhaps he should have asked, but he had been too upset to think very logically beyond the fact that he would raise Yukiko's child as his own. Tonight, he thought, he would ask her.

Tora came a while later to report on his visit to the Imagawa household. The matter of the silk purchase having been cleared up to their satisfaction, Akitada had to face up to the much more serious issue of Imagawa's abuse of the women in his household.

"The man's a coward and a bully," said Tora angrily. "Can't you find some excuse to arrest him and send him into exile? They'd all thank you for it."

"I wish I could, but you know very well that we cannot interfere in a man's family life. As a father and husband he has the right to discipline his wives and children."

"There must be something we can do. I was thinking that he may have killed Hiroko himself. Why not? Think about it! The fan seller said he walked her home. So she got home late and her father was waiting for her. He was angry that she'd been out so late and attacked her. Then, when he saw what he'd done, he tried to hide the murder by taking her body to that field. It belonged to Matsudaira and he hates them. He tried to blame the murder on Matsudaira's son when I talked to him."

"An interesting theory, Tora, but I don't see an angry father who is used to beating his womenfolk suddenly resorting to strangulation. It doesn't sound like him. If she had been beaten to death, I could accept the theory easily."

Tora sighed. "How will we ever solve this case? It's about as nasty a murder case as we've ever had."

"Did you share your information with Akechi?"

'Yes. Akechi thinks it was the fan seller. Because of the scratch."

"What scratch?"

Tora explained about Naganori's neck and the friend's cat.

Akitada frowned. "Strange place to get scratched by a cat. What did you think of the man?"

"He's a worm. Afraid to breathe in front of that wife of his. She accused him of going to the Iris Pavilion with a whore. Not that I would blame him if he did. She's hugely fat and very ugly."

"Perhaps she had good reason to distrust him. What was he doing, wandering around the lake that evening?"

Tora considered. "Well, the waitress in the Lake Restaurant knew him. She said he'd been there before and made a nuisance of himself with the waitresses."

"I think Naganori bears watching more carefully. Have you or Akechi checked his story with the friend?"

"I think Akechi probably did by now. I'll have a talk with him. Anything else?"

Akitada tried to think. His mind was not on this case. "The professor's son. From what you say, he has behaved very badly and doesn't seem to be heartbroken. Have Akechi send someone to Nagoya to ask some questions."

"His father isn't exactly a saint either. Instead of being shocked and sorry for the death of the young woman, he thought his son had done very well having an affair with Imagawa's daughter. He practically congratulated him in front of me. And the son jumps when the father tells him to. If he hadn't dashed off to Nagoya, she'd still be alive. Don't people have any feelings for others anymore?"

Akitada, so recently betrayed by his own wife, had no answer to this.

That night, the first storm of the season blew in from the sea, bringing torrents of rain and shaking the trees and the house roofs. After the family meal, which passed as painfully as the previous ones, though for once the children were distracted by the sounds outside and chattered away about rain and wind dragons and strange tales where people had been picked up bodily and deposited safely in faraway countries among supernatural creatures.

Yukiko was pale and ate little. Akitada thought again how this could not go on and decided to abandon the idea of family meals altogether. He informed the children that he would be too busy for a while to share their meals."

They looked a little disappointed, but Yasuko said, "Oh, well, as long as Yukiko is still here, we'll manage. Please stay longer, Yukiko."

Yukiko gave him a look and said, "As a matter of fact, I think I'd better leave a little sooner. This storm reminds me that the weather may delay my journey if I keep it too late."

This caused an outcry which Akitada stopped by saying quite firmly, "Yukiko is absolutely right. When you serve in the palace, a lack of punctuality is a very serious offense." With some relief, he saw that she, too, felt the awkwardness of their situation and wished to be gone. Alas, this would not change in their future life together. Not only was there no love left between them, they both wished for separate lives.

When he entered her room that night later, announcing himself softly at the door and being invited in, he said, "So you've decided to leave already?"

She shared her bedding with him, and his quilt lay ready some distance from hers, a symbol of their separation. She was sitting on her bedding, decorously covered with a robe and looked up at him. In the flickering light of the candle she looked positively ill, and he asked, "Are you feeling well? Is it the child?"

"I'm well, but this has been very difficult. It's, of course my own fault, but it will be better for both of us if we're apart. Besides, there is Hanae. She knows me too well. I think she suspects."

He took off his house robe, sat down on his quilt, and used the robe for a cover. "How soon do you wish to travel?"

"As soon as possible. As soon as the weather permits it."

"Very well. I shall accompany you."

"No, Akitada! Spare me." She practically wailed.

He sighed. Things were very bad. He said as gently as he could, "Tora and I both will come. I shall not trouble you any more than absolutely required. It would look bad if I didn't look after my wife."

She nodded reluctantly. "Yes, I can see that. Thank you." And after a moment, "I'm sorry, Akitada."

He said nothing and prepared to get whatever sleep might be possible.

The candle flickered, and the wind rattled the shutters. He wished he were alone again. At least then he had not been forced to look at her, to hear her voice, to know that she was close enough to touch.

Perversely, her confession that she had given herself to another man because she cared nothing for him had not stopped his desire for Yukiko. His body ached for her embrace, and he had been spending these strange nights, sleeping in the same room without holding her, recalling in most intimate detail their lovemaking in the past. He should be angry, and a part of him was, but this had done nothing to stifle his lust.

Between the sounds of the rain and storm outside and his equally violent fantasies, he could not fall asleep and eventually became aware that she was also restless. After a while, he asked, "Yukiko?"

"Yes?"

"When is the child due?"

"After the New Year."

"So soon?" He counted back. She must have sought the other man's bed very shortly after he had left. Well, what did he expect? Her anger with him had been strong enough to kill any love she might once have felt for him. And again he wondered how it had happened and about the man, but he would not allow himself to ask her again.

He said instead, "I'll try to get permission to come for the birth and I'll send Tora and Hanae to be there well ahead of your time. My tour of duty isn't officially over until the end of the month."

"That won't be necessary. I shall stay with my parents."

He sighed. His absence for the birth of the child would reflect poorly on him, but he did not want to force himself on her more than necessary.

"Very well. As you wish. We will prepare for you and the child. I suppose you and your mother will find a nurse?"

"Yes." Her voice sounded muffled, as if she were crying again.

He had not guessed that two people could make each other so very unhappy. This time, he said, "I'm sorry, Yukiko. We'll manage somehow."

She responded with another muffled, "Yes. Thank you."

Outside the storm tore at the shingles and gusts of rain rattled the shutters. They had nothing left to say to each other, and after a long while, things got quieter and both slept.

31

The Cat

The next morning was very rainy and windy, and the garden and most of the outside world were covered in debris and the first yellow and brown leaves. The weather was not yet promising for travel, and Akitada steeled himself for another day and night of pretense.

He did inform Saburo and Tora that Yukiko was eager to start on her homeward journey and that he had decided he and Tora would accompany her part of the way. Ono was gone and with him a good deal of work, and Saburo would be free to look after the tribunal in their absence. He estimated that they could be back in less than a week.

Tora was pleased. He had enjoyed the previous excursion and hoped for more excitement. Akitada just hoped to see Yukiko off as smoothly and quickly as was feasible.

"We'll leave tomorrow if it is dry enough," he said, looking anxiously up at the sky.

Tora's eyes narrowed. "What's the rush?"

"No rush, but it is the season for storms. I want to see my wife safely in her home again. Until then I'll have no peace of mind to deal with provincial matters."

"Oh."

"And speaking of the latter, what do you have to report?"

Tora told him about his visit to the Imagawa house. "The man's evil," he said. "He denied beating Hiroko or his wives and they lied for him. Nothing I could do about it."

"You should have expected it. They will hardly accuse him under the circumstances."

"Anyway, there never was any silk. Hiroko refused to pick it up and the second lady went instead.'

Akitada frowned. "You'd think you could have elicited that information when you talked to the silk merchant the first time."

"I didn't know. You remember they all said Lady Hiroko was getting the silk." Glossing over the uncomfortable silk episode, Tora added, "Imagawa's very angry with Matsudaira. He says the Matsudaira sons made advances to Hiroko and when he tried to get her married to the oldest, Matsudaira refused."

"Yes. We knew something happened between them. In any case, you have to finish checking the other merchant's story. That had better be done soon before he has time to make up more stories."

"You don't believe Naganori?"

"I don't know what to believe. Somebody must know something or have seen something. If Lady Hiroko was wandering about town alone, other people have seen her. You'd think Akechi would've come up with witnesses."

"It was getting dark."

"Yes, I know. Well, see what you can learn today. At the very least check the story of the scratches."

∞

Tora found Naganori's friend easily enough. Hankei lived in a tiny house in a street with other makers of tatami, reed shades, baskets, and cheap sandals. He was older than Naganori, quite bent and rheumy-eyed. He was sitting in his shop, weaving a mat with gnarled but quick fingers. When Tora walked in, he looked up from his work without stopping and gave him a toothless grin and a bow.

"Need some mats, sir? Mine are the best. Can't go wrong there. They'll last and last. And I can make you a good price."

"Are you Hankei?"

"I am. Did someone recommend me? My mats are known everywhere."

"Not exactly. You know a Naganori, right?"

"Oh, yes." Hankei cackled. "He cheats at go, but never mind that. What about him?"

"He says he was here on the ninth. Was he?"

"No idea. We have a game every second day of the week. He makes some excuse to get away from his wife for bit. She's a terrible woman."

Tora thought back. Yes, the ninth had been on the second day that week. "You have a cat?"

Hankei cackled. "Yes. His name's Tora. Orange cat with stripes. Fierce!"

Tora stared at him. "You named him Tora?"

"Right. On account he's a tiger and looks like one, you see."

Tora said weakly, "Yes. I get it, Where is this cat?"

Hankei, eyes twinkling, pointed up. And there, on a shelf near the ceiling, sat the biggest, meanest-looking cat Tora had ever seen. They stared at each other as if to gauge how fitting their names were. The cat opened its mouth, showing long yellow teeth, and gave a hiss.

Tora smiled and took a step closer. He said, "Here, kitty," and stretched out a hand to pet the creature.

"Oh, be careful," Hankei warned.

Too late. Tora, the cat, had already lashed out and sunk his claws into Tora's hand. Her jerked it back with a curse and sucked the blood from three nasty, deep gashes.

"He doesn't like strangers," Hankei explained and cackled again. "He's better than a watchdog, that cat. Naganori just leaned back and put his hand on his tail accidentally, and Tora nearly ripped his throat out."

Tora asked suspiciously, "Did he tell you to say that?"

"What?" Hankei looked blank.

"Did Naganori tell you to say that the cat attacked him?"

"Why would he tell me that? I was right there when it happened. Anyway, you want to be careful around Tora. Show him respect!"

Tora discontinued this odd conversation. "So what time did Naganori come that evening?"

"He usually comes after the evening rice."

"Listen carefully, Hankei. What time was it on the evening of the ninth?"

Hankei was offended. "Are you going to buy tatami or are you just wasting my time asking questions about my cat?"

Tora's fingers twitched to jerk Hankei upright and get right into his face. He controlled himself with an effort. "I'll pay for your time. Now answer!"

"How much?"

Tora counted out ten coppers, and Hankei pursed his lips. Tora added another ten. Hankei snatched them up and tucked them inside his shirt. "Now, let's see . . . the ninth . . . hmm . . . that was time before last. I think he was a bit late that night. Said something about doing a good deed. Surprised me. Naganori's not into doing good deeds, though he's all right otherwise."

"And that was the night the cat scratched him?"

"Could've been. Or maybe it was the time before that."

The scratches on Naganori's neck had been nearly healed, leaving only some red welts behind. Tora decided Naganori had probably told the truth.

He said bitterly, "Not much to choose between you and Naganori when it comes to doing good deeds."

They were again without suspects.

32

Farewells

The weather finally improved and roads dried out. Yukiko decided to leave the following morning. The final dinner was dismal enough, even though Akitada merely looked in briefly to remind the children to behave themselves in their absence the next few days. Yasuko had been crying and Yoshi complained about Tora not being able to take him hunting. Akitada noted once again that his children were no longer troubled by his own absence and came away as depressed as his family.

But the preparations at least went smoothly. Kosehira's men, having had ample time to sample the delights of a small provincial town, were eager to get home.

Their cortege was impressive. Kosehira's men, fully armed and carrying the Kosehira flag, rode ahead. They were followed by the palanquin holding Yukiko and her maid. Akitada and Tora, also fully armed, made up the end.

They left early and reached the border very late that night. Their accommodations this time were in a monastery, since Prefect Ikeda had lost his position and the new man was not prepared to entertain so large a retinue. Tora expressed his regrets at losing the pleasant services of Ikeda's maid, making Akitada wonder if she had treated Tora to special favors.

He shared a room with Tora and saw Yukiko only briefly to ask about her well-being. She looked tired but he saw that some of the strain of the past week was fading.

The weather held, and they reached Nagoya and the Owari tribunal the next night.

Fujiwara Michinori, having been forewarned of their arrival, did them proud. Akitada was touched by the festive meal he offered them, but this was again a strain as he had to hear commiserations that he and Yukiko had had so little time together.

Michinori, who had made Yukiko any number of compliments on her beauty and elegance, since this was permitted to a cousin, said, "What with all these separations, you and Akitada are practically still newlyweds. How very charming to see you both so much in love. I trust you made the most of it, my dears, for life will again become humdrum before you know it."

Like many governors, he had left his family behind in the capital and he added, "It is the separations that make us grow fond again. Ah, those reunions after a long absence are very sweet indeed." He raised his cup to Akitada and Yukiko.

Of course, Michinori had made sure that they shared a room that night. It was quite luxuriously appointed with silken bedding, candles, and a tray of sweets, just the sort of room a lover might prepare for the visit of his beloved.

Yukiko looked around and sighed. It was a sigh that pained Akitada, He took it to mean that she found their togetherness hateful, particularly after all the hints about their relationship that had been bandied about during the meal.

He said awkwardly, "I'm sorry, Yukiko. It couldn't be helped. If we had stopped at another monastery, your cousin would have been offended."

"I know." She undid her sash and took off her gowns, draping them over the clothes rack. As she stood there in her thin silk undergown and with the light behind her, Akitada saw the swelling of her belly. Perhaps he had avoided looking too closely before or she had managed to hide her condition. It told him their claim that the child was his would be problematic. Already her maid must know the truth. Hanae had suspected it. Could her own mother be unaware? And then, of course, there was his sister.

He saw no way to discuss the matter with Yukiko. They would simply have to take things as they came and hope that those close to them would keep the secret.

And so they spent another night together and yet apart,

He had planned to stay with Yukiko all the way to the capital and only turn around at the outskirts. By that time, she should be safe enough and he would hurry back to his duties.

In the end this was not necessary. During the night, another governor, passing through on his way to the capital with his wife and a large retinue, had sought shelter with Michinori. When they discovered this the following morning, Yukiko asked if she might join them. She was eagerly welcomed. Akitada saw that she was desperate to be rid of his company and accepted the invitation, expressing his gratitude.

He saw Yukiko only briefly as she got ready to be on her way. Her maid was with her, and he waited impatiently for the woman to leave the room. Finally they were alone.

"Yukiko," he said, "I worry about you. Are you sure you feel well enough to travel on? This long journey was not a good idea in your condition."

She did not look at him. "Thank you," she said, "but I'm perfectly well." After a moment, she added, "I . . . I had to come, Akitada. I was frantic." She swung around to face him. "I'm very sorry that I almost lied to you. And I'm truly sorry for what I've done to you."

The words hung between them.

Akitada said nothing. Reflecting that he would surely have recognized her pregnancy, had she in fact let him make love to her, he shrugged off the apology. He said, "Write to me. You haven't done so in the past, but I hope that now that matters are settled between us you may feel free to do so."

"Yes. And I shall look after your house."

"I hope you consider it yours also."

"Yes, of course. I only meant that I shall stay with my parents until you return."

He could think of nothing else to say. "Give my regards to your parents and siblings."

"I will."

She tried to smile, but faltered in the attempt. He was uncomfortably aware of the figure he must make when she had been used to handsome and wealthy men much younger than he and certainly far more entertaining.

Since all seemed to be eager to get on the way, Akitada and Michinori stood in the courtyard, watching Yukiko get into the carriage with Governor Tachibana's wife. The escort lined up, and a moment later, the now much larger procession of riders and carriages left the Owari tribunal and turned toward the west.

Michinori looked after them and said, "You should have turned down the offer. It would have given you a few more nights with that very fetching wife of yours. Poor fellow! Now you must go back to those same old duties without even the prospect of a warm embrace after a day's labors."

"This is much safer. You forget that Ono is about to present his charges against me. The less time I'm absent from my post the better."

"Ah. That reminds me. I meant to wait until you stopped by on your return. One of the men arrested with Tojo Muneyasu has talked, and now Tojo is also pretty vocal. He's bargaining for a reduced sentence by incriminating some local nobles who've been dabbling in piracy and robbery on the side."

Akitada congratulated Michinori, adding with a sigh, "I'd hoped to make some progress in Mikawa along those lines myself but we've found nothing."

"That's what I'm trying to tell you. You asked me about the Matsudaira. Well, there may be something. Are you interested?"

"Of course!"

"Then we'll pay a visit to our talkative prisoner."

33

The Matsudaira Connection

They took Tora along on their jail visit.

Akitada had come to like Michinori very much, but he was shocked by the conditions of his tribunal jail. The guards looked unkempt and brutish, the guard room was decorated with assorted whips, chains, and metal prongs. The latter were used to deal with rebellious prisoners. First a prisoner was knocked down and then pinned by the neck until he could be chained.

Tora looked as shocked as Akitada felt, a frown on his handsome face. He prided himself on keeping his own men spick and span at all times and did not permit unnecessary cruelty.

Michinori refused to visit the cells, a fact that suggested much about their condition. Instead he had Tojo brought out to be questioned in the guard room.

The fat man was no longer recognizable. He shuffled in bent nearly double, his face swollen and discolored. The guard kicked the back of his legs to make him fall to his knees. Tojo fell and remained nearly prostrate, his face on the dirt floor.

Akitada bit his lip. Clearly, Michinori had no qualms about the way criminals were to be dealt with. He reminded himself that Tojo was responsible for a number of murders, among them those of Gonjuro and Sadako's husband.

"Sit up!" Michinori told Tojo.

A whimper was the only response. The guard used his prong to poke Tojo in the side. The fat man squealed and struggled up. He looked at them from eyes that were nearly swollen shut and whimpered again. "I'm in pain," he mumbled. "I'm dying. I've told you everything. I know nothing more."

Michinori said, "We are interested in your comment about the Matsudaira. Repeat what you told me."

"Nothing to do with me. Just something I heard."

Afraid that the guard would engage in more painful encouragement, Akitada said, "We found a body washed up on the shore near Komachi. It belonged to a man who had a tattoo of the Matsudaira insignia on his shoulder. My assistant discovered that such a man worked in your stables and had gone missing."

Tojo peered at him and then at Tora. For a moment it looked as though he recognized them but he asked, "Who are you?"

The guard was about to hit him again, but Akitada stopped him with a gesture. "I'm Lord Sugawara, governor of Mikawa. I'm the one who stopped the attack on the pack train."

Tojo was silent for a moment. Then he said, "I will make a bargain. I have information. I'll tell you, if you let me go."

Michinori laughed. "Not a very good try, Tojo. You're charged with highway robbery, murder, plotting against the emperor and the nation, and assorted other offenses. That means you'll lose your life."

Tojo sagged and started weeping.

Akitada was surprised. Executions were exceedingly rare, though they did happen in distant provinces, presumably to instill fear in an unruly populace. Tojo's offenses had earned him the death penalty, but the emperor and court frowned on such punishment. It offended against their Buddhist beliefs. He glanced at Michinori and saw him wink back.

Tojo whimpered, "I'll do anything. Just let me live. You can condemn me to hard labor."

Michinori said, "Why don't we see how useful your cooperation is?"

Akitada, who had suffered the punishment dealt out to violent offenders, exile and hard labor in faraway and godforsaken places—he had worked in a gold mine on Sado Island—thought this probably a poor alternative to death, but he was often startled by how feverishly men clung to life. In his present mood it seemed even more pointless.

He said to Tojo, "Let's go back to the man who had this curious tattoo. A circle enclosing three leaves. That is the emblem of the Matsudaira clan. Do you know the man I mean?"

Tojo nodded. "He was my spy."

"A spy? You used spies?"

Tojo nodded. "To find out what goods were coming on the Tokaido."

"Did you send him to Mikawa?"

Tojo nodded again. "We heard a rumor about a shipment of tax rice coming from Izu Province by boat. I thought it might be transferred to pack train before Owari."

Such transfers were common. Where convenient, the goods were loaded on ships or boats and both Mikawa and Owari were places where they were shifted to the land route. Tojo's tale made sense. Tojo's man had come to Komachi harbor to ask questions and there he had run into trouble. But there must be more to the story.

At this point, Tora interjected himself into the interrogation. "There's an island off the coast close to the provincial capital. They call it Island of the Gods. You know anything about that?"

Tojo looked blank. "Never heard of it."

Akitada asked, "What do you think happened to your spy?"

282

Tojo sniffed and winced. "Not sure, but that's Matsudaira territory around your provincial capital and he used to work for them."

Michinori said, "Right. Now we're getting somewhere. Tell us all you know about the Matsudaira organization."

"It's my life to talk about that!" Tojo squealed.

Michinori laughed. "Don't be silly. Your life's lost already. You're trying to get another chance."

Tojo shifted on his knees. "They have an interest in piracy. Local fishermen work for them. Tomezo had their tattoo because they used to bring slaves down from up north to work on their land. They got the tattoo because they were their property. Some of them bought their freedom by working as pirates. This Tomezo was one of those. He ran away and came to me. I took him on because he was useful. He was a good stable hand, but he also knew things useful to the business. Anyway, I thought he could find out about this shipment and where they expected to unload. I guess someone recognized him and they caught him."

"In other words," said Akitada, "you sent him to do a very dangerous thing. You must have offered to pay him well."

Tojo made an attempt at grinning. "He didn't collect."

Tora said angrily, "They tortured him. That means he told them about your little business. I'm surprised they haven't come after you."

Tojo actually chuckled at this. "I guess they didn't have enough time."

Akitada and Michinori exchanged a glance. Michinori said, "That's enough for now, but we'll be back with more questions. You haven't earned your life yet."

Tojo pleaded, "Anything. Ask me anything."

As they returned to Michinori's study, Tora told the governor, "We must've caught your jailers on an off day."

Michinori asked, "Why?"

Akitada gave Tora a look and said quickly, "Thank you for letting us speak to Tojo. That was very helpful." He smiled a little. "Now I just wish I knew how to get proof of Matsudaira's activities, not to mention how to deal with him when I do. I'm told he keeps a small army of soldiers."

"Let him bring them on!" Tora said, rubbing his hands. "We'll be ready for them. My men are in top form," he added with a sidelong glance at Michinori.

Akitada said impatiently, "I'd like to avoid a war, Tora. And we don't have enough men."

Their host chuckled. "Sometimes you cannot avoid it, Akitada. In any case, I can offer you some additional people. You can also conscript some of your peasants."

"At this point, I'm not at all sure where their loyalties would be. But I thank you for your offer. I hope it won't come to it. Tora and I will have to investigate first."

The visit with Michinori ended on a more pleasant note with a fine dinner and a restful night before Akitada and Tora set out again to face the troubles in Mikawa.

34

The Companion

A surprise awaited Akitada when he reached
Komachi. Saburo greeted him with the news
that he had a visitor.

"A woman, sir," Saburo said, looking disapproving.

"Ah, Mrs. Iseya?" Akitada guessed.

"Yes, sir. She arrived alone, carrying her things in a
bundle. She said she'd come all the way from Totomi
by herself and she walked into the tribunal here. I gathered that she had traveled on foot for some of the distance. She said you'd sent for her."

"I did, Saburo. She's to be Yasuko's companion."

Saburo looked scandalized. "A common woman
like that? Are you sure, sir?"

285

Akitada was not at all sure. He had had second thoughts after dashing off his letter to her. Would a grief-stricken widow be good company for Yasuko who was already in very low spirits. But Saburo's objection startled him.

"I have met her, Saburo. She's perfectly proper, whatever you may think of her travel arrangements. She is very poor, I think."

"Oh. Sorry, sir. I cannot imagine her family letting her go off like that. The only women who travel all alone on the highways are common whores."

"Saburo! I shall not have you use this word in connection with Mrs. Iseya. She's a recent widow and has no family. I would have thought that your own life taught you not to judge people so quickly."

Saburo bowed his head. "I was wrong, sir. I apologize. Only, I was thinking of Lady Yasuko and it seemed . . . never mind. I shall not make this mistake again."

"Hmm. Where is she?"

"I found a room in the tribunal guest quarters, sir. I'm very sorry. I just didn't realize."

The guest quarters were intended for servants and attendants travelling with Akitada's guests and had most recently held the guards sent with Yukiko by her father.

"I'd better see her. Send to Hanae and have her prepare a room in the house. Tell her to make it close to Yasuko's."

Irritated by Saburo's mistake, Akitada left the tribunal and walked across to the service buildings. What must she have thought when she was put in a room meant for rough men?

He reached the guest quarters and, not wanting to burst in on her, stopped outside and called out, "Mrs. Iseya?"

She appeared quickly at the door, a slender, tall woman in a blue gown. Perhaps it was the same one she had worn the last time he had seen her. She came to meet him, looking a little unsure of herself but moving with the same elegance he recalled. Foolish Saburo, he thought. This woman was clearly quality.

She said a little breathlessly, "My lord," then corrected herself, blushing, "Your Excellency." And she bowed quite low to him before straightening up again and saying simply, "I came."

He said at the same moment, "Welcome!" And both paused. He chuckled and was pleased to see her smile.

"I'm very glad to see you," he said. "I didn't know if you would want to accept my offer."

"Oh, I was very glad of it, so glad that I came straight away." Again that small, deprecating smile. "I was quite without a home, you see."

"Saburo said you traveled alone. He was upset."

"He is a good man. He cares about people."

Saburo did not quite deserve her good opinion, but she was right.

"Shall we go to my residence and have a talk in my study? Then I'd like to introduce you to my children if you're ready."

"Yes, of course." She made a nervous gesture. "I do hope they'll like me. I'll try very hard to please them."

Akitada did not want her to try to please the children. He hoped they would please her. But it was clear that she was afraid to lose the position, and he marveled what it must be like to be suddenly all alone in the world with no home and no money and to depend on the good will of children. But he said nothing of this as he led her through the back gate into the garden of his residence.

"Oh," she said, looking up at the trees, "it's another world in here. How very nice for your family."

This reminded him of Yukiko and he said, "My wife serves at court. She was here for a brief visit and has just left again."

"Yes. Your secretary mentioned it. I have often wondered what it must be like to live close to their majesties."

"I can't recommend it," Akitada said bitterly.

"Oh? Yes, it must be difficult for you and your children."

"The children—Yasuko, your charge, and Yoshitada, Yoshi for short—are mine by a previous marriage. My first wife died." He thought to mention the expected child but decided not to.

She said, "It is very difficult to lose a loved one. But you have the children."

"Yes," he said. They had reached the chrysanthemums Yukiko had planted. They looked shriveled and brown. He felt this to be appropriate, a symbol of their marriage, and heaved a sigh.

She touched his arm. "I'm sorry," she said. "You must have loved her very much."

For a moment he thought she referred to Yukiko, then he remembered, and the old grief surfaced again and joined the new one and he stopped for a moment, staring sightlessly at the building ahead. What was he going to do?

She said nothing and waited. After a moment, he recalled himself and smiled at her. "Forgive me! Let's go and sit on the veranda of my study."

They did, and she remarked on his fish pond, another of Yukiko's installations. He offered her wine, which she declined.

The sun was setting and its rays slanted through the branches and fell on her face. It was a very pleasing profile, he thought, and she had lovely hands, long and slender like her body. She wore her hair twisted up at her neck like the last time he had seen her. He wished she would let it hang loose and tried to remember her from the few brief glimpses he had got before the attack that killed her husband.

He said, "Well, tell me about yourself. How did you manage since the last time we talked?"

She seemed grateful for his casual manner. "I returned to Totomi and packed up my husband's things. I had written his family, but there was no answer, so I sent everything to the capital. Then I was done. It did not take very long. We had been living in a house that belonged to the school where he taught and so we did not have many things."

Akitada frowned. "But what did you do? How did you live? Was there money?"

"Very little after I paid for shipping his things. And I had to leave the house. I was about to do so when your letter came. It was such a relief!"

"Dear gods!" muttered Akitada. "So you had no one?"

"No." She said it simply, leaving him aghast. Then she turned her face to him and added quickly, "I'm young and strong and quite healthy. And I can work very hard at whatever needs to be done. If you're not pleased with me as a companion for your daughter, or if she doesn't like me, then I can work as a maid or in the kitchen. I have no pride left."

He said again, "Dear gods!" and "How sad! No, of course not. I'm very glad you came. You see I'm also alone in a way and the children need more than my occasional attention. Do you read?"

"Oh, dear!" She chuckled and brushed away some moisture from her eyes. "I should have told you. Yes, of course. I have a good education. I read Japanese and a little Chinese. I write Japanese and I can paint some fairly ordinary things like flowers. I also play the *koto*, though I don't own one any longer. And I can sew clothes and cook a little."

He looked at her in surprise. "I'm amazed. Did your husband teach you? I recall he was a schoolmaster."

Her face tensed and she looked away. "No. I already knew all of it by that time."

The Island of the Gods

He had touched on some secret, an unpleasant one by her expression and he let it go. "Come," he said rising and giving her a hand, "let's go see the children now." He liked the way her hand felt in his, warm and strong yet delicate.

Yasuko was in her room, leafing through an illustrated book. Akitada had recently begun announcing himself before walking into Yasuko's room and she called out "Come in, Father."

He said, "I have brought a surprise, Yasuko. This is Iseya Sadako. She has come to be part of our family."

Yasuko's eyes widened as she took this in and looked at the visitor. "Say you're not taking another wife!" she cried, glaring at her father. "You just waited for Yukiko to leave and you brought in another woman! I hate you!" She burst into tears.

Akitada bellowed, "Yasuko! Stand up and bow to this lady immediately! I don't know when I have been so embarrassed by you. How dare you!" He raised an arm, perhaps to strike his daughter—he could not say afterwards—but Sadako put her hand on it and said quickly, "You made a mistake, Yasuko. I am merely to be a companion, a sort of servant. Your father sent for me to please you."

Yasuko, who had stood up and looked frightened all of a sudden, murmured, "Oh!"

"But you are very pretty and much more grown up than I expected. I thought you were still a little girl. Perhaps you will not like a companion?"

Yasuko sniffled and managed a smile. She bowed to Sadako. "Please forgive me. I behaved very badly. I did not mean it and I would very much like a companion. I've been very lonely since Yukiko left."

Akitada said to the woman beside him, "Yukiko is my current wife. I believe I mentioned she had to return to her duties. Please forgive this deplorable scene. I would have given anything to have spared you this." He turned to his daughter. "You and I will speak later. Where is your brother?"

"He's out exercising the horses with Yuki. I'm sorry, Father."

Akitada ignored this. "Perhaps then I may leave you together?" he asked Sadako.

She bowed. "Yes. Thank you, Your Excellency."

And Akitada fled.

35

Michiko's Bargain

Akitada and Tora had discussed Tojo's information on their journey back. Tora thought arresting Lord Matsudaira and questioning him was the quickest way to get at the truth, but Akitada wanted something more than the word of a confessed criminal to confront the man with. He was very uneasy about the reaction of the local clan chief. On the whole, he thought Matsudaira would have no choice but to attack with whatever manpower he could raise, and that would be much larger than the provincial guard. History had proved again and again that the appointed governors were pitifully weak against local strongmen.

I. J. Parker

Added to this was the fact that the peasants of Mikawa would throw in their lot with the local lords. These were ever present while the central government in the capital was far away. Eventually, the government would respond, of course. But it took time for news to travel, for generals to be appointed and armies to be gathered, and for these armies to make their way to Mikawa. By that time, he, his family, and a significant number of people would long be dead.

Michinori's troops were closer, but even they would take time to get here and were quite likely outnumbered by Matsudaira forces. Michinori had been blunt about this and Akitada had liked him for it.

In spite of being very tired after his journey, Akitada slept poorly. Between the unpromising beginning with his daughter and the new companion and the Matsudaira problem he tossed and turned.

Yasuko's behavior had appalled him on many levels. Her loyalty to Yukiko had, of course, caused her outburst against Sadako. Given his relationship with his wife, this promised a very difficult future for her as well as for her father. But he minded most what Sadako must have thought. She had already been afraid that she would be dismissed summarily. What must she have thought? It had been cruel to expose her without warning to a situation she could know nothing about. And what had possessed Yasuko to make such an assumption in the first place?

He found no solution to either dilemma but eventually slept.

In the morning he would have avoided facing Ya-suko and Sadako, but there was still Yoshi to be introduced formally to the new member of their household. He bathed, shaved, and dressed at dawn and sought out his son's room.

Yoshi was still fast asleep. He was young enough to look innocent and lovable in his sleep, quite different from the energetic and active child he was in the day time. Akitada gazed at him for a while, smiling to himself. He wished to hold him in his arms the way he had when he had been younger, but these days Yoshi would not allow such babying. Yasuko had remained gentler, but now she, too, had turned from him. Perhaps all parents suffered this sort of loss eventually, but Akitada felt it more acutely, felt the lack of close contact with another human being, missed touching another, holding him or her in his arms.

But he shoved these thoughts aside and bent to touch Yoshi's shoulder. "Yoshi?"

The boy woke reluctantly, was clearly tempted to roll over and sleep some more, but took in the fact that it was his father who had woken him.

"Father! You got back!" He rubbed his eyes with both fists. "Tora said you got back, but you'd already retired." He brightened. "Yuki and I had the greatest adventure!"

"I'm very glad to hear it," Akitada said with a smile. "You had taken the horses out, I believe?"

"Yes. And we rode all the way up to the promontory along the coast. It was great. Then we saw a bunch of fishermen with boats. They were busy moving things from one boat to another. I stopped to watch, and the rude men shouted at me. Yuki said we should go, but I told them we had a perfect right to be there and that I was the governor's son. That's when some of the men came after us, and, Father, they had long knives. I wished I'd brought my sword. But Yuki screamed at me to come away, and then he hit my horse with his whip and it shied. I couldn't stop it for the longest time. Oh, I was so mad at Yuki! Father, you must go and punish those men right away."

It all poured out in a rush and Akitada's heart nearly stopped at the danger the boys had been in. This business of fishermen shifting goods was likely a case of piracy and their attack on the boys proved as much. But he calmed himself and said, "You took a foolish chance, son. Yuki was right. For that matter, neither of you should have been out so late with the horses. The men you saw would have killed you if your horse had thrown you."

Yoshi looked deflated. "I'm a good rider. I wouldn't have fallen off. And I would have fought them."

"With what?"

The boy had no answer.

"Well, never mind. Come, I'd like you to meet Yasuko's new companion."

He helped his son to put on his clothes and retied his hair. Then they set out for Yasuko's room.

Invited in, Akitada found to his relief that all seemed to be well between his new servant and his daughter. They sat side by side, studying one of Yukiko's many books.

Sadako, still in the same blue dress, rose immediately and made him a deep bow. "Good Morning, Your Excellency," she said. "I hope you had a good rest."

"Yes, thank you." He hesitated, not sure whether he should address her by her first name or as Mrs. Iseya.

Yasuko solved the problem. "Sadako and I are going to practice poetry later. We were just studying some very fine poems in this book. Sadako knows all about it. I'll make a poem about autumn and if Sadako likes it, I'll send it to Yukiko." She recalled herself and added, "Good morning, Father. Good morning, younger brother."

Akitada made the introductions and left for the tribunal.

∞

It had been decided that Tora should try to get more information about the mysterious island of the gods. Consequently, he put on ordinary clothes, a blue robe with a dark sash, and went to pay a visit to Michiko.

Auntie Haru received him with a broad smile. "Tora! Got another girl for me?"

"No, Auntie Haru. I came to see Michiko. How's she working out?"

"Working out good!" Auntie nodded several times. "Hard worker. And the men like her a lot. She'll have enough to buy herself out in no time."

Tora was not sure whether he should be glad that Michiko apparently spent most of her time on her back. He said, "I'd like to talk to her. If she's free."

"Sleeping. But for you I'll get her."

I. J. Parker

No doubt the girl needed her sleep, but Tora had more important things to think about.

Michiko appeared a few moments later, rosy-cheeked and wrapped in a beautiful red and purple silk gown. "Tora," she cried and flung herself into his arms, the gorgeous robe falling open as she did. "Tora, my rescuer, my hero, my beloved Tora! Where have you been?"

"Busy." Tora disentangled himself, noting the Michiko was quite naked under her fancy wrap. "Auntie Haru says she's very pleased with you."

"So she should. I'm her hardest worker and I make her more money than any of the others."

Tora frowned. "But . . . are you happy?"

"Happy? Of course, silly. Nobody beats me, there's delicious food, I have lots of nice money, and beautiful clothes," —she stroked the red and purple silk lovingly— "and I get so many compliments." She paused, suddenly serious. "And my father no longer beats me."

Tora relaxed. "Good. I've been worried." This was not completely true, though he had not been altogether happy with his decision to turn a very young girl into a prostitute. Apparently it had worked out all right.

"You've worried? Oh, Tora, I love you. Come, let's go to my room and I'll show you how much. I've learned so many things, Tora. You've never had anything like it before."

"No, thank you," he said stiffly. "I'm here about that island of the gods again."

Her face fell. She frowned. "I'm not going back there. Not even for you."

298

"Come on, Michiko. What could happen? I'll be with you."

Her pretty face softened a little. "Sorry, Tora. If my father sees me, I'm dead. And most likely you'll be too. Stop thinking about that place. It's cursed."

Part of this made no sense at all. Tora focused on it. "Your father can't do anything to you or me. For one thing I'm going armed, and for another he wouldn't dare attack the captain of the provincial guard."

She turned away. "You don't understand. Trust me, even you'd be a dead man. People who go to that island either die or they're killers."

"We can go at night. Your father won't see you then and neither will anyone else."

"My father often goes over there at night and so do bad people. And besides, the island has eyes. I feel it."

"What?"

"There's something horrible there. It's not human."

Tora had a fear of ghosts and other supernatural creatures and this gave him pause. "How do you know?" he asked.

"I know. My father knows. He told me. I wasn't supposed to take you over there at all, but I thought you just wanted to see the shrine and nothing else."

"Your father goes there?" This raised new possibilities. "What if I arrest your father on some charge? We could go once he's in jail."

She looked uncertain. "He wouldn't find out about me?"

"Not if I can help it. But you've got to give me something I can charge him with. Has he done anything illegal?"

Michiko gave a bitter laugh. "Of course. Only there's no proof."

"Then how do you know?"

"I found a lot of blood in the bottom of his boat once. He said it was from fish, but he hadn't brought back any fish that day. And he threatened to beat me if I talked about it."

"You think he killed someone?"

She looked uncertain. "I don't know. But he'd probably hurt someone. He hurt me enough."

Tora studied her thoughtfully. "You really hate your father, don't you?"

"Of course. He beat my mother until she died. And the only reason he kept me was so I could cook and work for him."

"Hmm. But he didn't want you to sell your body."

She laughed that bitter laugh again. "Oh, Tora! How do you think I learned that men will pay for it? He's had me lying down to men for a few coppers ever since I was ten. He didn't beat me for that. He beat me because I went into business for myself and kept the money."

Tora was nauseated. But at the same time he felt an enormous wave of pity wash over him. "Come here, girl," he said softly. "She slid over on her knees, a hopeful smile starting. Tora took her in his arms and held her. "Poor girl," he muttered into her hair, freshly scented and quite soft and clean. "Poor, poor girl."

The Island of the Gods

Michiko clutched him, buried her face in his neck and cried. They sat together like this, she sobbing, he rocking her like a small child he was consoling after a fall.

Eventually she stopped and just sat quietly in his arms.

He said, "I've been blaming myself for bringing you here, but I suppose it worked out all right."

She looked up at him then, black paint smudged around her eyes and her nose pink from crying. "You silly man," she said softly, lovingly, "you saved my life and you gave me a way to earn a very good living. I loved you before, but now I'm yours, body and mind. Forget what I said. I'll go with you. We'll go together, and maybe when you have what you want, you'll make love to me."

He started to shake his head, but she stopped him with her hand. "Just once, Tora. Please. Just once. I want to be loved by you just that one time, and then I won't mind whatever happens to me."

He pulled her close. "Silly girl," he murmured in her ear, "I'm probably older than your father. My hair is gray. What could you possibly see in me?" Much against his will, his heart was pounding and he felt himself flush. Worse, his body signaled arousal, and Michiko, wise in such matters, knew it and moved seductively against him.

"Come, lover," she whispered. "Now and again later, after I've done what you wished."

He disentangled himself. "No," he said hoarsely. "Not now. Afterward. When can you go?"

She half pouted and half laughed at his discomfiture. Becoming serious, she said, "I've loved you since the first time I saw you. I'll wait, but not too long. How about tomorrow night if there's no moon?"

"It's a deal," said Tora, feeling thoroughly ashamed but also excited by the prospect.

36

The *Koto*

The newest member of his small family not only caused Akitada unease about whether she would get along with Yasuko. He also found himself very curious about her. He knew next to nothing about her background and had been embarrassed about his ignorance when he had questioned her about her education. The recital of her formidable skills had taken his breath away. How had such a paragon ended up abandoned by family and friends? There must be a secret there, and this secret again worried him in case it might turn out to be harmful to his children.

Consequently, Akitada spent the next day looking in on his children in hopes of learning more about Sadako.

She had become Sadako very quickly. Both Yasuko and Yoshi addressed her by her first name. It struck him as a little unsuitable, but apparently she had urged it herself. It made him think her younger than he had before.

Her appearance remained extremely modest. Perhaps this was due to the fact that she had arrived with only the one small bundle of clothing. Her gown was always the same, simple and not of silk; her hair was always tied up at the back of her neck; and she wore no make-up whatsoever. All of this should have made her appear older—he had no idea what her real age was—but there was something in the way she moved and the way her face lit up when she smiled that made him think of her as a young woman. Not as young as Yukiko, of course, but younger than Tamako had been when she had died. But she had lost two husbands and led a hard life. Such things mature both men and women quickly. He realized that it was probably the fact that they had both loved someone and lost this person that drew him to her. They surely both knew loneliness.

He found himself thinking of ways he might make her life under his roof more comfortable and pleasant. She must have more clothes, of course, but his first present was to be a *koto*. He thought this very appropriate since it could be passed off as something she would need as Yasuko's companion.

Consequently, on the day after her arrival, Akitada set out in ordinary clothes to shop in town—something he had not done in a long time. It gave him pleasure that he was not recognized and he took his time

304

strolling about the market and peering into various shops. He saw Naganori's shop, his name painted on its door curtain, and entered out of curiosity.

An unimpressive little round man with a black eye approached, bowing, and asking what the gentleman might like. Akitada said he had not decided but wished to look around.

A shrill voice from the back bellowed, "Naganori! Get in here!"

Naganori called back, "We have a customer, my treasure!"

A moment later, a very fat woman appeared and stared suspiciously at Akitada. "I'll take care of the gentleman," she told her husband. "You go back in the kitchen and sweep the floor."

Naganori sighed, bowed to Akitada, and left.

Akitada had never quite seen such a reversal of roles. Women were supposed to be subservient to their husbands. Here it was the other way around. Master Kung-fu-tse would predict that no good could come from changing the natural order of things. Then he remembered Yukiko. He had not felt shame before, but now it struck him that in most men's minds he cut a pathetic figure. And far too many people knew it or would know.

He transferred his sudden anger to the fat Mrs. Naganori and glowered at her. "You treat your husband abominably, woman!" he snapped.

She gaped at him. Her pasty face flushed an ugly red. "W-what?" she gasped.

"Sweeping floors is woman's work. And you do not tell your husband what to do. He tells you."

In the back Naganori had crept to the doorway, his face wreathed in a smile.

She said defensively, "He cheats on me and goes off with loose women, leaving me to run the shop and take care of the house."

"Do you have children?"

"No, thank the gods! I could never deal with him and them, too."

"Then you're useless as a wife. If he has any sense, he'll divorce you and marry someone who is a better wife to him." He glanced toward Naganori and saw a look of utter astonishment on his face.

She caught his glance and turned. Fury seized her and she pointed. "He's useless as a husband. Maybe I'd have had children to look after me when I'm old, but he wasted his seed on sluts. He's always chasing them. We barely have enough to eat because he pays for high-priced whores. But he's about played out. They don't want him any more when something younger comes along. Isn't that right, Naganori? Isn't that what happened?"

Naganori was red with embarrassment and Akitada had had enough. He turned around and left. But his anger did not leave as easily and he walked for quite a long time until he had calmed down enough to remember his errand.

He returned to the market, found a shop that sold musical instruments and walked in.

"Do you have a *koto*?" he asked the old man who greeted him.

"Yes, sir." The old man bowed. "In fact I have a very nice one. I've had it for quite a long time. It isn't cheap and nobody in Komachi wants to spend much money on an instrument that isn't useful to street musicians."

The *koto*, or zither, he produced was indeed of very good quality. The old man said, "See, sir, it's the finest paulownia wood, lacquered and with inlays of mother of pearl."

Akitada admired the decorations. They formed tendrils and leaves at one end of the fairly large musical instrument. In fact, it was almost as long as he was tall and about a foot wide. The *koto* rested on short feet and was strung with thirteen silk strings, each supported by a movable ivory bridge. It was usually played by women who plucked the strings with several picks attached to their fingers.

Akitada asked, "Does it have a good sound?"

The old man found the picks and slipped them on his fingers. He said with a smile, "I restrung it myself. The silk was getting old. Listen!"

Akitada was enchanted. The old man played a melody he had played himself on his flute. It had been too long since he had last made music. Yukiko played the *koto* but preferred the *biwa*, or lute, and had taught Yasuko on it. He thought that they would have quite a little orchestra now if Sadako played the *koto*, Yasuko the *biwa*, and he his flute. It would be an excuse to bring out his flute again and spend some time with his daughter. He should probably start teaching Yoshi how to play the flute so he could take part as well.

"I'll buy it," he said, when the melody faded and the old man looked at him expectantly. "And do you have any simple flutes also?"

Another pleasant exchange occurred next as Akitada tested flutes and looked at flute music. In the end, he added the flute and several books of music to his purchases and had them sent to his residence.

The old man blinked at the instructions and said, "Dear me! I think you must be the governor himself. Your Excellency, sorry, I didn't realize." And he knelt immediately.

Very pleased that he had not been recognized before, Akitada said, "There's no need. Please get up. I enjoyed your explanations very much. Thank you."

He walked away, smiling. He had not been in such a cheerful mood in many months. The fact was he looked forward with pleasure to these musical gatherings. Suddenly his life no longer seemed so bleak.

37

Sadako

Tora awaited him in the tribunal office. He looked unusually tense. Tora rarely ever worried about anything, so Akitada felt a twinge of uneasiness. He sat down and asked, "What's the matter?"

"I'm going back to that island," Tora said. "The girl I told you about, the fisherman's daughter, will take me. She knows how to get to those caves. I know the answer to Tojo's tattooed spy is there. And that should tell us not only what happened to him and why, but also who ordered his torture and death."

Akitada did not like the sound of this. "You're going to walk into the tiger's den with nobody but a young girl?" he asked.

"I doubt anybody is there unless they have business. Can you think of a better way to get what we want?"

Akitada thought. ""You could take armed men."

"That will alert the Matsudaira and they'll be quick to cover up or else they'll raise their armies. If I go with the girl, maybe whoever is there will think we're just a pair of lovers." Tora grimaced slightly.

"Why the face? You never used to mind such a role."

"She's being silly about it."

"I don't understand."

Tora cast up his eyes and said bluntly, "She didn't want to go unless I promised to lie with her."

This situation struck Akitada as funny. He laughed out loud and said, "You're not serious? What? Is she repulsive?"

Tora snapped, "She's a beauty!"

Still grinning, Akitada said, "So you agreed to make the ultimate sacrifice?"

Tora glowered at him. "I'm a married man with a family, and she's fifteen."

"Oh!"

"I'm surprised at you, sir."

"I'm sorry. It's just that it doesn't seem like you."

"That's because you've always had a very low opinion of me."

"You're right. Forgive me. So will you find a way out of your dilemma?"

Tora looked glum. "I don't know if I can."

"Well, this little problem doesn't change the fact that you will both be doing a very dangerous thing. Does she know that?"

"Yes. That's why I had to promise."

"We'll need to talk to Saburo about this. He may have an idea or two."

Tora said, "Don't mention the girl."

"We'll have to mention her, but I won't say anything about your bargain."

Tora nodded.

Saburo appeared promptly and greeted them both cheerfully. He looked more rested and Akitada felt guilty again for having put him through Ono's visit. As if he had read Akitada's mind, Saburo asked quickly, "Any news about Lord Ono's report, sir?"

"No, nothing. I got the feeling that he had calmed down quite a lot by the time he left us. Thank you again for working with him."

Saburo grinned and sat down beside Tora. "I think her ladyship convinced him to go easy on you."

Akitada remembered the day Yukiko had arrived. He had found her with Ono and Saburo. And Ono had seemed unusually courteous subsequently. Curious, he asked, "How did she do that?"

"As I recall, she informed him that she served Her Majesty and that the empress had taken a great interest in your work." Saburo smirked.

Tora laughed. "Good for her! Now why didn't we think of that? Her ladyship was smarter than all of us. You're a lucky man, sir."

Akitada did not feel lucky. In fact, he did not feel particularly grateful to Yukiko. He would much rather rely on his own efforts than depend on the gossip of women, no matter how powerful. But he said nothing of this. Instead, he explained Tora's plan, adding, "I should have mentioned it before, but I didn't like the adventure the boys had a few days ago. They were exercising the horses and ran into some hostile fishermen. I suspect that those fishermen were involved in some illegal activity. You may recall that Tojo expected a tax shipment to be landed in Mikawa for transfer to the land route."

Tora nodded. He said, "Yuki said nothing to me. He knows better than take Yoshi into danger of any sort."

"It was nothing, Tora. The boys weren't hurt. But there may be something going on and your expedition may be more dangerous than you think."

Saburo listened, frowned, and said to Tora, "So you're going back to that island? Let me go! You might alert whoever is there, and you have no idea how many armed men there may be. You're just one, and the girl doesn't count."

"The girl knows the island."

"I know something about the island too. You left out things when you talked about it. Just what does she know?"

The fact was that Michiko had not revealed much beyond the fact that there were caves and that evil men and her father sometimes went there. Tora said, "I just want to take a look at some caves if nobody is there.

The pirates can't be there all the time, and the place isn't big enough for a lot of people. We'll be very careful."

A brief silence fell, then Akitada asked, "What do you know about it, Saburo? I don't recall discussing it with you."

Saburo sat a little more stiffly. "I took the liberty to do some checking when you assigned Tora to the murder of the tattooed man. I found out the place has a bad reputation and the local fishermen don't talk much about it. I thought it sounded suspicious, but then you and Tora dropped the investigation."

Akitada realized that Saburo had grown a little resentful because he had given Tora all the assignments while Saburo had been relegated to tribunal duties. But he said nothing and instead told Tora, "Very well, you can go, Tora. But you must be careful and you must not alert them unnecessarily. If you see anyone there, you must turn back. We'll find another way."

Tora nodded.

∞

Akitada was very uneasy about Tora's plan, but Tora was experienced and he forced himself to trust him. The *koto* and flute were delivered that afternoon, and Akitada carried them immediately to his residence.

He found his daughter and her companion singing on the veranda outside Yasuko's room. Yasuko had a very pretty voice, but it was nothing compared to the strong, full sound of Sadako's. They were unaware of him, as he stood and listened with pleasure. His earlier sense of joy returned. It was good to hear music again.

When they finished, he walked out on the veranda and presented the *koto* to Sadako with a bow and a smile. "You said you played, so I bought this."

She blushed, then knelt quickly and bowed. "Oh, your Excellency. How very nice! Look Yasuko. It's a large and very beautiful instrument. You will enjoy such a very fine *koto* all your life! I shall be happy to teach you."

Yasuko frowned at the instrument. "It's very big, Father. I don't want to learn to play it. It looks very hard."

Akitada cleared his throat. "A misunderstanding, Yasuko. I bought this for Sadako so she can play with us and we can have a little orchestra. I also bought a flute for Yoshi."

Sadako went pale and then red. Tears shone in her eyes. She looked from him to the *koto* and clasped her hands, apparently overcome by the gift.

Yasuko spoiled the moment by laughing out loud. "Yoshi play the flute? You're being silly, Father. He'll never touch anything that isn't a weapon or a horse."

Akitada ignored her. "Sadako?" he asked softly. "May I call you Sadako?"

She nodded without looking up. Her hand stroked the *koto*. "It's the most beautiful instrument I've ever seen," she murmured thickly. "I'll play it for you, sir, but you must keep it for Yasuko. Or perhaps for your lady."

Yasuko, still pouting, said, "Yukiko has her own. It's more beautiful than this one."

Akitada shot her a sharp look and snapped, "That was extremely rude! Go inside."

314

Yasuko muttered, "Sorry, Father," and scurried off.

Akitada sat down on the veranda beside Sadako. "As you can see, my daughter badly needs your guidance. I apologize."

She finally looked up. Her eyes were a little moist but she smiled. "Don't blame her too much. She's not used to me yet, and your making such a gift to a complete stranger has shocked her."

He smiled back. "Ah, but we're not strangers. It gives me great pleasure." On an impulse he added, "In fact, finding the *koto* and thinking of you has lifted my spirits amazingly. Will you play a little for me?"

She blinked and blushed rosily. Akitada felt quite warm, sitting there in the autumn sun and looking at her delight in the instrument. She bowed a little, pulled it closer, adjusted the bridges, then placed the picks on her fingers. "It has been a very long time, but I shall try. Please forgive my poor performance. Do you have a favorite melody?"

He thought a moment. "Do you know 'The cuckoo sings'?"

She said eagerly, "Oh, I love that," and bent over the *koto*, strumming a few strings softly and adjusting a bridge or two, then began.

He thought she played enchantingly and very well. Again he wondered: where she might have learned such an aristocratic skill. Perhaps she had been in service to a noble family.

When the last note died away, he sighed with contentment. "Thank you. You are an expert, I see. Where did you learn to play like this."

Her smile faded and she looked down. "It wasn't very good. I'm badly out of practice. You see, I haven't had a *koto* in such a very long time." She added softly, stroking the instrument, "Or anything else of this kind."

"That doesn't answer my question. What happened? How did you become so completely destitute when you clearly had a very different life at one time?"

She did not look at him. "Life brings all sorts of changes. We must bear them as best we can." Then she raised her head. "You've been very good to me, sir. That wasn't anything I could have expected. My life would have been . . . horrible, I think, if you had not written. I'm very grateful. It was my karma to lose my parents and two husbands and everything in the world I ever owned, and it was also my karma that you found me on the Tokaido."

This moved him and also frightened him a little. Had their meeting been foreordained? He did not like to think that his life was being arranged by some force outside himself. He said, "It was an accident. I only did what anybody else in my position would have done. And you did me a great favor by accepting the position as Yasuko's companion."

She smiled and shook her head a little.

He added quickly, "No, I mean this sincerely. I was at my wits' end. You see, I lost the mother of my children a few years ago. In the darkness of the soul that followed I have neglected them. Then I married again, unsuitably you might think, but hoping that a new family might draw us close. Only my wife serves at court,

316

and I found myself alone again. I'm very glad I found you."

The oddness of this speech struck him immediately. He felt himself color with embarrassment. Clearing his throat, he got up abruptly. "Thank you for the music," he said and walked away quickly, before he might say something else stupid.

38

The Island

Tora felt excited about the night's work. He dressed in old, dark clothing—much to Hanae's concern—and shoved a knife in his sash.

"What are you going to do?" his wife asked, her eyes narrowed.

"Nothing very dangerous," he assured her, though he was not at all sure himself. "The knife is just because you never know who might be out after dark."

Hanae frowned. "You didn't answer my question."

"Oh. You remember the body that washed up on the shore a few weeks ago? I'm going to walk down to the harbor and see if anything unusual is going on." This was not far from the truth.

Hanae was not altogether reassured. "Can't some-one else do that? It seems to me after all these years you still haven't learned to order your men to carry out these supposedly not very dangerous duties. Does the master know what you're doing?"

"Yes, he does. And I'm not going alone."

That stopped the questioning. She said, "Well, be careful."

Michiko was waiting for him behind Auntie Haru's. She, too, wore dark clothes and she had a lantern. Having seen Michiko blossom in her recent finery, Tora grinned to see her in short pants and a loose shirt and with her braid hanging down her back.

She frowned. "I look ugly," she complained.

"You look ravishing," he said gallantly.

She came closer. "Hold me, Tora. I'm afraid."

He held her, patting her back awkwardly. "There's nothing to be afraid of. "I'm here. But put down that lantern. We'll have to manage without."

She detached herself and left the lantern near the wall. "Let's go and be quick about it. And don't forget what you promised."

"I haven't forgotten."

She stood on tiptoe to kiss him on the mouth, murmuring against his lips, "Make love to me now, Tora. Please. I swear I'll keep my promise."

He put her away. "No. Business first, pleasure later."

She sighed. "All right."

They walked quickly through the dark streets and to the even darker harbor. There were very few lights to be seen and no people were about. What they had not bargained for was the fact that even with a cloudy sky the water remained strangely luminous even though there were neither stars nor a moon tonight. The island seemed to float in the luminescence like a black hole, an opening into even greater darkness.

Michiko muttered something.

"What?"

"I told you the island has eyes. It will see us coming." Her voice was tight with fear.

Tora's hair bristled, but he shook off his fears of the supernatural. There could, of course, be human eyes watching, but that was extremely unlikely when the pirates could not know their secrets were known. He said staunchly, "Nonsense. Everybody's asleep by now and there won't be anyone on the island." Tora tried to speak with conviction, but the idea of an island having eyes was sufficiently spooky to make him nervous. It could not be helped. This was something that had to be done and he had done many more dangerous things before. This fear was just another sign he was getting old.

Her father's hut was dark.

"See," Tora said. "Fast asleep. Let's get in the boat."

The boat, however, was not in its usual place. Michiko said, "He must be out in it. What if he went to the island?"

"I told you, I can handle your father. In fact, I hope he's there. It's time he paid for what he did to you. But what about a boat?"

She took his hand. "I love it when you're fierce, my tiger. Come. I know where there's another boat."

This one turned out to belong to another fisherman and was slightly larger and steadier than the one they had used before. Tora rowed while Michiko steered. The physical exertion felt good. Tora drew energy and courage from it. He was not quite over the hill yet and would show those pirates a few things, if any were hanging about. But he doubted that very much. Michiko's father he did not fear.

They tied up the boat at the landing place. The island did not seem quite so dark now that they had arrived. They could make out the steps leading to the shrine on top and some of the dense forest near the shore. The tide lapped rhythmically at the rocks and a light wind rustled the branches. Otherwise there was no sound.

Tora said, "No sign of your father's boat. You worried for nothing. There's nobody here."

"Sshh!" Michiko whispered urgently, "Be very quiet. Maybe the island is sleeping. Come along."

Tora decided this was good advice, though her words reminded him again uncomfortably of the watching eyes.

Instead of heading up the steps, she turned right, walking along the shoreline. A thin strip of sand ran between the edge of the forest and the sea, though it could not be called a path. In several places they had to delve in among the trees because the water reached their roots. Now and then, Tora glanced toward the land. It lay dark and mountainous against a slightly lighter sky. An occasional glimmer of light showed where Komachi was.

322

A rustling in the branches made them both jump. Michiko gasped and flung herself into Tora's arms. He listened a moment and said, "Just the monkeys."

She cuddled against him and kissed him. The kiss almost cost him his footing. He gasped at the expert way she managed to arouse him.

"Let's make love now," she pleaded softly. "I want you so much." She tugged at his sash.

Tora put her away from him. "That's a good way to be caught unawares," he muttered. "Let's get the work done. How far to those caves?"

She shuddered. "Not far."

They plodded on and rounded the island. The land disappeared and before them lay the open sea, black water as far as the eye could see with a slightly lighter sky above. The vegetation receded and they reached a small beach. And here Michiko's father's boat lay on the sand. Beyond it was a small landing stage, and there a larger boat with a sail was tied up.

Tora pulled her back into the cover of the trees. "Somebody's here," he said unnecessarily.

"It's my father! Let's go back." Michiko pulled his sleeve.

"I want to see what's going on," Tora said, freeing himself. You can wait here. I'll come back when I've seen what I came to see."

"I'm not leaving you." She clutched at him with both arms. "Come away, love. We can come back another time when nobody's here. They are bad men. They'll kill you."

"You don't have much faith in me. Besides I'll be careful," Tora told her. "And you made a promise."

She gave a small moaning sound and let go of him.

"Just show me where the caves are. I'll take it from there."

She pointed. "Just past the boat landing. A path starts among the trees."

As he left her, she whispered after him, "Come back to me!"

He decided to move along the tree line rather than across the open beach and found the path easily. It led to the landing and was clearly well-traveled. Unfortunately in the other direction it became lost in the darkness of the brush and trees.

Tora proceeded slowly, trying to make no sound. Once he was under the trees, his eyes adjusted a little and he could see the path. Moving a little more easily now, he saw a darker, more solid mass ahead. It must be some sort of rock formation and that meant he was close to the caves. He paused.

What with the boats on the shore, he thought at least three people were on the island. That was, if they did not keep someone here at all times. "The island has eyes," Michiko had said. Most likely they were the eyes of whoever guarded the caves. And that meant the caves contained something worth guarding.

There again the obvious answer was that pirated goods would be stored here, or at least the portion that the pirate boss collected as his share. Could it be Matsudaira himself? Probably not. This sort of business seemed too rough for such a great lord.

Tora realized that he was wasting time. What lay ahead was dangerous and he was postponing it. Ashamed of his cowardice, he moved ahead more quickly.

He reached the rocks and peered up and ahead. The cliff was tall and almost sheer. Below, the trees receded somewhat, leaving a small open space. The path led to it, and Tora assumed that the cave opening was there. He could not see it because the cliff jutted out just there. So far, he had neither seen nor heard anything. He had no idea what the cave was like, but if it was large, they might be deep inside and not likely to hear him coming.

He moved along the path as quietly as he could, rounded the cliff, and saw the cave gaping dark in its wall. The blackness of this opening made him shudder. He bit his lip and went in.

For a moment he wondered if it was empty, but then he saw a light just ahead. And there was the faint sound of male voices in conversation. Whatever was going on seemed peaceful enough. At least no one was being tortured tonight.

Perhaps he should turn around now. What he had so far might be enough to bring the tribunal guards to take a look. But he still had nothing to implicate Matsudaira or anyone else, and without some form of proof they could not prosecute. Instead they would give warning to the villains to hide their activities, or worse, prepare for battle. If he could just see the men or perhaps hear what they were doing he would have enough for his master to decide.

Touching the wall of the cave he moved along it toward the light. He was patient, putting one foot softly before the other to make sure he would make no noise when he shifted his weight forward. And he felt for his knife.

The cave curved and after what seemed like an eternity, he finally could look into a larger space lit by torches and by assorted lanterns that the men must have brought with them. There were five of them, sitting on the floor. They seemed to be waiting for something. Their faces were turned toward an area Tora could not see. Four of the younger men, Tora did not know. The fifth must be Michiko's father.

At that moment, someone spoke to them. "You'll be paid the usual," he said. "One hundred pieces of silver. Forty for the four of you, and twenty for Oyoshi."

Tora knew that voice. He had heard it not too long ago; it was slightly high and nasal, and definitely the speech of one of the good people.

But who was it?

He leaned forward to catch a glimpse of the man, lost his balance, and stepped on a dry branch that broke with a loud, snapping noise.

39

Maple Leaves Falling

Akitada was quite aware of the fact that Sadako had not really answered his question about her birth. He knew little more about her background than he had before. She had lost her parents and two husbands, but that surely did not mean she had no family whatsoever. If she had been raised as one of the good people, and her education seemed to prove that, than she belonged to a large clan. Even if she somehow lost parents and siblings, she would have been looked after by relatives. It was the duty of the clan chief to make certain that orphaned children were attached to new families within the clan. He himself held that position and, though the Sugawara clan had shrunk pitifully over the centuries, there were distant cousins who had a claim on him. Besides, he would also feel responsible for the children of his two sisters, even though they now belonged to their fathers' clans.

So what had happened to Sadako? The only explanation he could come up with was that some extraordinary crime or offense had been committed by someone close to her, and that this had dismantled the entire family structure. She would keep such a secret to herself out of fear that he would dismiss her.

Again he felt pity welling up inside him. Surely someone so lost deserved a helping hand. Surely whatever had happened in her past was not something that would harm his children. But the fact was that she made him very uneasy.

So that evening after his duties in the tribunal were done, he walked out into his garden to ponder the mystery of Sadako.

There was a slight chill in the air, but one cicada was still singing. Soon it would be winter and the cold would creep into every nook and cranny of his residence. He would huddle over a brazier and wear extra robes to keep warm. And while the snow would bring brightness and beauty outside, all the shutters would be closed against the sharp north wind and everything would be dark inside.

When he was younger he had enjoyed brisk walks in the white, sparkling world outside. He and the children had had snowball fights, and they had eaten steaming hot soups and stews afterwards. And at night he had

slipped under warm covers to hold Tamako in his arms
and perhaps make love to her.

He paused on this thought. He had spent winters
with Yukiko also. Why was it always Tamako who came
to his mind when he thought of the past?

He had come to a halt in front of the maple and was
looking down at a carpet of brilliantly red leaves. The
color was beautiful, yet it was the color of blood and of
death. The coming cold snatched at lives, destroying
what had filled life with joy.

Stirring the leaves with his black slippers, he sighed.

What must be in Sadako's mind? So newly bereaved in this season, in a strange household and with
no hope for her future? Without volition his feet carried him deeper into the garden and in the direction of
his daughter's room. When he was close, he called out
to her. There was no answer.

He stepped quickly up the steps and into the room.
It was quite empty. He was about to turn away again
when he heard a small sound. It had come from behind
a screen. Walking across, he moved it aside, and there
was Sadako, cowering on floor, her hands over her face.

"I beg your pardon," he said quickly. "I didn't know
anyone was here."

She rose then and turned to him and he saw that she
had been weeping. Appalled, he said, "Forgive me. I
had no right. But . . ." He paused, unsure what to say.

"No, please forgive me. I . . . your daughter went to
visit Hanae and I was at loose ends and . . . " Her voice
trailed off.

He said nothing for a moment. He should leave, he thought, leave her to her private grief. But something stopped him. He touched her arm and said, "It's the sadness of the season. I was just now in the garden thinking of my late wife and then of you. Can we not sit together for a little and cheer each other up?"

She dabbed at her eyes with her sleeve and smiled. "Of course, my lord. I was just being foolish."

He felt the warmth of her arm through the fabric of her gown and drew back his hand quickly. She was moving away, bending for two cushions and placing them side by side at the open doors. Then she stood waiting, her eyes downcast.

He went to sit down. "I've been worried about you," he said.

Her eyes widened. "About me? Why? I'm nobody."

He lifted an eyebrow. "Do you really believe that?"

Her lips quirked a little. "No. You've found me out. I'm much too proud for my own good. But what I am has nothing to do with what people consider of interest. As you know, I'm very poor and I have nobody to use his or her influence to help me on in the world. I only have myself. But I do take a foolish pride in that."

He smiled. "Good. I found you in tears and thought perhaps Yasuko or someone else had been unkind."

She looked shocked and shook her head. "Oh, no! Everybody has been more than kind. And Yasuko is a joy. You have a charming daughter. No, I was thinking about Heishiro."

So he had been right. She had been grieving for her husband, grieving as he used to and still did, for the one person she had loved more than anything. He said awkwardly, "Believe me, I know how you feel. When I lost my wife I couldn't find my way in the world any longer. It seemed that I was erring in some dark place that would never release me. But in time the darkness lifted."

She sighed. "Yasuko said her mother died more than four years ago and you still grieve."

"Yes."

They sat silently for a while, looking out at the changing colors of the leaves and the empty blue sky.

The season reminded him of something else. "It will soon be winter. Forgive me, but how will you keep warm? You brought no clothes."

She looked startled, then chuckled. "You are the kindest man to think of that. I have some trunks waiting in Totomi. You see, I was so very anxious to get the position you offered that I set out right away. But then I was afraid you might not want me, so I've been waiting to send for my things."

He was both startled and flattered that she should call him kind. It had seemed very familiar but it pleased him. She had a very strange way sometimes of speaking to him like an equal. He said, "You relieve my mind. Then will you please send for them? I have no intention of dismissing you."

She blushed a little. "Forgive me for being so forward, but I warned you. I do have this foolish pride that makes me say things that are quite improper. I promise you I shall guard my tongue better in the future." Then she bowed. "Thank you for your trust. I shall not disappoint it."

"Good! Then let us both cheer up and make the best of things. Do you think we might meet after the evening rice and make some music?"

She smiled and nodded, and he rose and went back out into the garden.

As he passed the maple, he looked up at its branches. Quite a lot of its leaves still remained and just then the setting sun lit up its top. The tree blazed with crimson fire. Life was still very beautiful.

40

The Broken Pact

There were shouts, and then they burst from the inner cave. Before Tora could run back outside, they were upon him in the murky outer chamber.

There were four of them.

Three had short swords and the fourth a coiled rope.

Tora had no time to wonder if there might be more because he was surrounded by ugly brutes with bared teeth and death in their eyes.

"Hold it!" Tora extemporized, raising his hands. "I bring a message for your master."

They hesitated.

"Who from?" asked the bearded one.

"From Tojo."

The thin one snapped, "Oh, no, you don't. Tojo got caught. You're a liar. And a dead man." He raised his short sword and rushed Tora, aiming the point of his sword at the middle of Tora's chest. Tora snatched out his knife and parried the attack. He moved back a bit more.

The one with the beard blocked his way. "Wait," he said to the others. "Let's find out who he is. He looks familiar."

Tora did not wait. He jumped and buried his knife to the hilt in the thin man's belly. He roared with pain, doubled over and fell to his knees, dropping his sword at Tora's feet. His screams tore at Tora's eardrum and reverberated in the narrow space. Tora snatched up the sword and turned on the bearded man who had been blocking his retreat, but he was ready and knew how to use the short sword. They circled each other warily, while Tora tried to keep him between himself and the other two.

When he saw the bearded man's eyes move toward his right shoulder, he twisted aside.

The one with the rope attempted to catch his head or sword arm tossing it. The rope whistled past, just brushing his shoulder, and Tora used the moment to shove his own sword into the rope man's unprotected side.

Before he could recover his weapon, the bearded man had slashed at his thigh. Hot blood poured down to his foot and his leg became stiff, but Tora turned fast and swung the sword back-handedly at the bearded man. It caught his neck, stopping short of decapitating him but leaving a slash that gushed blood. The bearded man's knees buckled and he fell.

Suddenly Tora was the only one standing. Barely standing. He was swaying and feeling light-headed from blood loss. The man with the wound in his belly still screamed. Tora used his sash to make a rough bandage for his leg, wrapping it as tightly as he could. It was too dark to see much, but he had a good idea how bad it was. Michiko would have to row them back.

He did a quick check of the four dead or dying men. They were complete strangers.

Then whose voice had he recognized?

And where was Michiko's father?

He grasped the bloody sword more firmly and limped toward the lighted area ahead. The cave widened into a room that was almost round. In its center was a rickety table. On the table stood an oil lamp shedding its yellow light on piles of gold and silver. And behind the table stood a short, gray-haired man with one of the burning torches in one hand and a knife in the other.

Michiko's father.

They stared at each other.

Then the familiar voice said urgently, "Kill him, Oyoshi! Now!"

Michiko's father did not seem to be inclined to obey. Of course not. Men who beat women were cowards. Tora tried to see past the brightness of the torch. Someone stood behind Michiko's father.

Dragging his injured foot, he took a couple of steps forward and stopped in surprise.

Surely that was . . .

"Tora!"

Tora swung around. Michiko stood in the entrance, wide-eyed and pale. "Go back!" he shouted.

"I want to be with you. I'm afraid."

Her father finally moved. Roaring, "You bitch!" he ran forward, dropping the torch but swinging the knife. Tora slashed at him with his sword as he passed but missed. Michiko screamed and ran.

Torn, Tora looked at the last man in the cave. The Matsudaira heir cowered against the cave wall, his eyes on Tora's bloody sword.

"Don't touch me!" he squealed. "My father will kill you if you lay a hand on me. My father will kill all of you. You and your master."

Disgusted, Tora swung around again and tried to run after Oyoshi and Michiko. Both had disappeared, but then he heard her screaming again. Cursing his weakness under his breath, he shuffled after them, half falling a couple of times, supporting himself against the wall.

It was lighter outside but the night was still dark. It took him a moment to orientate himself. Then he heard a sound from the pier. Michiko's father was getting into the small boat. He was alone.

Tora shouted, "Michiko," and scanned the open area between the cave and the woods and finally saw her. She lay slumped among the trees. Only her pale face showed up against the uniform blackness of the shrubbery and her clothing.

"Michiko!" He limped to her. She lay on her back. Her eyes were open and for a moment he thought she was just resting. Then he saw the thin line of blood crossing the hand that clutched her chest and he knew she had been stabbed.

By her own father!

Her lips moved. "Tora?"

He knelt beside her. "Where are you hurt?"

"Tora," she said again and tried to sit up. Blood welled up between her fingers and she fell back. "I love you."

"Don't talk. Let me see."

He tore off his shirt and folded it. Then he gently lifted her hand and parted her shirt. Blood welled up from a deep chest wound. There was a second wound a little farther down in her abdomen. He pressed his shirt to the chest wound and heard her breath rattle. Too late. She was dying.

"Hold me," she whispered.

It was an awkward business, but Tora lay down beside her and took her into his arms. She nuzzled into his neck and kissed it. He said, "I love you, Michiko," and thought she smiled.

He did not know when she died. But it was dawn when he realized that her face was cold against his. They had made a pact, and he had not paid off. He wished now that it had been otherwise. That she had lived, and that he could have made love to her.

Or that he had made love to her earlier when she had asked him to. He had been a fool. He had rejected a priceless gift. He wept and was not sure if it was for her death or for his own stupidity.

When he tried to get to his feet, he found he was too weak. Never mind, he thought, I'll stay here.

We'll stay here like this.

41

The Arrest

They made music that night and it was as pleasant as Akitada had hoped. Yoshi, hearing them from his room, had crept out on his veranda and sat listening. Yasuko had played her lute much better than Akitada had expected and the combination of the sounds from the zither and the lute was charming.

He himself had played tentatively, feeling out of practice and afraid to embarrass himself, but once or twice he thought his flute added just the right touch at the perfect moment.

Of course they made mistakes, but those produced giggles from Yasuko and smiles from Sadako. They were all happy for a while, so much so that Akitada finally realized that the watchman's call from the tribunal meant it was the middle of the night and sent the children to bed.

Sadako busied herself with slipping the koto into a sort of bag she had made for it, and he stood watching her.

She looked up, bowed, and said, "Thank you, sir. I shall always remember this night."

Perhaps it was the remembered music or the faint light from the candle inside—the night was unusually cloudy—that cast a golden hue on her face and her slender hands. She appeared suddenly like a being from another, more perfect, world, both remote and desired.

He stood a moment longer, wanting to hold on to this feeling somehow, then he bowed, murmured, "Thank you for a very pleasant evening," and hurried away.

∞

The next morning he woke feeling very foolish for the strange thoughts he had been entertaining about his daughter's companion. He decided to put her from his mind. Whatever her secret was, it could not matter the least to him. And the musical evenings were quite pleasant, but he must guard against showing too marked an interest in them. It was quite improper.

Having settled the matter to his satisfaction, he set about getting dressed. In the midst of this, he heard Hanae's voice outside his room, calling out softly, "Sir? Are you awake?"

He went to open the door and saw that Hanae looked very worried. In an instant the memory of Tora's plan to visit the island surfaced and his heart sank.

Hanae said, "Tora hasn't come home. It's not like him. And he went out on some undertaking he said you had approved. I wanted to ask if you thought he was safe."

Akitada said, "Sometimes things get complicated. He is probably just running late, but I'll go immediately to check on him."

Hanae bowed. "Thank you, sir."

Akitada did not bother to wash and shave. He walked quickly across to the tribunal where he found Saburo waiting.

Saburo said, "He hasn't come back, sir. With your permission, I'd like to go see what happened."

"We'll both go. And take ten armed men with us. Find us some swords and horses. And be fast."

For such a rushed order, the ten guardsmen who presented themselves armed and mounted did Tora's training proud. The cavalcade clattered through the sleepy morning streets of Komachi to the harbor, where Akitada confiscated enough boats to take them across the water to the island.

Saburo spoke up and directed the boats to head for the back of the island, causing Akitada to send him a questioning glance. Saburo explained, "I have mentioned, sir, that I did some checking earlier. The main landing stage is behind the island, and that's where the caves are. I thought it would save time."

"Yes. Of course. Thank you."

Akitada sat impatient, staring at the island as it grew quickly and then slid past them. As Saburo had promised, there was the landing place. A good-sized boat had come untied and bobbed some distance away, but the shore was empty.

They tied up and disembarked. Akitada's eyes had found the path heading into the woods and he hurried up in this direction, shouting, "Tora!"

Saburo ran after him. "Sir! Wait. Look. Over there." He pointed.

Some distance from the path, Akitada could make out two bodies. He held his breath and ran.

The bodies were those of Tora and a young girl. Tora was shirtless. The young girl lay in his arms. They looked like lovers. There was something protective about the way Tora's arm went around her, holding her close. And she had nestled her face against his and clasped his head with one of her arms.

Where they lay, the sand had soaked up their blood. There had been an awful lot of blood. It had soaked their clothes, covering them and then pooling around their bodies. Their faces looked strangely peaceful, their eyes closed as if they were merely asleep.

"Oh, dear gods!" Akitada felt so powerful a physical pain in his chest that his legs buckled and he fell to his knees beside the bodies. "Oh, Tora!" he groaned and laid his own head on Tora's chest next to the girl's.

The sounds of the guards arriving and gathering about them seemed far away. Nobody talked, but Akitada wanted them to go away. Far away.

Saburo, somewhere above him, said, "Sir?" His voice was strangely tight as if he too were overcome.

Akitada groped for one of Tora's hands that clasped the girl's body. It resisted.

The fact meant nothing at first. Then Akitada raised his head. The hand, covered with dried blood was not cold. Neither did it have the stiffness of death.

Quickly he inserted his fingers under the girl's hair to touch Tora's neck . . . and felt a flutter. A faint flutter that meant hope, meant everything.

"He's alive," he told Saburo.

Saburo squatted, checked, and nodded. He checked the girl also and shook his head. Together, they moved Tora's arms to take the dead girl out of them. There was the same resistance, and then . . .

"No!"

They stopped and looked. Tora's eyes had fluttered open. There was no recognition in them. "No!" he said again, a little louder.

"Tora," Akitada leaned over him, "you must let her go. She is dead. You are wounded and we need to see how badly."

"What?"

Recognition came slowly and with it memory. They saw it in his face. There was a moment's relief when Tora tried to raise his head. Then his eyes fell on the girl in his arms. He closed them again and let his head fall back with a deep moan.

But Tora was alive. That was all that mattered. Between them, watched by the ten warriors, they managed to lift the girl's body and lay her on the ground beside him. Then they checked him for wounds.

"Just the thigh, I think," said Saburo, "but he must have lost an awful lot of blood."

"It doesn't seem to be bleeding anymore," Akitada commented. "Do you think we can move him?"

Tora's eyes fluttered open again. "Take Michiko, too. She's my responsibility." This long speech clearly exhausted him, because his head fell back again. After a moment, he added, "Her father killed her."

Akitada looked at the slight figure of the young girl. She was no more than fifteen, Tora had said. Younger than Hiroko. He did not understand how any man could abuse and kill his own child, and a helpless girl at that. "Dear gods," he said again.

He rose and told the soldiers, "Find something that will serve as a litter. We'll put them both in the boat and go back."

Tora said, "Matsudaira's in the cave. He set his pirates on me."

Akitada thought he had not heard right. "Did you say Matsudaira?"

Tora grimaced. "The kid. Not the father."

Akitada thought Tora might be hallucinating, or at least be confused about the events of the night, but he directed two of the soldiers to take a look around. Then he crouched beside Tora again. "How do you feel, brother?" he asked. "Do you feel up to going home?"

Tora's lip twitched. He seemed unable to get the words out. After a moment, he muttered, "Hanae'll be mad." Akitada took this as a hopeful sign.

The Island of the Gods

The litter was produced. The men had taken boards from the abandoned boat at the landing stage and lashed them together. With the greatest care Akitada and Saburo shifted Tora onto it, having refused the men's help.

Tora grimaced with pain and looked anxious. "Michiko?"

"We won't leave her." Akitada wondered why Tora showed such care for a mere fisherman's daughter who had become a prostitute. But he asked no questions.

They were close to the landing stage with their burden when they heard a shout. Akitada looked back. One of the soldiers had come from the woods and was waving his arms.

"Saburo, see to Tora. I'd better have a look." Akitada was already hurrying up the shore and to the soldier.

"Four dead men and one live one," said the man. "He says his name's Matsudaira and we're on his land. He wants us to take him back to Komachi. The others are watching him."

"Let's see what it's about."

The entrance passage was reasonably well lit during the day. As the man had said, four bodies lay about. They looked like rough characters and had been armed. Tora had fought hard against them.

Akitada could see light up ahead and walked into a larger cave. His soldiers stood with drawn swords near a table. On the table was an impressive amount of gold and silver, and behind it sat the youngest Matsudaira, the arrogant youngster who had confronted them near the back gate of the Matsudaira garden.

Akitada searched his mind and said, "You're Kinto. What are you doing here?"

The youngster tried to bluster. "I have a right to be here. You don't. I want to leave."

"Ah. But unfortunately there's the matter of four dead men, a dead woman, and my severely wounded retainer, Captain Sashima."

"I know nothing about that. Take me away with you."

"How did you get here?"

Kinto searched his mind. "A servant brought me and went back."

Akitada strolled over and handled the piles of gold and silver coins. "Is this yours?"

"Yes." Kinto reached for the money.

"How exactly did you come by it?"

"None of your business." Kinto gathered the coins and looked for something to put them into.

Akitada shook his head regretfully. "I'm afraid the money is confiscated. It looks like contraband to me. And you're in quite a bit of trouble. I am charging you with piracy, conspiracy to commit piracy, conspiracy to engage in highway robbery, murder. You're under arrest."

Kinto gaped at him. Then he laughed. "You can't do that. My father will not permit it."

But Akitada was tired of him. He told the soldiers, "Chain him and take him back to the tribunal jail. Send someone later for the bodies. The gods of this island must be very angry with the desecration."

42

The Final Truth

Tora's condition outweighed everything else and Akitada did not have time to deal with his prisoner until the following day. By then Doctor Oyama had been called to deal with the deep wound in Tora's thigh. The young physician had tutted over it, probed, and then remarked, "It's deep, but it's quite clean. The main thing is to nourish the patient's life force which has apparently left him almost completely."

It was true. Tora was pale as death and weak as a kitten. After his initial effort to protect Michiko's body and his mention of the Matsudaira heir, he had become nearly completely unresponsive and slept mostly.

Hanae, Saburo and Akitada sat with him through the long first night. Hanae prayed and wept silently. The following morning, Tora opened his eyes and asked for water. After quenching his thirst, he asked, "Michiko?"

Akitada said, "She has been taken to the monks. Her funeral has been paid for. Her father is still a fugitive."

Tora nodded and closed his eyes again. Hanae had become still when Tora asked for Michiko. Akitada took her aside and told her that Tora felt responsible for having caused the girl's death. He did not mention how they had found them. What had happened between them was a mystery to Akitada, but it seemed best not to talk about it.

The doctor returned and declared himself satisfied with the looks of the wound and declared the patient still free of fever. Akitada and Saburo went to the tribunal to deal with the events of the previous day.

At the tribunal, they found Lord Matsudaira waiting for them. Somewhat to Akitada's surprise, Matsudaira was uncharacteristically subdued. He rose when they came in, looking anxiously at Akitada, and said, "I was told that you have arrested my son. My younger son."

"Yes. We found him on the island the local people call the island of the gods. Your son was with a number of criminals who attacked Captain Sashima. Captain Sashima was severely wounded. Most of the others are dead except for one man who escaped. Your son could not account for his presence there so I had him arrested."

"I see." Matsudaira seemed surprised, as if he had expected something else. He said, "The island belongs to my family. I cannot speak for Kinto's companions, but I assume my son had no hand in the violence?"

Akitada had foreseen this. Kinto had not laid a hand on Tora, though he probably had ordered his men to attack him. Tora was in no condition to answer questions yet so Akitada was hard pressed to hold on to his prisoner even when he was convinced that Tora had walked into a meeting between pirates and their master. He said, "It's too early to know exactly what role your son played. The incident only happened last night."

"I trust Captain Sashima will recover?"

"We hope so."

"I'm glad. Can you release Kinto to me? I'll promise to produce him when needed for questioning."

Akitada smiled. "I regret it isn't possible until we know what he was involved in."

Matsudaira sighed. "Kinto is a foolish boy. He's nothing like his older brother. He has been a great disappointment to me, but I am his father and I love my children. I think he has fallen into bad company again and the men he was with may well have been criminals. But you must understand that Kinto is not at heart bad. He is spoiled perhaps, but I've tried to correct that. The trouble is that he envies his older brother. Kintsune is just the sort of son a man could wish for. He's obedient and studies hard. And now he is rising in the government in the capital. Kinto on the other hand was always slow and couldn't keep his mind on his studies. I had to dismiss his tutor when he failed every examination that would have admitted him to the university. That's when I told him he could not go to the capital like his brother but must remain here. He was very upset." He paused. "On top of this he had fallen in love with the Imagawa girl but she wouldn't have him. Her father tried to make a match between her and my oldest, but I decided, given Kinto's infatuation, that was a bad idea. Still, you can see the boy has had disappointments which caused him to rebel against my authority."

It was a long speech, and Akitada did not doubt the truth of it, but people had died and Tora might still succumb. He did not feel that the spoiled brat should get away with the trouble he got into on this occasion.

He said, "I'm sorry that you have been disappointed in your son, but I must insist that he stay here at least until this matter is cleared up."

Matsudaira heaved another sigh and rose. "Very well. Thank you, Governor. You will keep me informed?"

"Of course." Akitada got to his feet as well, and both men bowed.

When Matsudaira had gone, Saburo said, "Well, that was surprising."

"Yes. I thought he'd be furious and threaten us."

"I think he knows his son and he knows he's guilty."

Akitada frowned. "Perhaps. But we have assumed all along that the whole Matsudaira clan is involved. Or at least, the father. But if that were the case, wouldn't he fight like a tiger to protect himself and his son?"

"Maybe he isn't involved."

Akitada sighed. "I suppose it's possible, but we need to proceed carefully. I want to know everything about Kinto's reputation. He's very young to be involved in piracy, torture, and murder on his own. And we have to find the girl's father. He's our only witness against Kinto. I think we'd better find him fast, because Matsudaira probably realizes the same thing and may make sure he doesn't live to talk."

Saburo nodded. "I'll get busy right away."

"Get Akechi involved also. You cannot do this alone."

"Akechi hasn't exactly shown himself very efficient in the previous investigation."

"True, but the more people are going about searching and asking questions the better. The guard will also be useful. They are outraged at what was done to Tora."

Saburo departed and Akitada sat in his office staring at documents and letters that awaited his attention. It all had to wait. The game had changed overnight. The meeting with Matsudaira senior suggested that the father might not be involved in some grand piracy scheme. It was in fact altogether possible that Kinto had indeed fallen into bad company and had been financing operations from the island. If he was jealous of his brother's success, then it was likely that he would do something of the sort to gain money that was not likely to come from his father in the amount he expected.

Then there was still the unfinished case of Hiroko's murder. Strange how she had been entangled with the Matsudaira family from the start. He was impatient to get answers. Saburo and the others were employed in asking questions in the city and scouring the place for Michiko's father. He could not sit here waiting. On an impulse, he decided to send for Imagawa.

Hiroko's father arrived, looking drawn. Akitada greeted him briefly, then asked, "What do you know about Matsudaira Kinto?"

"Kinto? Why?"

"I wondered if Hiroko had spoken of him."

"Not to me. When the marriage between his brother and my daughter fell through, Matsudaira had the nerve to propose that useless puppy as a substitute. I was so angry I showed him the door."

"Why was Kinto unacceptable as a husband for your daughter?"

"That should be obvious. He's a younger son. I won't have a useless good-for-nothing without prospects palmed off on my daughter."

"I see. In what way is Kinto a good-for-nothing?"

"His reputation smells to high heaven. He lives only for drinking, whoring, and gambling. His father is forever paying off his debts and hushing up brothel scandals where he abuses the women."

Akitada stared at Imagawa. It took one to know one, apparently. Still, it might be true that Kinto had a violent streak even if he had played the coward on the island.

Imagawa narrowed his eyes, "You suspect Kinto of killing Hiroko?"

"No. We just arrested him for piracy. I'm trying to understand his motive."

Imagawa laughed bitterly. "Money, of course. He is always in debt and has expensive tastes."

Akitada thought it a strange conversation, one he should have had much earlier. Was it possible that Kinto was also involved in Hiroko's murder?

What he had learned was certainly suggestive. All those brothel visits and Kinto's reputation with the women. Perhaps they had been asking the wrong questions.

Suddenly filled with new determination, Akitada dismissed Imagawa and decided to visit the business quarter of the city.

Naganori was in his shop, dusting the objects that filled the shelves. There was no sign of Mrs. Naganori but Akitada assumed she was watching her husband from the backroom. Naganori was a silly man but he had to be pitied. As it was, he was in an excellent position to answer Akitada's question.

Naganori recognized him and was instantly in a dither. "Welcome back, sir," he squeaked, bowing deeply. "Wh-what may I do for you?"

As expected, his wife's round face peered out from the back, but when she saw Akitada, she withdrew again quickly.

"Naganori," Akitada said, "I need a bit of information about you and the murdered girl."

Naganori paled. "The m-murdered girl?"

Akitada realized that Naganori could not know that Tora had reported to him. "You told Captain Sashima of the tribunal certain things," he said. "The captain reported to me. It's my understanding that you found the young woman standing by a lake and were afraid she might drown herself. Is that right?"

Naganori nodded, speechless.

"You also said you felt sorry for her and offered to take her to her home."

Naganori nodded again. Behind him, his fat wife was creeping closer.

"What happened when you parted company?"

"She must've gone home, sir."

"How do you know? She was still quite a distance from her home, wasn't she?"

Naganori, looking frightened, said again, "She must've gone home. Where else would they have gone?"

"They?"

Naganori frowned. "Well, she and her brother. Seeing that she was safe with him, I went away."

Mrs. Naganori snorted. "Don't you believe it, sir. The whore went off with another man, leaving my foolish husband standing there."

Akitada looked at her. "I do recall that you mentioned something about the young woman going off with someone else." He turned back to her husband. "Lady Hiroko has no brother. What did this man look like?"

Naganori's eyes grew round. "He wasn't her brother? But he knew her and she knew him. She went with him." He suddenly gasped. "Was he the one who murdered her?"

"Most likely."

"Amida! That's terrible."

"Yes."

"He was young, sir. It was pretty dark so I couldn't see him well, but he was quite tall and strong and he looked angry. He made a fist at me and told me to get lost. I . . . I'm afraid I left."

Akitada was certain now that Hiroko had met her killer. "Where exactly did they meet?" he asked.

"It was a little past the Iris Pavilion."

Naganori's wife cried, "I knew it. You'd been to that whore house."

Naganori threw up his hands. "No, my precious. I swear."

Akitada gave the woman a look and asked her husband, "Why didn't you tell Captain Sashima about the man?"

Naganori hung his head. "I . . . he didn't give me a chance."

His wife snorted. "A fine tale. I bet you were afraid of him. You're lucky he didn't kill you, too, for trying to steal his woman."

Akitada ignored her. He said to Naganori, "I'd like you to come with me to the tribunal and take a look at a prisoner."

43

Fathers

kitada was so certain he had found Hiroko's killer that he had Kinto brought to his tribunal office to confront Naganori. He sat behind his desk with a scribe in place to record the event and Saburo as a witness. Naganori waited in another room.

Two guards led the chained Kinto into the office and remained beside him. Akitada saw that the young man was both tall and muscular and therefore quite capable of killing a slight young woman and disposing of her body in a nearby field. It was easy to see Kinto as the willful and spoiled son of a noble family. Both the coward and the bully resided in this young man. Kinto was only nineteen, a very young age to be in this much trouble and there was little excuse for it. Unlike Imagawa, Matsudaira senior seemed to care for his children. This one apparently had expected to get his way in everything and when he had been denied, he had lashed out. The fact that he had not fought for his freedom and escape on the island had proved he was a coward.

Now he stood before Akitada and complained.

"This is outrageous, Governor. I'm a Matsudaira and was arrested on my own land. I demand that my father be notified this instant. He will not tolerate this."

Akitada said, "Your father has been informed."

Kinto's eyes widened. "He knows?"

"Yes. It appears he regards your behavior as shocking and your arrest as well deserved."

Kinto's defiance deflated. "I'm innocent," he wailed. "You told him lies. I did nothing. I'm not responsible for what those fishermen did."

"Why were you in their company and how do you account for the money that was found?"

"How should I know what they were doing? I don't know them."

"What were you doing on the island?"

Kinto opened his mouth and closed it again. His look had become haunted.

Akitada told a servant, "Bring in the merchant Naganori."

Kinto fidgeted. "I don't care what people say about me. They're lying. I've done nothing illegal."

Akitada said nothing.

Naganori came in and bowed to Akitada. Akitada told him, "Turn around and look at the prisoner."

Naganori turned and looked. "That's him, you honor. That's the man who called her name and threatened me."

Kinto frowned. "I've never seen him before in my life."

"Oh, yes?" Naganori cried. "Weren't you coming from the Iris Pavilion that night? And didn't you call the young woman 'Hiroko'?"

Kinto paled. "B-but . . ." he stammered. "What nonsense is this? What does this have to do with the island?"

Akitada compressed his lips. "Nothing at all. This concerns quite a different crime you're accused of. According to Mr. Naganori you encountered him and Imagawa Hiroko in the city. He was walking her home. It happened on the ninth day of the month sometime after sunset. You forced him to leave and walked away with the young woman. Where did you take her?"

"No where! I never saw them that night. You're not going to pin her murder on me."

Akitada studied him for a moment. No question about it: Kinto was frightened.

"Show me your arms!" he ordered.

Kinto shook his head. "No!" His chains rattled as he folded his arms across his chest.

"Guard!" Akitada said sharply.

Both of Kinto's guards seized his arms, pulled them apart, then ripped open his full sleeves. Both of his lower arms showed long red scars."

"How did you get those?" Akitada demanded.

Kinto struggled, but he said nothing.

A lie would have been simple, but he had not been prepared for questions about Hiroko.

Akitada asked quietly, "What happened? I assume you planned to take her home to her family. Perhaps there was an accident?"

Kinto said sullenly, "She wasn't at all grateful. She's a spiteful girl."

"You argued?"

He nodded. "She's never liked me. She used to mock me. I told her I'd seen her go into the Iris Pavilion and that I knew she was meeting a man there. I called her a whore. She was a whore. I'd asked her to be my wife and she'd turned me down and then she'd gone to meet men in the Iris Pavilion. I know because I followed her there."

"I can see where that might be upsetting. What did she say when you told her this?"

"She hit me."

At first Akitada wasn't sure he heard right. "Hiroko hit you?"

Kinto, red with anger, glared. "Yes. She hit me. I was just walking her home, asking her what she'd been doing in the Iris Pavilion, in a brothel. And when she tried to deny it, I called her a lying whore. That's when she hit me."

This cleared up a number of missing details. Hiroko, unaware that their love nest was in fact a brothel, and still overcome by her lover's betrayal, had lashed out at Kinto. And Kinto was not the type to take this well, not when she had rejected him.

"What did you do?"

"I don't know. I was angry. I think I shook her. She ran away, but I chased her. When I caught her, she fought me and suddenly went limp."

"Then what did you do?"

"It was dark and we were near the open country. I picked her up and took her to some field and put her among the rice plants."

"You murdered Imagawa's daughter, your sister's best friend." Akitada summed up the confession.

It suddenly struck Kinto that he was in trouble. "I didn't mean it. She hit me first. I was just trying to calm her down." He could see from Akitada's face that he did not believe this. "You can't charge me with this. It was an accident, as you said."

Akitada said, "You will sign your confession. Then you will be returned to your cell until we can sift through the other charges."

Kinto wailed, "My father will help me. I insist you send for my father."

Akitada said, "You may be quite sure he will be informed."

After they had taken Kinto back to jail, and Naganori had pressed his seal on his statement and left, Saburo said, "How did you know, sir?"

"A lot of small things. We should have suspected him earlier but there were too many false clues. Luckily I stopped in Naganori's shop and recalled what that shrew of a wife had said about her husband's girlfriend going off with another man. Naganori hadn't mentioned that important bit of information. At least he made up for it by coming and identifying Kinto." Akitada sighed. "It might have been a good deal harder if Kinto weren't so certain that his father would save his hide as he has probably done in the past. Well, I'd better go and inform both fathers about the confession."

∞

Akitada went to speak to Imagawa first.

The majordomo received him. He bowed, then asked, "Any news, sir?"

Such a question from a servant was improper, of course, but Akitada recalled the man's worry about Hiroko's maid and answered, "Yes. We have a confession. The young man claims he was provoked."

The other man nodded. "Thank you, your Excellency. I'm glad it was no one in this house. We were quite fond of Lady Hiroko."

Akitada thought he knew where the majordomo's suspicions had fallen, but he said nothing.

Lord Imagawa came in quickly. "You have news?" he asked.

"Yes. A young man has confessed."

Imagawa nodded. "Foolish girl. She should never have gone off by herself. But he did not rape her?"

Akitada regarded him with distaste. "No, though he may have tried to. Lady Hiroko fought. He bears the scratches on his arms."

"Good! That should settle the matter then. Thank you for letting me know."

"You did not ask who the killer is."

The Island of the Gods

"It doesn't matter. Some low-life scum no doubt."
He sighed. "The disobedience of children is a terrifying
thing, governor. Be careful to guard yours well."

"I think you know that your abusive treatment of
Lady Hiroko is known to me. If she was disobedient it
was because she wished to escape this house and hoped
that a young man she had met would take her to wife.
She had gone to meet him."

"I did not abuse my daughter and if she went without my knowledge to meet a man then she chose her
fate. There is a certain justice in this. We parents attempt to rear our children strictly precisely to protect
them from taking such chances."

Akitada bit his lip. "The killer is Matsudaira Kinto,
by the way. Not the young man she had fallen in love
with. I believe you encouraged that relationship."

Lord Imagawa stared. "Kinto? That cannot be. They
were practically raised together. Hiroko was supposed
to marry his brother."

"It appears it was Kinto who wanted her, but she rejected his advances."

Imagawa clenched his fists. "So!" he said through
clenched teeth. "First they insult me and then they kill
my daughter. We'll see about this."

Akitada knew it was an empty gesture. Neither
Imagawa nor his clan were wealthy or large enough to
take on the Matsudaira. He did not really care what
happened to Imagawa, but he hoped his household
would not suffer more. In any case, he had another call
to make.

His reception at the Matsudaira mansion was quite different. He was taken to Matsudaira immediately, almost as if he had been expected. To his further surprise, Matsudaira looked as though he had not slept. He rose and bowed when Akitada was shown in.

"Governor, some wine or refreshments?" he offered in a distracted manner, all the while searching Akitada's face.

"No thank you. I'm afraid I bring unpleasant news."

Matsudaira sat down heavily. "Tell me."

"Your son has confessed to killing Lady Hiroko."

Matsudaira put his face into his hands. His shoulders slumped.

Akitada said, "I'm sorry. It appears he encountered her in the city . . ."

Matsudaira lowered his hands and looked at him. "Don't bother, governor. I know. He told me."

"He told you?"

"Yes. Kinto is still like a child. He has tantrums and when he's in trouble he runs to me. It seems I cannot help him anymore." He looked down at his hands. "It is too much. How much can a father cover up? I used to think he'd grow out of his fits of violence. He was always sorry afterward."

Astonished, Akitada asked, "He has killed before?"

"No. Or at least not another human being. He killed his dog and his sister's cats, and he broke his horse's leg so that it had to be put down. What should I have done? What would you have done?"

"I don't know. I suppose I would have punished him, hoping he would never do such a thing again."

"I did, though it broke my heart. But it was as if he knew how much I loved him."

The spoiled child. And perhaps in this case a child with an evil, twisted disposition. Half afraid, Akitada asked, "What will you do now? He asks to see you."

Matsudaira shook his head. "There must be an end somewhere. I will not see him. Do as you wish. I now have only one son. Kinto is dead to me. I told him it was over when he confessed about Hiroko." His head sank to his chest again, and tears glistened on his face.

Akitada left quietly.

44

Justice

Lieutenant Akechi managed to find and arrest Oyoshi, thereby salvaging his reputation to some extent. Oyoshi was crucial to prosecuting Kinto's piracy enterprise. He knew who worked for Kinto and for how long the raids on shipping had been going on, what had been taken, and who had killed Tojo's spy.

To Akitada's relief, the organization had always been only Kinto's. His father was never involved.

Since Oyoshi had resisted arrest rather desperately, he was not in very good shape when Akechi delivered him. He had a broken leg, a dislocated shoulder, a broken nose, and missing teeth. Doctor Oyama had a look

at him, declared most of the damage not life-
threatening, but shook his head at the way Oyoshi
wheezed.

In any case, Oyoshi's interrogation began and he became quite cooperative.

As it turned out, the pirate enterprise was relatively
recent, dating roughly to the time when Kinto's father
had refused to allow him to go to the capital and reduced his funds.

Kinto had decided to augment his income in his
own way. The island had played a role in this. It belonged to the Matsudaira, who had found little use for
it. From time to time it had been used by pirates in the
past. It was convenient in that it was close to Komachi
but offered a hidden landing place. As it turned out, it
was also an excellent place to pass messages about
shipments or meetings. These were written on paper
strips and tied among the prayers left at the shrine. The
men encountered by Yuki and Yoshi had been part of
the gang and had been moving captured goods. Altogether there were some fifteen members, all of them
local fishermen and all were arrested.

Of course a good deal of time passed as they built
the case against Kinto and Oyoshi.

Tora improved slowly, but he was able to attend
Michiko's funeral, though he was taken in a sedan chair
and supported into the temple by leaning on Akitada
and Saburo. By the time of Oyoshi's trial, he was walking on his own and watched the proceedings grim-faced.

Oyoshi, who was dragged in more dead than alive,
confessed his crimes, and no one had looked too close-

ly into the methods that had produced his compliance. The judge found him guilty of the murders of Tojo's spy and of his daughter as well as of engaging in piracy. The second of these charges alone brought a sentence of exile. Oyoshi died in prison before he could be transported.

Kinto's case was another matter. He, too, was questioned, but he denied everything, even when confronted with Oyoshi's testimony. Nothing in all the questioning of Oyoshi had pointed to any involvement of Matsudaira senior or any other members of the family. Akitada was glad their fears of a major uprising of the Matsudaira clan had come to nothing. Kinto did not deny killing Hiroko but insisted that it had been an accident. He had only meant to shake Hiroko because she had hit him first. Nobody believed this for a moment and he was eventually found guilty of both charges, but because of his birth the records of the investigation and the trial came under review in the capital.

Kinto's father remarkably applied no pressure on Akitada or anyone else to dismiss the charges. Neither did he attend the trial or visit his son. The outcome of Kinto's fate was that the court in their wisdom decided that a son of one of the most powerful clan chiefs was best employed by being assigned military duty. Kinto was shipped off to the far north where General Minamoto Yoriyoshi, the governor of Mutsu province, was putting down a rebellion. Matsudaira Kinto died in the fighting there shortly after.

During the peaceful weeks that followed, a letter from Yukiko arrived, informing Akitada of her safe arrival in the capital. He found that he no longer missed her. His life had become circumscribed by his work and by the time he spent with his children and Sadako. He was frequently reminded of his days with Tamako, with their sense of being settled and content in an ordinary life far from the excitements of the court scene or worries about advancement.

With that time in mind, he had made one resolve and that concerned the kind of father he wanted to be to his children. The events he had witnessed so recently had struck him with horror at the way some fathers treated their children. Master Kung-fu-tse and all the books of the Ancients stressed the duties owed by children to their parents. These lessons were reinforced early by instructive tales about the lengths good children went to in serving and protecting their aged parents. There was a need for this kind of instruction, he knew. It was all too easy to reject the elderly when they became feeble and a burden. But where was the duty of the parent to the child?

He would soon be a father again and was not sure how he felt about this. The failure of his marriage depressed him, but he had made up his mind that this child should never know he was not its father. He would give it the same love and care as the other two.

Of the men he had come to know in the course of the investigation, Matsudaira had turned out to be the most decent father. He had struggled with Kinto and ultimately failed, but it had not been for lack of love.

372

This made all the more repulsive the other two fathers, Imagawa and Oyoshi.

Little troubled by grief for Hiroko, Imagawa had swallowed his pride and not attacked the far more powerful Matsudaira, but he had demanded blood money for his daughter. Matsudaira had paid and added a handsome apology.

Matsudaira had not visited his son or seen him off when he left for the northern frontier, but Akitada thought he probably grieved for him.

As for Oyoshi: his behavior defied comprehension, though poverty and greed probably played a role. Tora never spoke of Michiko, but Akitada was sorry to see that his friend had become subdued and serious. He missed Tora's flashing teeth and his jaunty manner.

Still there was much to be grateful for. The children were well; Sadako had settled in and become a graceful part of his family; and Ono had duly filed a report that had cleared Akitada of all malfeasance.

HISTORICAL NOTE

Heian Japan (794-1185) predates the age of shoguns and samurai. The country was still under a central government by an emperor and his court nobility. The court nobles served as administrators in various departments of the government in Kyoto and as provincial officials appointed to administer distant parts of the country

The system had originally been adopted from China but soon all vestiges of a meritocracy disappeared. The ancient Japanese clans still existed, but the power rested almost exclusively in the hands of one, the Fujiwara family who filled all important posts and provided the empresses, thus extending their powers to include the emperors.

The control of the provinces through court-appointed officials soon weakened. Governors served for four years and then were reassigned. While they arrived with their own staff and the police chief was appointed from the capital, they relied on local men for the running of the provincial headquarters and for administering the various districts of the province. Besides, the governors relied heavily on local powerful landowners for military support in case of unrest and war. This arrangement eventually meant that the military power of the country fell exclusively into the hands of a few powerful provincial families, which effectively led to the rule by shoguns at the end of the twelfth century.

Even in the eleventh century, the time of this novel, there was already considerable uneasiness about the interests and powers of local families. Rebellions were frequent, and governors were by no means secure in their person or position. Occasionally, the governors themselves rebelled.

The administrative network of the time relied on a road system that connected even the most distant provinces to the capital. There were seven official routes and circuits. Of these, the Tokaido was probably the most important. It connected the eastern provinces to the capital. The roads were administered by the government, and each province was responsible for the section that passed through it. Maintenance was carried out by corvée labor and post stations were maintained with provincial funds. Centuries later these stations still existed, famously collected in Hiroshige's prints of the 53 Stations of the Tokaido.

Post stations offered rental horses, lodging, and food to travelers. Officials on government business carried tokens that would cover their costs, but everybody else paid. Perhaps most importantly, the stations provided a way for the central government to control travel. The roads were mostly paved, about seven meters wide, and with stations every twelve miles or so.

But travel was by no means safe. Highway robbers abounded. And sea voyages were subject to pirate attacks. The greatest temptations for these gangs were government transports of tax goods such as rice, silk, and horses, and the goods sent by private landowners from their estates to the capital.

Something should be said about religious practices. The native Shinto religion and Buddhism, an import from China, coexisted peacefully. The Shinto gods, or kami, were closely connected to the imperial descent, the rice culture, and the land. As Shinto abhors death, Buddhism, powerfully supported by the aristocracy, was in charge of funerals and most religious observances connected with the human life cycle. It was opposed to killing, a fact that made executions extremely rare in early Japan.

Finally, the relations between men and women in early Japan differ somewhat from those in western cultures. Men who could afford it practiced polygamy. They could divorce their wives by simply informing them of the fact. Most noblemen had several wives, ranked by their fathers' position and by whether they produced heirs. They might, in addition, maintain concubines and mistresses. Peasants and the poor usually were monogamous. During the Heian period, Japanese women had more rights than later, because they could own and control property. The episode between Akitada and Yukiko was suggested by an incident in the eleventh century novel Genji, where Genji also accepts the child of another man as his own. The situation was probably not as startling in Japan because the marriage bonds were not as sacred as in the west and no particular blame was attached to unfaithfulness. It would generally have been rather rare for married women of the aristocracy because they tended to live withdrawn from the world in their private apartments. This apparently did not apply to women who served at court, as evidenced by the diaries of Japanese court ladies.

About the Author

I. J. Parker was born and educated in Europe and turned to mystery writing after an academic career in the U.S. She has published her Akitada stories in *Alfred Hitchcock's Mystery Magazine,* winning the Shamus award in 2000. Several stories have also appeared in collections, such as *Fifty Years of Crime and Suspense* and *Shaken.* The award-winning "Akitada's First Case" is available as a podcast. Many of the stories have been collected in *Akitada and the Way of Justice.*

The Akitada series of crime novels features the same protagonist, an eleventh century Japanese nobleman/detective. *The Island of the Gods* is number sixteen. The books are available on Kindle, in print and in audio format, and have been translated into twelve languages.

Books by I. J. Parker

The Akitada series in chronological order
The Dragon Scroll
Rashomon Gate
Black Arrow
Island of Exiles
The Hell Screen
The Convict's Sword
The Masuda Affair
The Fires of the Gods
Death on an Autumn River
The Emperor's Woman
Death of a Doll Maker
The Crane Pavilion
The Old Men of Omi
The Shrine Virgin
The Assassin's Daughter
The Island of the Gods

The collection of stories
Akitada and the Way of Justice

Other Historical Novels
The HOLLOW REED saga:
Dream of a Spring Night
Dust before the Wind
The Sword Master

The Left-Handed God

Please visit I.J.Parker's web site at www.ijparker.com
You may contact her via e-mail from her web site.
The novels can also be ordered in electronic versions.
Please do post Amazon reviews. They help sell books
and keep Akitada novels coming.

Thank you for your support.